ANY WITCH WAY YOU CAN

A WICKED WITCHES OF THE MIDWEST MYSTERY
BOOK ONE

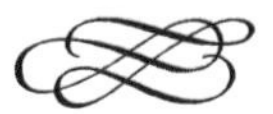

AMANDA M. LEE

WINCHESTERSHAW PUBLICATIONS

Created with Vellum

To Lillian Avery – You are missed

ONE

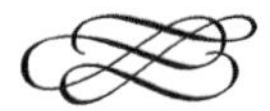

"She should just shoot him!"

The vehemence of the statement took me by surprise. It wasn't just the veracity of the words – but the person who was saying them, as well.

"Who are we talking about?" I wracked my brain trying to remember what we had been idly chatting about mere moments before. The problem is, when I'm talking with Edith, I try to tune out rather than in. She has a tendency to ramble, and I have a tendency to zone out. It's a dangerous combination.

Edith sent a disdainful look in my direction. With her sharp features and severe bun, she looked like a disgruntled nun more than anything else. The clothes didn't help. Her vintage pencil skirt hit the mid-calf length and her crisp white shirt was buttoned up to the very top.

"Don't you ever listen to me?" Edith whined.

Not really. "Of course," I lied. "I was just focusing on the files for a second. I'm sorry."

Edith sniffed. She was clearly still put out by my lack of attention. "I'm talking about Sonny."

"Who's Sonny?"

Edith emitted what could only be described as a disgruntled growl. "Sonny Corinthos," she seethed.

"Did he just move to town?" I'm often lost during conversations with Edith – she meanders from topic to topic at a fantastic pace – but this was ridiculous.

"He's not real," Edith practically bellowed as she gestured emphatically toward the television.

I glanced up from my place on the floor. I was sitting cross-legged and I had about twenty different files opened and scattered around me. The two of us were in the file room at The Whistler, Hemlock Cove's lone weekly newspaper. We were looking for a list of the area's haunted houses and corn mazes – which I had accidentally lost. I was hoping beyond hope I'd just shoved it in another file and not actually misplaced it for good.

When my gaze rested on the television that was perched on the countertop, I realized Edith was talking about a character from her soap opera.

"He's the mobster, right?"

Edith nodded. She'd become distracted by the television again. "In my day, young lady, you didn't worship mobsters and treat them like heroes. In my day, the true heroes were the soldiers risking their lives for our country ... and professional baseball players."

I internally snickered. Edith always did have a soft spot for professional athletes. Baseball and golf, that is, never basketball and football.

"If you don't like him, why are you watching?"

Edith seemed to consider the question seriously for a second. I found it entertaining that she was giving a query about fictional characters on a daytime soap as much thought as she would one about the history of women's suffrage. I didn't give my laughter any volume, though.

"I just think the show would be better without mobsters as heroes," she finally said. "It is called *General Hospital*, after all."

"There's a lot of other stuff you could be watching," I suggested. "There are whole channels dedicated to cooking shows – if you're bored, that is."

"Young lady, when you get to be my age, you're always bored," she said. "Why would you think I would want to watch a cooking show? It's not exactly a talent that I can utilize."

This was true.

"Sorry, I didn't mean to offend you."

Despite myself, I found I couldn't stop glancing up at the television, though. "Who is that blond guy?"

Edith smiled to herself at my question. "That's A.J. He came back from the dead a couple of months ago."

"And why is he fighting with that little guy?"

"They share a son."

"Oh, they're gay?" Soaps were getting more and more progressive.

"No. Sonny stole A.J.'s son and raised him as his own."

"Huh. I could have sworn they were gay given the hair gel issues they share."

If Edith got my humor, she didn't let on. Instead, she'd apparently decided to ignore my soap opera commentary. I didn't blame her.

After a few more minutes of shuffling through folders, I found what I was looking for. "I found it," I crowed.

"Good for you, dear," Edith said absentmindedly as she distractedly waved me off. She was fully entranced with the soap again. It was probably because the two men in question were arguing shirtless. It was a little distracting.

I packed the files back up and carefully placed them in their proper positions in the file cabinets and then took the small stack of papers I'd been looking for back out into the empty newsroom. I'm one of only two full-time employees at the paper – and we work different shifts – so we don't overlap all that often.

Hemlock Cove is a small town in northern lower-Michigan. About twenty years ago, seeing the writing on the wall when it came to the town's survival in a flagging economy, the town officials decided to do something drastic. They rebranded the village as a tourist community that appealed to paranormal enthusiasts. I'm not making it up. Honest.

Hemlock Cove was a beautiful small town, after all, but it had no manufacturing base to build an economy on once the local tire factory shut down for good. That left the people in the area with a tough choice: Stay behind and struggle or move on.

Essentially, with the rebranding effort, town officials thought they would be able to sell Hemlock Cove as a vacation destination for the horror movie crowd. A lot of the townspeople voiced their concerns – but their religious objections ended up taking a backseat to the town's survival. It was fake, after all. They convinced themselves it was no different than a movie.

The town is unique, even for Michigan. We had minor access to Lake Michigan and a quaint downtown that was more cobblestone than asphalt. Some of the older Victorian homes in the area were turned into bed and breakfasts while many of the shops were converted into kitschy herbal remedy stores and porcelain unicorn peddlers.

Because of the town's location, we also had a local resort that was thriving – as long as it was during the winter for skiing or the summer for golfing. Luckily, given the location of Hemlock Cove, the fall was also a busy time thanks to the ever-changing color of the expansive forests that swallowed the small community.

In essence, the town had turned itself into a little Salem, Massachusetts – and they did it without burning anyone at the stake. At least to my knowledge, that is.

Enough about the town, though. Let me introduce you to myself. My name is Bay Winchester – and I'm a witch.

After what I just told you, I would wager you think I'm a "witch" to fit in with the town's rebranding.

The truth is, though, I really am a witch. My whole family is full of them. We're not dark witches, with warts on our noses and conical hats on our heads, who ride around on brooms. We're also not good witches who dress in some satin concoction that's akin to Pepto Bismol and bless people with sparkly wands either. No, we're the kind of witches who draw our power from the earth. We don't curse people – unless they really deserve it – and we don't bestow wishes like fairy godmothers. I guess it's fair to say that we're all Earth witches – not wicked witches.

You might ask yourself what it's like to be a real witch in a town that glorifies witches. You would probably think it's great. Well, the truth is, it's not.

Not only does everyone in town know my family is inundated with actual witches – but they also wish they could burn us at the stake. No joke. Okay, maybe it's a slight exaggeration. They don't want to burn us at the stake; they just want to chase us with pitchforks.

It's often said that people fear what they don't understand. The town understood that it had to rebrand itself – and the best way to do it was find a niche and go with it. Sure, they picked a supernatural niche – and it paid off. That didn't mean they were going to embrace the actual witches in the town, though. Fake witches are good, real witches are bad.

That's why, after I graduated from college, I moved down to Detroit to be a 'real' journalist. For a couple of years, I fed off the violence and non-stop action that the city offered. I perfected my craft and embraced the urban atmosphere.

I loved the city – but I often felt my heart being pulled back to my country roots. Then, the economy bottomed out, and I found myself on the unemployment line. I tried to stay in the city as long as I could, but there were no jobs to be had.

So, five years ago, I moved back home and started working at a small weekly with an average circulation of 15,000 readers. Some people might think it's a step down. Me? I just thought of it as a lateral move. There were no exciting murders or ghoulish traffic accidents, but I was home. I felt more settled in the shade of the elm trees that had nurtured me as a child. I didn't think of it as a loss. It wasn't really a win, though, either.

When I was a kid, I was embarrassed by the disdain I felt emanating from the townspeople. I used to think they were just scared of us. And, to an extent, they are. It's more than that, though. The townspeople fear what they don't understand, but they also covet what they can't have. They think we have power – and we do – but it's not the power they would wish for.

What they don't realize, is that sometimes these powers are a curse as much as they are a blessing.

What I'm truly grateful to the city for instilling in me is a thick skin. The townspeople don't bother me anymore. They can't. Now I pretend I don't hear their whispers – and mostly I don't. I take power from their disdain. I have become what they truly fear – empowered.

Of course, I'm also ridiculously co-dependent where family is concerned and often browbeaten into doing something stupid by a well-meaning but meandering relative who doesn't know any better. We're like *Duck Dynasty* – without the millions and the non-stop hunting. Oh, and the rampant sexism, of course.

"Bay," Edith had wandered through the open door into my office. The nameplate on the front door said "editor." The truth is though, in a paper this size, I was an editor, photographer, editorial assistant, and reporter all rolled into one.

"Is your soap over?"

"Yes," Edith replied. "I just wanted to make sure you found everything you were looking for."

Now she cared? "Yes, I found it."

"Is that going to be the main story on the front page this week?" Edith was looking over my shoulder as I compiled the list.

I grimaced as I nodded. Only in a small town can you get away with a roundup of holiday happenings and call it a banner story. Small towns may have their perks, but they have their weaknesses, too. The sad thing is, the town would revolt if I didn't publish the annual list – and I had to keep the advertisers happy.

Edith must have read my mind. "Don't worry. People like these kinds of stories."

"I don't have much of a choice," I admitted ruefully. "I can't manufacture news, and other than Nell Towers' new baby, absolutely nothing of note happened in Hemlock Cove this week."

"Well, a list of haunted houses and mazes is just what everyone needs to get them into the spirit," Edith said cheerfully. "People love that sort of stuff."

"They do," I nodded.

Edith bit her lower lip as she thought about the statement she had just uttered. "Do you like that stuff?"

"What stuff?"

"Haunted houses and corn mazes?"

"As long as they're done tastefully," I admitted.

"Meaning?"

"Meaning, I don't like it when it's overly gory – or when they use chainsaws. I hate it when they use chainsaws. They freak me out – even though I know they can't really hurt me."

Edith looked horrified.

"Chainsaws? Why would they use chainsaws?"

"You know, to dismember people."

Edith had turned as white a sheet – which was an impressive feat.

"And they let children go to these?"

"I don't think all parents take their children to them," I cautioned.

"Just the bad ones?"

"Just the more adventurous ones," I clarified.

"Well, I think it's downright ghastly," Edith announced. "Making fun of death is not funny." Edith started to flounce out of the room and then stopped. "I should know," she added as she floated through the wall. "It's no fun being a ghost."

I didn't have the heart to tell her that I doubted she had much fun when she was alive, either.

TWO

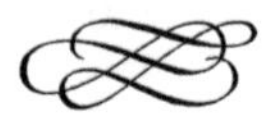

I didn't stick around The Whistler for too long after Edith's outburst. I was used to her histrionics. There's nothing worse than a high-strung ghost.

I had met Edith when I started working at The Whistler. You might think meeting a ghost would be traumatizing. It really isn't. Ghosts are just like people, really. You have good ones and you have bad ones.

I'd been able to see ghosts for as long as I can remember – so it didn't seem odd to me. As a child, I would hold entire conversations with them out in the yard – never realizing I was the only one who could see them. It made me the weird kid in class – I was likened to the strange girl who sat in the back corner eating her hair – but at home it was a coveted "gift."

The witches in my family embrace the weird – and I was definitely weird. Still, in the grand scheme of things, we were pretty harmless. Okay, sometimes we get a little rambunctious – and the older generation of the Winchester witches does get a perverse pleasure from scaring people – but in general we're pretty normal. I just happen to be able to talk to ghosts. The technical term is post-cognitive – but I don't really think in technical terms. I just have the ability to see more people – or what used to be people – than everyone else.

As I wandered down Main Street in downtown Hemlock Cove, I breathed in the crisp autumn air and exhaled slowly. I always needed to cleanse my aura a bit after being with Edith. If you're not careful, a ghost can actually darken your aura. Not on purpose, of course. Edith isn't a bad ghost. She's just wrapped a little tight. When she died in the 1960s, she had been the relationship columnist at the newspaper. Kind of like Ann Landers. Except, for Edith, all of her advice essentially told women that sex was the work of the devil and it was only good for procreation. She'd been a ghost for almost fifty years – and even though the times had changed, Edith really had not. She looked at my short skirt (anything above the knee is unacceptable) and calf-high leather boots as a call to sin. Since I was the only one who could see her, though, she had to put up with me if she wanted to talk to anyone. And Edith? She loved to talk. She didn't even care what subject – just as long as she could register her complaints about the world today.

Hemlock Cove is a small town that looks like it has been untouched by time. That's deliberate. When the town went the tourist route, the town leaders took out the lone traffic light and tried to hide any hints of modern technology. That doesn't mean the denizens don't have laptops – and iPads and iPods – but we just don't flaunt them. We try to keep the town looking antiquated – for lack of a better word. I actually like the feeling of the town – even if many of the townspeople cross the street when they see me coming.

The foibles of the Winchester women are well known in Hemlock Cove. The town leaders would never admit that we were the inspiration to turning Hemlock Cove into a "witch" town. We were, though. Most people would prefer the town didn't have actual witches. In other words, Hemlock Cove treats us like trash. It bothered me to the point of distraction as a child, but I'm used to it now. I still don't like it, but I'm better equipped to handle it.

The streets of Hemlock Cove are littered with specialty stores. Mrs. Gunderson – one of the few women in town who embraces my family and doesn't shun it – runs a small bakery. Mrs. Little, the town's self-appointed moral compass, runs a small pewter store that has a scary amount of unicorns in it. Mr. Wharton, a kind old man who has a crush on my Aunt Marnie, owns a small hardware store that boasts old-fashioned reeves and scythes in the front window – even though he sells the normal nails and hammers you would expect inside.

The town is really an entity of its own – and I love it.

I made my way to the corner of Cauldron Court (yes, all the streets have ridiculously cheesy names) and found myself outside Hypnotic. Hypnotic is brightly painted – purple with yellow trim – and has a low-hanging eave that is decorated with a variety of different hanging vines (which were now starting to wither in the autumn weather). The hand-painted window promised Tarot readings, the biggest selection of herbs in town and a variety of power crystals for the practicing Wicca. There was also a handmade wooden sign that boasted, "If you want to curse someone, we can help." I smiled to myself. That was new.

When I entered Hypnotic, I heard the familiar clang of the wind chimes hanging by the front door and felt a sense of calm settle over me. I was comfortable in this environment. It was as much of a home as my actual home was.

"Welcome to Hypnotic, how may we assist you?"

I looked up and smiled as I saw my cousin, Clove, enter the main part of the store from the back room – which was set apart by some colorful green curtains.

"Oh, it's just you," Clove sighed.

"Good to see you, too."

"Sorry, I'm just cutting herbs in the back. If I knew it was you I wouldn't have stopped what I was doing. I don't want to forget what I'm doing. It would be a disaster if I mixed up the Agaric and Ague Root."

Since Agaric was for fertility and Ague Root was for protection, she definitely had a point.

Clove and I look nothing alike. While I'm fair and blonde, Clove has olive skin and dark black hair. She's also a whole half a foot shorter than me. While I'm not tall at 5'6", Clove is downright tiny at 4'11". She was dressed in an ankle-length skirt – which had sparkly flowers all over it – and a simple black tank top. She looked the part of a witch effortlessly. Since she really *was* a witch, though, I wasn't that impressed with her clothing choices.

"Cool skirt."

"Mom made it," she said simply. Clove's mother was my Aunt Marnie. She ran a bed and breakfast with my own mother, Winnie, and their other sister, Twila. They were all a lot more adept than we were when it came to sewing – and cooking – and meddling in everyone's lives.

I threw myself on the comfortable couch in the center of the store. "How's business?"

Despite the herbs in the backroom, Clove joined me on the couch. She could be easily distracted. I had a feeling she was looking for any excuse to get out of work – like always.

"Pretty good," Clove answered. "This time of year is our bread and butter."

"People like to be scared," I said.

"We aim to please," Clove said brightly.

"Speaking of which, I like the new sign."

Clove smiled mischievously. When she smiles, she has a dimple in her left cheek that comes out to play. Her brown eyes sparkled as they turned to the window sign briefly. "That was my idea."

"I figured."

"Not everyone thinks it's a good idea."

I pondered it for a second and then shrugged. "As long as you're not really cursing people, I don't see what the problem is. I think it's a good idea. It will bring people in – even if it's just out of curiosity."

"That's what I said but . . . ."

"Don't encourage her!"

I shifted my gaze up to the curtains that covered the backroom again and smiled when I saw my other cousin Thistle step from behind them. While Clove and I looked nothing alike, Thistle was a whole other thing entirely. She was taller than Clove but shorter than me. We had a lot of the same facial features, but her hair was cropped short to her head – and dyed bright blue today. When I saw her yesterday it had been red.

"New color?"

"It matches my mood," she said bitterly.

"What's wrong with you?"

Thistle stomped around from behind the counter. She was dressed in a pale blue sparkly halter-top that showed off the bevy of tattoos that scattered across her chest and shoulders. I was particularly fond of the blue dahlia on her chest. It just matched her personality for some reason. She was wearing skin-tight ripped jeans, though. She shunned skirts – and only wore them for special events at the store.

"What do you think is wrong with me?" Much like her mother, Twila, Thistle was prone to exaggerated outbursts. I was used to them. Instead of finding her grim demeanor intimidating, I found it endearing.

I noticed that Clove was steadfastly studying her fingernails – which she had painted black. Clove and Thistle are as close as sisters – which means they fight like cats and dogs.

"You don't like Clove's sign, I'm guessing," I said. I was used to their little spats.

"What's to like about it? It makes people think we're evil."

"No, it doesn't," I protested. "Tourists will just think it's funny. It will draw people into the store. And the town? Half of them already think we're evil anyway. The other half isn't going to be swayed by a sign."

Clove smirked triumphantly at Thistle. Thistle shot her the finger. Ah, our maturity knows no bounds. "You always take her side," she grumbled.

"That's not true. I just don't happen to think it's a big deal."

"The townspeople are going to think we're doing horrible things."

"They already think that," Clove supplied.

Thistle threw herself dramatically in the chair across from us and leveled a dark glare on Clove. "We don't have to encourage that type of thinking."

"Since when? You purposely mess with them all the time."

"I do not!"

"You do, too."

"Whatever."

I found it suspicious that Clove had been mostly silent during the argument. We were all equally close to one another – but since Clove and Thistle worked together, she usually got off on arguing with her. She knew a secret.

"What aren't you telling me?"

Thistle quickly averted her gaze. We're masterful liars when dealing with strangers. When dealing with each other, though? We suck.

"You're hiding something." I can smell a story a mile away.

"Why do you say that?" Thistle made an effort to meet my gaze, but it was a weak effort.

"Answering a question with a question is a sure sign of guilt," I offered.

Thistle met my gaze solidly. "I'm not hiding anything."

Clove finally opened her mouth. "She doesn't want Marcus to think we're evil."

"Who's Marcus?" I asked curiously, grabbing a wrapped candy from the end table.

"He's no one," Thistle mumbled.

"He just bought the livery," Clove said slyly. She really is evil when she wants to be.

"The livery? You mean the horse barn?"

"It's not just a horse barn," Thistle barked.

Ah, I knew where this was going now. "People go there to rent horses to ride around on the trails. It's a horse barn. Is Marcus that good-looking blond I saw working there the other day?"

"He's Mr. Richmond's nephew," Clove was clearly relishing doling out information now. "We met him the other day when we were buying feed for the horses out at the inn."

"So, Marcus bought the place from his uncle?" I couldn't help it. I liked watching Thistle squirm, too. She was usually so sure of herself; I couldn't help but find the sudden reddening of her cheeks funny.

"Yeah," Clove said devilishly. "When we went into the barn to pick up the feed we ran into him – and he didn't have a shirt on."

"Impressive sight?"

"You have no idea," Clove giggled. "He looks like one of those guys on the fliers for the gym in Traverse City."

"He looks gay?"

Clove snorted. "He's definitely not gay. He about fell over himself when he saw Thistle."

"He was very professional!" Thistle raged suddenly.

I bit my inner cheek to keep from laughing out loud. "Did he ask you out?"

Thistle started picking at her frayed jeans distractedly. "No."

"Why not?"

Thistle shrugged.

"I think he's shy," Clove answered for her. "Of course, Thistle was so flustered she practically dragged me out of the store before he could really talk to us anyway. She didn't give him a chance."

"You think you know everything," Thistle said malevolently.

"He was definitely interested," Clove said.

"How do you know? Did you read his mind?" In certain circumstances, Clove can actually hear what people are thinking. That's her "gift." It doesn't always work, but it is pretty accurate when it does.

"Let's just say that the first thing he thought about was what she would look like naked."

I giggled despite myself. "What was Thistle's reaction?"

"Pretty much the same as his. You could actually feel the temperature rise in the room. I was afraid all that hay would suddenly catch on fire."

"You're making that up!" Thistle argued vehemently. "You can't read my mind."

This was true. No matter how hard she tried, Clove could never read the thoughts of other witches. I turned to her curiously. "How do you know what she was thinking?"

"You don't need to be a mind reader to recognize the smell of sex in a room," she snickered.

This is true.

Thistle looked uncomfortable. She kept shifting in her chair. I realized I hadn't seen her this interested in someone in a really long time. She was more the 'love them and leave them' type. I suddenly felt sympathy for her.

"You could ask him out."

"Maybe," she said noncommittally.

"You have a reason to go back. We always need feed. I think the aunts are using it for more than feeding the horses."

"They're probably using it for spells," Clove agreed. "There's no way four horses use as much food as they order."

"Speaking of which, we have family dinner tonight," I remembered.

Thistle and Clove groaned in unison. I felt their pain. We all loved our mothers. We all loved our aunts. We all really loved our Great Aunt Tillie – even though we often wondered if she hadn't gone completely round the bend in recent years. Family dinners, though, were more work than anything else. The women in my family were witches also – obviously – but they were also spastic at times. Much like Clove, Thistle and I, they were ridiculously close. It didn't help that they ran the bed and breakfast together – and were constantly on each other's nerves – and at each other's throats.

"I wonder what they'll be fighting about tonight," Clove wondered aloud.

"The same thing they always argue about. Who is the best cook, who is the best gardener, who is the smartest …?"

I smiled to myself as I pictured the scene that was sure to unfold this evening: Utter chaos.

"We could say we're too busy to go?" Even as I uttered the words I knew how ridiculous they were.

"Yeah, they'll believe that. It's a small town. They know we're not too busy," Thistle said.

"I like family dinner sometimes," Clove admitted.

"I do, too," I said hastily. "I'm just always so tired from the arguing afterward."

"It is exhausting."

Thistle fixed a no-nonsense gaze on both of us. "There will be no Marcus talk tonight," she said. It was a statement, not a plea.

"Of course not," I agreed. It was one thing for the three of us to rag on one another. It was quite another thing for the aunts to do it. They would be down at the livery casting love spells before dessert hit the table if they had even an inkling anything was up. It had become the standard between the three of us: No lies for the younger crowd, but nothing *but* lies for the older crowd. These are wonderful women – don't get me wrong – but they are the four biggest busybodies you have ever met. They never met a life issue they didn't want to weigh in on. Or a romantic interest they didn't want to horn in on.

"What time are you going up to The Overlook?" Thistle asked me.

"I still can't believe they renamed it that after the renovation," Clove muttered.

"We tried to tell them," I said. "We told them that was the name of the hotel in *The Shining*, but that only made them more resolute. We told them to keep the old name, but you can't argue with them when they make up their minds."

"They think it will make tourists want to stay there."

"It's worked so far," I admitted.

"Yeah," Thistle blew out a breath "It's still creepy. I expect to see ghosts around every turn, like a self-fulfilling prophecy." She turned to me expectantly. "You've never seen a ghost there have you?"

"No," I shook my head. "That's been our family home since it was built in the 1600s. Witches don't usually become ghosts."

"I didn't know that," Clove said. "Why is that?"

"I don't know either. I've just never met a witch who became a ghost and didn't move on."

"It's probably because witches usually finish their business before they die," I said.

"In the case of our family, it's usually because witches finish everyone else's business, too," Thistle snickered.

I laughed pleasantly on the outside– but on the inside I shuddered. Wasn't that the truth?

THREE

I gossiped with Clove and Thistle for another half an hour before I made my way back to The Whistler. I had to file the holiday happenings roundup before dinner. It wasn't exactly taxing work, but given the makeup of the town, it was a lot of work. Every business had some sort of event happening over the next couple of weeks and if I missed one, then I would be accused of purposely omitting it.

It took me about two hours to do the write-up and send it to the layout people via email. The edition would be printed tomorrow, so I had gotten the article in just under the wire. I was happy to see that Edith had apparently forgotten her discomfort with the populace's fixation on gruesome deaths and was back to being her usual snippy self.

Thankfully, I was alone in the office this afternoon so I didn't have to explain to anyone why I was talking to thin air. Usually, I just told the handful of part-time workers who filtered through the newsroom that I was talking to myself and planning the latest edition of the newspaper. I'm not sure – given the stories that flew around the town regarding my family – if they believed me. I really didn't care, though.

I was beyond worrying what other people thought about me. The city had taught me that.

When I was sure everything was set – and I'd marked the mockups accordingly and left them on the paginator's desk – I left the office. I had about a half an hour before dinner and if I wanted to make it to The Overlook in time, I would have to hurry. Lateness was frowned upon in the Winchester house. So was swearing, burnt dessert, and sarcasm, quite frankly.

I had walked to work that day. It was only a mile and I wanted to enjoy the fall colors and warm weather while I still could. When the snow hit, walking wouldn't be an option. The town was beautiful in the winter, with all the twinkling lights and decorated Christmas trees, but even when plowed, the roads were largely impassable.

The Overlook is the biggest house in the county. It's an old Victorian that the Winchester family built in the early 1900s. Actually, to be fair, it started out as a ramshackle shack long before that, only taking on a life of its own as the family grew. It has grown throughout the years, with each generation adding something new to the house. Now it boasts twenty guest rooms, a four-bedroom core where the family resides, a huge greenhouse and adjacent stables. There's also a large guesthouse on the premises where Clove, Thistle, and I reside together. It's not technically part of The Overlook – but that doesn't stop my mom and aunts from coming and going from the guesthouse whenever they see fit. We can't really complain, either, since we live there rent-free. The lack of privacy is disturbing, though. Thankfully, the aunts only make their presence known about once a week – just long enough to comment on our housekeeping skills.

When I got to The Overlook, I stopped at the guesthouse long enough to drop off my purse. Thistle and Clove weren't there, so I figured they had already made their way up to the main house without me.

When I got to the main house, I let myself in through the back door. A few months ago, the house had undergone a massive renovation to make the core of the house – where my family resided – more separate from the rest of the building. After the renovation, the aunts decided that they needed to rename the property. Hence, they now live in The Overlook.

The family living quarters are located at the back of the house and include four bedrooms, a living room, a library and a warm den where my mom and aunts take their evening tea – and gossip sessions. The family living quarters are attached to the rest of the inn via a stairwell and through the large kitchen.

When I entered the house I couldn't help but smile when the tantalizing smell of stuffed cabbage hit my nostrils. My favorite. My family may be out there – but there are no better cooks in the county. If you hear them talk, there are no better cooks in the world. They might be right. I never told them that, though. I didn't want to encourage them.

I could hear the steady stream of chatter from the adjacent kitchen. Everyone must be in there, I figured.

"You're late," my mom admonished me when I entered the warm room.

I looked up at the clock on the wall and sighed. "One minute is not late."

"It's not on time."

My mom, like her sisters, is short. She's about five feet, three inches tall and still has the same blonde hair she had when I was a kid. She claims it's natural – but I have my doubts. I never voice those doubts out loud, though. I know exactly how that conversation would go.

Clove was sitting on the counter munching on a cookie. Her mother, Marnie, was standing on the floor in front of her with her hands on her hips and glaring at her disdainfully. "Who taught you to sit on the counter? That's what heathens do."

Clove sighed dramatically and hopped off the counter. Standing next to her mother, the resemblance was startling. Marnie was the same height as her daughter – and she had the same expansive bust. Like my mom, her hair seemed untouched by time. I knew for a fact she dyed her hair, though. I'd seen the empty dark dye bottles in the trash. Marnie owned her color jobs, though.

My Aunt Twila was stirring something on the stove as she talked to Thistle. "Blue dear? I don't think it's flattering to your coloring."

I could see Thistle bristle at the comment. She was fighting the urge to argue with her mother. She knew it was a fruitless endeavor. We all knew that. That didn't mean we didn't engage in fruitless endeavors from time-to-time – or from minute-to-minute, for that matter.

I stifled a smile. My Aunt Twila's hair had always come out of a bottle for as long as I had known her. A bright red Ronald McDonald bottle. She had the same coloring as my mother and I had – that Thistle had naturally – but she never embraced it. She liked to be different. Her hair, much like Thistle's, was cropped short. Marnie and my mom had chosen to keep their hair longer – and they often swept it up in messy buns to keep it under control. Twila never had that problem.

"I like the color," Thistle argued.

"The color is fine in a blouse – not on you though, it washes you out – but it's not okay for hair. Hair should be natural."

"Your hair isn't natural."

"My hair is natural for *me*."

"Maybe this is my natural color."

Twila regarded her daughter contemplatively for a second. "No, dear, it's not."

I pulled Thistle away from her mother before she could say the words that were dying to come out of her mouth. I didn't want the yelling to start until *after* I had gotten the stuffed cabbage in my stomach to sustain me.

"How was work today?" My mom asked.

"Fine. Same old, same old."

"And how is Edith?"

"The same."

"So she's still a frigid old biddy?"

Every head in the room turned as my Great Aunt Tillie entered the room. If Marnie and Clove were tiny, Aunt Tillie was miniscule. She was four feet, eight inches of raw power – and general disdain for everyone. She reminded me of a hobbit – without the hairy feet. Actually, I don't ever remember seeing her feet – so it was entirely possible they were hairy. She had dark hair and olive skin like Marnie and Clove – while her sister, our grandmother, had been blonde and fair before she died a few years ago. She had long ago given up the battle to keep her dark hair intact, though. She'd embraced the gray a long time ago. I didn't actually remember her without the gray hair. I had seen pictures, though.

"She's not a frigid old biddy," I argued. "She's just stuck in a time long since passed." Like most of the town, I thought.

"You forget, I knew Edith when she was alive," Aunt Tillie pointed a gnarled finger in my direction. "I know *who* she was – *what* she was."

"And what was she?"

"She was a nasty woman who tried to ruin my life."

I sighed heavily. *Here we go.*

"She tried to steal your Uncle Calvin from me, you know?"

My Uncle Calvin had died thirty years ago and my Aunt Tillie still acted like he was going to come through the door at any time. He had died before I was born, but from all the stories I had heard, he was a wonderful man. How he put up with Aunt Tillie was a mystery to us all. I loved the woman, but she was mean – and she could hold a grudge like nobody's business.

"Well, I'm not sure I believe that," I started to argue with Aunt Tillie. We were like oil and vinegar. All of our interactions always evolved into an argument – and sometimes a slap fight.

"Are you calling me a liar?"

"No. I'm just saying that maybe you are exaggerating."

"I don't exaggerate."

Thistle and Clove snorted. Aunt Tillie turned on them with speed that belied her eighty-five years. Thistle and Clove immediately stifled their reactions. They were more scared of Aunt Tillie than anything else – including wild animal attacks and mismatched socks. They were in self-preservation mode. Aunt Tillie was more ferocious when cornered than any animal ever could be.

"She used to bring your Uncle Calvin cookies all the time," Aunt Tillie had turned back to me.

"Was she naked when she brought him the cookies?"

Aunt Tillie looked scandalized. "Of course not."

"Than why do you think she was trying to steal Uncle Calvin?"

"Why else would she make him cookies?"

"Maybe because she knew you couldn't cook." I hadn't meant to actually say it out loud, but I did. The truth was, while my mom and aunts were accomplished cooks – kitchen witches each and every one of them, like my grandmother – Aunt Tillie was known as something of a disaster in the kitchen. She couldn't boil water – and when she tried, she burned it.

"I can too cook," she growled. "I just choose not to. I'm an old lady. I shouldn't have to cook."

The truth is, Aunt Tillie is only old when she doesn't want to do something. When she wants to do something dangerous – and we remind her of her age – she tells us she's old, not dead.

"Fine, she was after Uncle Calvin. It obviously didn't work."

"Not for lack of trying," she huffed. "The only thing that stopped her was the fact that she was murdered."

"You didn't do it, did you?" I asked suspiciously.

"Of course not."

"Than how do you know she was murdered? I thought she was found slumped over her desk and everyone thought she had a heart attack?"

"I never believed that," Aunt Tillie sniffed. "And that was before I knew she was a ghost."

Aunt Tillie was post-cognitive, too. She could see ghosts and talk to them. "Did you ever ask her about it?"

"Of course not. Why would I want to help the woman who tried to steal my husband?"

"I don't know, to do the right thing?"

"Have *you* ever asked her?" My mom was trying to ease the conversation before Aunt Tillie hexed me with some horrible curse. Don't scoff. She's done it before. When I was a teenager, she gave me a big zit on the end of my nose right before the prom – I swear it was her. When I was in college, she once made it so I could only turn to my left for an entire week. It made getting to classes a nightmare – and a long ordeal – on a daily basis.

"I have, but she doesn't remember anything," I finally answered my mom. I couldn't help myself from arguing with Aunt Tillie – but I also didn't want to try and cover a story when I could only make left turns. People would think I was stranger than I already was.

"Well, you should help her find out so she can move on," my mom clucked.

"I offered," I admitted. "I don't think she wants to move on. I think she's generally happy as she is."

"She's not happy, she's miserable," Aunt Tillie admonished me.

"Maybe she's happy being miserable? I know some people like that," I said pointedly.

Marnie hurriedly ushered everyone into the dining room. I think she was trying to head off a big showdown between Aunt Tillie and myself.

Clove, Thistle and I helped carry dishes into the dining room – where a handful of inn denizens were milling about and waiting for the meal. One rule that held fast in The Overlook was that dinner was served at 7 p.m. sharp – and everyone ate together. If you wanted food before or after that, you were just fresh out of luck. Despite that, the legend of the Winchester women and their cooking was enough to keep the inn at capacity most of the time. The curiosity factor is enough to draw in a lot of people.

After everyone had taken their seats – Thistle, Clove, and I always sat together as a show of unity for each other– everyone began passing the dishes around the table. The guests were chatting away happily. They all seemed enthralled with Hemlock Cove – and they couldn't stop talking about the magic that abounded in the small hamlet. They also couldn't stop raving about the food – which always made my mom and aunts happy.

Occasionally, they would ask questions. We had been trained to answer them politely – and honestly.

"Did you ever have any witch burnings here?" The woman who asked looked to be about twenty-five or so. She was here on her honeymoon. I could tell she just liked the *thought* of horror. She didn't really want to *hear* about any horror.

"Not to my knowledge," I answered.

She looked a little disappointed at my answer.

"Of course, the records from back in the day were destroyed in a fire in the early 1900s, so there's really no way for us to know for sure."

My mom beamed at my answer. The woman nodded thoughtfully. "They might not have written it down if they did it."

"They might not," Clove said with a smile. "You should never write down your misdeeds." She'd learned that from personal experience when Aunt Marnie read her diary when she was a teenager. She'd been grounded for a month over the dalliance under the bleachers with the quarterback.

"That's for sure," Aunt Tillie muttered as she sipped from a glass of wine. I frowned when I saw her doing it.

"I thought the doctor said you weren't supposed to drink anymore?"

"Red wine is good for you," Aunt Tillie argued.

"Yes, but the doctor said one glass a day and I know you've had more than one glass."

Aunt Tillie glowered at me. "You mind your own business. All you reporters, you're so nosy."

I thought that was rich coming from any woman in this family, but one look at my mother's frown told me that pointing that out would be a mistake. Instead, I turned back to the inquisitive woman.

"What are your plans while you're in town?" I feigned interest – if only to keep my mother off my back.

The woman – I learned her name was Emily – seemed to glow under my attention. "We're going to go out to a corn maze tomorrow."

"The one at Harrow's Bluff?"

"I think that's where it is. It's new."

"I'm going out there tomorrow to do a story on it."

"Maybe I'll see you there?"

I smiled brightly at the suggestion, but inside I was hoping I would be able to avoid her. Tourists can be a pain.

Emily had glommed on to me, though. She monopolized the conversation for the duration of dinner. I continued to answer her questions throughout the meal – and then quietly excused myself to the kitchen when there was finally a break in the conversation. I was surprised to find Aunt Tillie there. I hadn't noticed her leave the table, which meant she had done it sneakily – and she was chopping up something on the cutting board.

"What are you doing?" I asked suspiciously.

"Nothing."

"It doesn't look like nothing." She had pushed her stool up to the counter so she could reach it easily. She obviously meant business.

"I'm just chopping herbs."

I tried to peer over her shoulder, but she actively tried to block my gaze. That only made me more suspicious. When I finally got a glimpse of what she was doing I grabbed her wrist.

"That's belladonna," I admonished her.

"So?"

"What are you planning on doing with that?"

"I'm putting together a sleeping potion. I've been having trouble sleeping."

I'd once seen Aunt Tillie fall asleep at a parade, so I knew she was lying. "What are you mixing up?"

"I told you," Aunt Tillie wrenched her wrist free from me. "I'm making a sleeping potion."

"For who?"

"None of your business."

"I'm telling mom," I warned her.

"Go ahead tattletale. You always were a bothersome little pain in the ass."

"You could hurt someone with that if you give them too much."

"I never use too much."

"Just tell me who you're planning on drugging."

"It doesn't matter." Aunt Tillie seemed to be growing in height as her anger at my interference blossomed.

"It matters to me."

"Why?"

"Maybe I don't want to see you spend your final years in jail?" Just locked in a home where she couldn't do any real damage.

"Since when? You've never liked me."

"That's not true. I love you. You're just always up to something." That was also the truth.

"I am not always up to something. That would be you and your two cousins. The three of you were nothing but trouble since the moment you could walk. Before then, you were cute. After that, though? You were always into everything."

"That's what little kids do." I realized she was trying to distract me. She was good at that. "Who is the potion for?"

Aunt Tillie let loose with a long-suffering sigh. "I'm just going to put a little in the tea."

"What tea? Your tea? Mom's tea?"

"Everyone's tea," she finally admitted.

"Why?" I narrowed my eyes as I regarded her.

"So they'll go to bed early."

"Why do you want them to go to bed early?"

"So I can get some peace and quiet." She was lying. She had something else in mind. I just couldn't figure out what it was.

Aunt Twila had entered the kitchen and was regarding us curiously. "What are you two doing?"

"She's mincing up belladonna to put in the tea." I don't like being a tattletale, but I also don't want Aunt Tillie poisoning the guests. She was unpredictable – and that made her dangerous.

Twila wandered over cautiously. "Why?" She had grown up with Aunt Tillie so she was understandably nervous around her when she was plotting something. She knew the extent of the damage Aunt Tillie could wreak when she set her mind to it – which was fairly often.

Aunt Tillie threw up her hands in defeat. "Can't a body have any privacy in this place?" She clamored down from the stool, cast a disdainful look in my direction – which promised retribution at a later date – and then flounced back out to the dining room, leaving the mess for us to clean up.

Twila started absentmindedly brushing all of the herbs into the open garbage can on the floor. "I'm worried she's starting to lose her mind."

"Starting?"

"That woman is our family," Twila reminded me. She always was the kindest of her three sisters – which meant she was also the most easily manipulated.

"That doesn't mean she's not crazy."

Twila regarded the belladonna remains ruefully. "No. She's definitely crazy. She's still family, though, and in this family we don't chastise the crazy, we embrace them and love them for their eccentricities."

Truer words were never spoken.

FOUR

With the joys of another family dinner behind us, Thistle, Clove, and I made our way across the property toward the guesthouse. I had told them about Aunt Tillie's weird behavior in the kitchen – but they didn't seem as worried as I was.

"She was just looking for attention," Clove protested.

"Yeah, but her ways of seeking attention could leave a body count in her wake."

"She wouldn't do that again," Clove said.

"Again? What again?"

Clove bit her lower lip. I could tell she had let something slip she hadn't planned to. "We were told not to tell you."

"By who?" I asked suspiciously.

"Everyone," Clove admitted.

"What did she do?" I swung around to ask Thistle – but she was caught in her own little world and holding a conversation with herself.

"Blue washes me out? Blue washes me out? This from a woman who is trying to make Ronald McDonald's color palette look good. I don't know why I even listen to her. She drives me crazy. Crazy! She does it on purpose, too. I don't know why I listen to her! She named me after a remedy for people who drink too much. You were named Bay. Clove was another herb. So she wanted to follow the pack. So what did she do? She looked at a bottle of vitamins – not even an herb really. Okay, it's kind of an herb – and read milk thistle on it – and thought Thistle was a great name? So how she thinks she can say that my hair looks bad is beyond me."

Yeah, there was no talking to Thistle when she got like this. I swung back to Clove expectantly. "What did she do?"

Clove took a deep breath as she regarded me. "I'm going to tell you, but you can't, you know, pull a 'you'?"

Pull a 'me'? What could that possibly mean? "I promise. I just want to know what she did."

"It happened like eight years ago – when you were in Detroit – so it's really not a big deal," Clove cautioned. She was stalling.

"What did she do?"

"It really wasn't a big deal when all the dust settled," Clove was still hedging telling me. It was driving me crazy.

"I'm going to wrestle you down and make you eat dirt if you don't tell me," I threatened.

"That hasn't worked since I was ten," Clove argued.

"That's not true," Thistle finally piped in. "It worked last year when you borrowed her favorite boots and then lost one – which I still don't understand how that happened – and then you refused to replace them because you won't buy leather products."

Clove glared at Thistle. "Well, other than that time. You just had to bring that up, didn't you?" She hissed.

Like I had forgotten about the boots.

"I didn't mean to bring up the boots," Thistle said sincerely – although I had my doubts that she was speaking the truth. "I just wanted to point out that whenever she makes you eat dirt, you fold like a bad gambler."

"Well, at least my hair doesn't wash me out," Clove shot back.

"It doesn't wash me out! My mom is crazy!"

"I like your hair," I admitted. What? I like the color blue. I like purple better. I wonder how she would look with purple hair. Wait. I was letting them distract me. "Back to the subject, though. What did Aunt Tillie do when I was in Detroit that everyone thinks is too bad for me to know about?"

Clove averted her gaze again. She still wasn't sure she wanted to tell me.

"Oh, good grief, it's really not a big deal," Thistle finally said. The more they said it wasn't a big deal, the more I was convinced it was a huge deal.

"Then tell me what it is," I challenged her.

"She poisoned everyone at the Senior Center."

Never what you expect. "And how did she do that?"

"She mixed up some concoction and put it in the coffee."

"Why would she do that?"

"She was convinced that they were cheating at euchre and she wanted to teach them a lesson," Thistle answered simply.

"All of them?"

"She was convinced they were all in on an elaborate plan to make sure she always lost at euchre when she was there," Thistle said.

"Well, that seems plausible – or not," I sighed. "And she killed people?"

"She didn't kill people," Clove interjected. "Most of the people were fine. There were only like twelve who had to go to the hospital – and most of them were out within a few days."

"And she wasn't arrested for this?"

"The chief let it slide when your mom asked him to," Clove admitted.

The chief had always had a crush on my mom. Actually, I think he had a crush on Marnie and Twila, too. It all depended on who brought him baked goods that week. "Is that why they still take him cookies and pie every week?"

"Probably."

"Does everyone in town know she did that?"

"I don't think they know," Thistle said. "I think they just suspect. They can't prove anything."

"Well, great, that makes it all better."

"Don't be sarcastic," Thistle chastised me. "People hardly remember it anymore, especially since she held the autumnal equinox celebration in the buff last year. That hurt a lot more people than the belladonna incident did."

I shuddered involuntarily. Yeah, I was one of those people.

The next day, I was still irritated by the fact that my whole family had conspired to keep a secret from me. Thistle and Clove could tell I was bothered when they handed me my usual cup of coffee in the morning.

"Just let it go," Thistle warned me. "You're not going to get anywhere if you confront everyone and pull a ... well, a 'you.'"

Why does everyone keep saying that?

Instead of going to the office, I decided to go straight to the new corn maze on the north side of town at Harrow Bluff. It was opening today and it would be one of the front-page stories in next week's edition of The Whistler. It's a small town. Sue me. A new corn maze is the height of sophistication and interest in Hemlock Cove.

Since it was a corn maze, I dressed in comfortable jeans and a simple top. That's the one good thing about working in a small town – and being the editor – you can get away with dressing any way you want to.

It took me about ten minutes to get out to the corn maze – and I was surprised to see that there was already a crowd milling about. Only in Hemlock Cove can a ribbon cutting for a corn maze draw half the town.

I parked next to the rest of the assembled vehicles, grabbed a notebook from the glove compartment, and exited my car.

I ran into several people I knew – most weren't openly hostile to me – and I pleasantly smiled at them. I reminded myself I didn't care what they thought. Oh, who am I kidding, no one likes being feared – unless you're Stalin or something. I just didn't feel the sudden urge to cry like I did when I was a teenager.

I made my way up to the concession stand and helped myself to a cup of free cider and listened as a couple of townspeople chatted amiably.

"This is just great," one of them said. "I love seeing everyone come out to these types of things."

"It's so great," the other woman enthused.

I saw them both fix their gaze on me. "It's even nice that the press managed to come out and report on something good for a change."

"When do I report on something bad? Nothing bad ever happens here?"

The women didn't answer me. Instead, they shuffled away. I could hear hints of whispers as they left. I could only imagine what they were saying. One of the wicked witches of the Midwest was here and she wasn't to be trusted.

I didn't have long to consider it, though, because my attention was suddenly diverted elsewhere. There were loud, raucous voices emanating from the far side of the corn maze. I couldn't tell who was speaking – but the voices were definitely raised. I saw two elderly women hurry from that end of the corn maze, and they both looked disturbed.

"What's going on?" I asked curiously.

"Hoodlums," one of the women muttered. "Hoodlums."

I wandered around the corner of the maze and was surprised by what I found. There were four men standing there with open beers in their hands. A couple of them were idly leaning against ornate motorcycles. The men themselves weren't easily recognizable – what with all the leather they were clad in. I realized pretty quickly that they looked like some sort of gang from a bad movie.

One of the men looked to be in his mid-fifties – and he was clearly the leader of the little rabble. He was dressed in denim pants, a white T-shirt and a leather jacket that looked to be older than I was. He also had on leather motorcycle chaps over the jeans. He looked like a walking mid-life crisis.

The other men were dressed similarly and I could see that skulls and crossbones were emblazoned across the back of the jackets. This would be normal in a city setting – but I'd never seen anyone dressed like this around Hemlock Cove. The fact that they were all drinking was even more curious. I'm sure there are people who drink at 9 a.m. in town – they just don't do it in a public setting.

What the hell?

The men saw me looking at them and turned to face me curiously. "Can I help you?" The ringleader asked.

He was obviously trying to be intimidating. It didn't work on me. I was doubtful they'd do something to me with the entire town in attendance. "Who are you?"

The ringleader looked me up and down and smiled slyly. "The man of your dreams?"

"You don't look like Chris Hemsworth to me." I always think before I speak. I can't help it. It's a family trait.

"Who is Chris Hemsworth?" One of the sidekicks asked the question, but I didn't turn my attention from the ringleader.

"He's Thor."

I turned to see who had spoken, only to find another leather-clad figure moving toward me. Despite being dressed like his cohorts, he was somehow different. I could tell immediately. He had long black hair, which fell just below his shoulders, and his skin was rich and tan. While his face was sculpted with some very appealing angles, his eyes were his most striking feature. They were ice blue and piercing. I felt a shock pulse through me when my gaze met his. I just couldn't figure out why.

"Who are you guys?"

"Who are you?" The newcomer joined his friends, but his gaze never left my face.

"My name is Bay Winchester. I'm the editor at The Whistler."

"The newspaper?"

I nodded mutely, swallowing hard. I couldn't tear my gaze away from the newcomer. He was only about six-one – but he seemed to suck all the air out of the field with a very large presence.

"Why are you here?"

"To cover the opening of the corn maze," I found my voice, but it sounded alien to my own ears, almost hollow.

"This is news?" The newcomer's eyes crinkled at the corners. He was clearly amused.

"It is in Hemlock Cove."

The newcomer seemed to consider that for a second. Then he extended his hand to me in greeting. "Well, Bay Winchester, I'm Landon."

I shook his hand nervously. I still couldn't figure out why they were here.

Landon proceeded to introduce his friends. I rolled my eyes when he pointed at Diesel and Gunner in turn. I'm betting those weren't their given names. They were probably really known as Norman and Myron. When he got to the ringleader, though, I forced my attention to him. "This is Russ."

I nodded warily at Russ, who was still mentally undressing me with his eyes. "You still haven't told me why you're here," I prodded.

"Just wanted to see what all the hoopla was about," Landon shrugged, accepting a beer from one of his friends and popping the top off it.

I narrowed my eyes when I saw Landon toss the beer cap onto the ground next to him. I stepped forward and picked up the beer cap and tossed it in the garbage can a few feet away. Landon smirked at my frown.

"Sorry," he said simply. "We'll try not to make a mess."

"That would be great," I said sarcastically.

The initial shock – okay, rampant physical attraction – I had originally felt was starting to fade. The only thing I was feeling now was suspicion.

"Where are you from?"

"Around," Landon said evasively.

"Around where?"

"A little bit of everywhere."

"So, you're from nowhere?" I raised my eyebrows confrontationally.

Landon chuckled to himself. "I guess you could say that."

"Well, that's great!"

"Something tells me you don't actually think that's great," Landon smiled winningly.

"Perceptive."

"Maybe we got off on the wrong foot here," Landon started. Russ interrupted him, though.

"Why are you so interested in us?" His question was forceful. I could tell he was used to people quaking in fear at his presence.

"I'm interested in everyone who visits our quiet little town," I lied.

"I don't see you questioning everyone else here," he said pointedly.

"I already know all of them." Well, all the residents, at least. Tourists come and go. There was really no reason to get to know them.

"You want to know me? Is that what you're saying? I'm flattered."

I let my gaze lower to Russ' extended beer gut – gross – and then drew it back up to his eyes. "I'm just curious why you're here."

"We just wanted to see what all the excitement was about," he said.

"And you brought beer?"

"It's a party, isn't it?"

"It's not that kind of party."

"Maybe you wouldn't be so rigid if you had one yourself?" Russ grabbed a beer out of the container at his feet and handed it to me.

I took a step back involuntarily. I didn't want him invading my personal space for some reason. "Thanks. I'm good. It's a bit early for me."

Russ shrugged as he slipped the beer back in the case. "Your loss."

Even though I was still curious about what these guys were doing here, I noticed that the maze was now open and the crowd was starting to filter into it.

Landon noticed my attention drift.

"I have to go," I said finally. "Welcome to Hemlock Cove – whatever it is that you're doing here."

"Have fun in the maze," Landon smiled.

I didn't answer him as I drifted off to the opening of the maze. Mrs. Little was standing at the opening when I got there. She'd been watching us – and she wasn't happy by what she saw.

"Who are they?"

"They didn't really say," I admitted.

"They look unsavory."

"They don't seem to be doing anything," I said noncommittally, even though I agreed with her.

"They're drinking in the morning," Mrs. Little said disapprovingly.

"Keep an eye on them," I urged her.

"Oh, I will." She started moving in their direction purposefully.

I couldn't help but smirk to myself as I pictured the conversation Mrs. Little would have with the men. I hoped they had some knowledge about pewter unicorns. They may think they're scary – but they didn't know scary. All five-foot-two of it was stomping its way toward them, though. They were about to find out.

I tried to put the men out of my mind – all of them – as I made my way into the maze. It really was well constructed, I mused to myself. Instead of just the simple walls of wilting corn, they had set up walls throughout the maze that were constructed of stacked hay bales. It forced visitors to stay on certain paths – and not cut through the corn and risk getting lost. They'd even put lights in all the corners so people could take twilight walks after dark. That was a nice touch. The tourists would love it.

The maze was about a mile long – and there were a lot of turns that took you absolutely nowhere. After about a half an hour, I'd only made it to the center of the maze.

I stopped to snap pictures with my iPhone camera as I took in the morbid tableau they'd set up in the center of the maze. There were a number of grotesque scarecrows – with one even being crucified on a cross in the center. I moved up to it, snapping a few pictures as I went.

When I looked up at the scarecrow, I couldn't help but cringe.

"This thing is very realistic, isn't it?"

I turned to find Emily, the woman from the inn the night before, standing beside me. "It's gross," I admitted.

Emily reached up to touch it and shrank back. "It feels so real."

I turned my attention back to the scarecrow. Something just wasn't right about it. I glanced around at the other scarecrows and frowned. They didn't look anything like this one. This one had a weird Mardi Gras mask affixed to it. One of those ones with the colored eyes and long, beaked noses. The rest had simple bags with holes cut out for fake eyes. You could see the hay poking out beneath them.

Emily was equally transfixed as she regarded the scarecrow on the cross. She reached up and touched the Carhart glove on its hand.

I don't know why I did it – even as I was doing it my mind was telling me to walk away – but I ignored the warning in my brain and reached over to strip the glove off. I was expecting to find it stuffed with straw – like the other scarecrows. Instead, I saw a real human hand – stained with blood – in its place.

For a second, I thought the screaming I was hearing was coming from my own mind. I realized, though, that it was Emily and she'd come to the same conclusion I had.

This wasn't a fake scarecrow. It was a very real body.

FIVE

Emily's screams drew a crowd quickly. Despite her horror fascination the night before, she was quickly dissolving into rampant hysterics. I handed her off to one of the teenage boys working the maze who had come to see what all the fuss was about.

"Take her to the front of the maze and give her some cider to calm her down," I instructed him. "Don't let her leave, though."

As he moved to walk away, I grabbed his wrist. "And call the chief," I said in a low voice. "Get him out here right away."

The boy looked at me questioningly. "Is that a real body?"

"Yes."

"Who is it?"

"I don't know. We can't touch the body. That's for the police to do."

The boy swallowed hard and then determinedly grabbed Emily and dragged her from the center of the maze.

I corralled the other two teenage workers who had come to the scene – despite the fact that I felt like I could pass out at any minute – and instructed them to cordon off the center of the maze. "Don't let them wander in here. They'll ruin the evidence," I instructed.

Both boys listened to me without complaint. I think they were in shock.

Once the boys had moved everyone out of the center of the maze, I remained rooted to the ground. This wasn't the first body I had ever seen. I saw plenty when I was covering the police beat in Detroit. I didn't expect it in Hemlock Cove, though. Even in the rare cases where there was a murder around here – they usually almost always stemmed from domestic disturbances. The bodies never showed up in the middle of a corn maze.

Despite my initial surprise, I tried to get a good look at the body without getting too close. I didn't want to ruin any evidence – although, if I had to guess, this would be a nightmare of a crime scene. People had been traipsing throughout the maze for the past half hour. Excluding suspects wasn't going to be easy – especially for a police force who had absolutely no experience with murders like this.

The body – how anyone could have mistaken it for a scarecrow was beyond me – was hanging limply. As the temperatures started to climb, I saw that flies were starting to buzz around it. Still, given the fact that they were just arriving now, I figured the body couldn't have been here all that long.

"Is that what I think it is?"

I jumped in surprise. I thought I'd been alone with only my thoughts to keep me company. I turned to find Landon had moved up beside me. His gaze was riveted on the grotesque scarecrow.

"What are you doing here? I told them to keep people out until the police arrived." I was a little out of my element here. My conversation skills were taking a monumental hit.

"I just wanted to see if what everyone said was true," Landon was staring at the body grimly.

"It's a body," I said simply. "I think it's a male."

"I think you're right," Landon agreed. "A young man would be my guess."

I slid a gaze suspiciously in his direction. "You didn't do this, did you?"

Landon frowned. "You think I killed him?"

"You guys showed up out of nowhere and now there's a body. It's convenient timing."

"Do I look like a killer?"

I shrugged. "I don't really know you well enough to say. You don't look like you belong here, though."

"Neither do you."

What was that supposed to mean? "I grew up here."

"You didn't always live here, though, did you?"

"No. I lived in Detroit for a few years. How did you know that?"

"Everyone out there is freaking out because they've never seen a body before. You're a little too calm."

I didn't tell him I was fighting not to lose my morning breakfast on the evidence in the area and further contaminate the scene. "I'm not calm. I'm composed. There's a difference. This isn't the first body I've seen, though."

"You get a lot of bodies strung up in corn mazes?"

"That's not what I said," I protested vehemently. "I just said that I've seen other bodies before."

"In Detroit?"

"Yes."

Landon raised a hand and placed it reassuringly on my shoulder. "Well, you're doing a good job of pretending to be in control."

"Someone had to take charge," I argued.

"I get the feeling you have to be in control, no matter what situation you find yourself in."

I wasn't sure, but I thought I'd probably been insulted. I didn't get a chance to find out, though, because I could hear voices coming through the maze. I turned to see Chief Terry making his way through the remnants of the crowd who were still milling about the corridor. "Go out to the front of the maze," he ordered. "My officers have some questions for you."

Chief Terry's gaze met mine as he entered the cleared area where we were standing. "Bay," he greeted me with a nod. I saw his gaze wash over Landon. He didn't speak to him directly, though. Instead, he asked me the question that was clearly banging around in his head. "Who is this?"

"I'm Landon," Landon stepped forward to shake Chief Terry's

hand. Chief Terry, who stood about two inches shorter than Landon – and five inches wider – steadfastly ignored it.

"Who is he?" Chief Terry raised his gray eyebrows as he pointed the question at me, instead of Landon. He was obviously trying to put Landon in his place.

"I don't know," I replied. "They were outside of the maze drinking beer before it opened."

Landon looked like he wanted to say something but then wisely clamped his mouth shut.

"Is it really a body?" Chief Terry asked finally. He hadn't made a move toward the scarecrow.

"Yeah," I said. My mouth was dry and the single word came out as a rasp.

"Do you recognize him?"

"I didn't touch the mask," I said. "I figured you would have a forensic team here to do that."

"A forensic team? This isn't the city."

I hadn't thought of that. Chief Terry had exactly three officers at his command. He didn't have the resources to investigate something like this. "Maybe you should call the state police?" I didn't want to offend him, but I didn't want him to bungle this either. Chief Terry had been the head of the Hemlock Cove Police Department for as long as I could remember. That usually entailed citing underage drinkers, random cow tippers and the occasional drunken driver. I don't think he'd ever seen anything like this before.

"I already did," he said, running a hand through his salt and pepper hair. "They'll be here in a few minutes."

Chief Terry moved over to my side protectively. He was still regarding Landon warily. "Why are you here?" He finally addressed Landon directly.

"I heard the screams," Landon said.

"And you wanted to run to the rescue?"

"Something like that," Landon muttered.

"You don't look like a guy who runs to the rescue of others."

"Meaning?" Landon had placed his hands on his hips and was now facing off against Chief Terry aggressively.

For his part, Chief Terry didn't look intimidated. He moved around me and stood in front of Landon, placing his own hands on his hips and adapting an equally confrontational stance. "Meaning you look more like the type of guy who causes trouble."

"I heard screams and wanted to make sure no one was hurt," Landon said, casting a sideways glance at me. "I didn't realize that made me a criminal."

Chief Terry slid a questioning glance toward me and realization dawned on his face. "You came in here to make sure she was all right." Chief Terry jerked his thumb at me when he said the word "she."

"I just met him," I protested.

Chief Terry ignored me. "She makes an impression, doesn't she?"

Landon didn't answer the question, but a small smile played at the corner of his lips.

"The whole family does. You should see her mother. And her aunts. Her beautiful mother and aunts. Well, not her Aunt Tillie, not that she doesn't make an impression," he said hurriedly. Even Chief Terry didn't want to run the risk of offending Aunt Tillie.

Landon quirked a smile. "I see you know the family well."

"I've known her since she was a kid and I don't like ruffians – especially ones who look like you – sniffing around."

"He's not sniffing around," I interjected. "I really did just meet him a few minutes ago." I don't know why I felt the need to stand up for Landon – but I did.

Chief Terry was still pretending he didn't hear me – even though I knew he did. "Why don't you go join the others out front," he ordered Landon. "Don't leave, though. My officers are going to want to interview you."

Landon glared at Chief Terry, but he did as he was told. He cast a glance back at me as he left, but he didn't say anything. I was relieved when I saw him disappear back into the maze.

"I don't need you to protect me," I told Chief Terry, even though I was touched at his concern.

"That is not the kind of man who you should be spending time with," he said, his warning clear.

"I told you – three times now – I just met him," I snapped. "I'm not spending time with him."

"Just keep it that way," Chief Terry grumbled. "I don't think your family would like him."

"Who do they like?"

"They like you," he replied quickly. "And they don't want to see you get hurt."

I wasn't sure about Aunt Tillie, but he was right about the rest of them. "What makes you think I'm going to get hurt?"

Chief Terry opened his mouth to explain, but he was interrupted by a contingent of state police who were suddenly descending on the area. I wanted to stay and see what they found, but I was ushered out of the area quickly.

Once I was back at the front of the maze, I found myself surrounded by the townspeople who usually made a point of shunning me.

"Who was it?" Mrs. Little asked in alarm.

"I don't know," I admitted. "I didn't see his face."

"You're sure it's a body, though?"

"I'm sure."

One of the teenage boys who had been in the maze earlier brought me a cup of cider. I thanked him and sipped it mindlessly. I don't even like cider – and yet it tasted good.

The police questioned everyone in the area. Most people were released quickly. After about an hour, only a handful of people was left. One of them was Landon. I watched as he made his way over to me.

"How are you?" He seemed genuinely concerned – and that puzzled me.

"I'm fine." I glanced around the front of the maze and realized that his friends were gone. "Where are your little buddies?"

"They didn't like all the police, so they left," he said.

"Why don't they like police?"

Landon shrugged. “Lots of people don’t like the police.”

“And how do you feel about the police?”

Landon looked down on me and smiled despite himself. “I think that police serve a purpose.”

“Have they had to serve a purpose with you before?”

Landon chuckled. “I get the feeling you don’t trust me.”

“Why would I?”

“Why wouldn’t you? Because I drink beer at nine in the morning?”

That’s as good of a reason as any. “No. I just don’t know you.”

“So you’re suspicious of everyone you don’t know? You only trust family?” Landon was baiting me. He was trying to get a reaction.

“Oh, I’m suspicious of my family, too. That’s because I know what they’re capable of, though. I have no idea what you’re capable of.”

“Maybe you’ll find out?”

I realized he was flirting with me and felt a rush of warmth wash over me. Then I remembered where I was.

I turned to see Chief Terry exiting the corn maze. He made his way over to me. “It’s a teenage boy,” he said heavily.

“One of ours?” I felt as if the air had been knocked out of me.

“I don’t recognize him.”

That was a small relief. Not for his family, though.

“They’re going to get dental records and see if they can identify him.”

“He didn’t have any identification on him?” Landon asked the question, but Chief Terry directed the answer to me.

“He didn’t have a wallet on him. They’re still looking around the maze to see if they can find any of his belongings.”

I swallowed hard. “How was he killed?”

“He was stabbed in the heart and it was … removed.”

“Removed?” My eyebrows practically shot off my head. “Why would someone remove a heart?”

“I don’t know,” Chief Terry admitted. “It’s sick. The state boys say it’s ritualistic.”

“Like a cult?”

Chief Terry shrugged. "I don't know. We'll have to wait and see what they find out. I know about as much as you do right now."

"Where will they take him now?"

"The state lab."

We lapsed into silence for a few minutes and watched as the state police wheeled a body bag on a gurney out of the maze. I felt sad for the unidentified boy inside. What a horrible way to die. I could only hope he'd been dead before his heart had been cut out.

Chief Terry turned back to me briefly. "I'll let you know what we find out."

"Thanks."

I started to move away, but Chief Terry stopped me. "Bay, they did say one other thing."

"What?"

"They said if it is some sort of ritual thing, this might only be the beginning."

SIX

When I left the corn maze, I was still shaken by Chief Terry's parting words. Only the beginning? More murders? More teenagers with their hearts cut out? I couldn't even imagine that. Why here? And why now?

I found my hands shaking as I drove and pondered what had just happened. This was Hemlock Cove. Things like this weren't supposed to happen here. The most distressing thing to happen here on a regular basis was gossip.

I stopped at the paper to see how the layout for this week's edition was going. It wasn't exactly rocket science, but it was still important. This was the town's only source of local information, after all. And, even though the townspeople made fun of the paper, they would be lost without it.

I went into my office, closing the door behind me, and opened my laptop. I started Googling ritual murders – and was disturbed by what I found. To be fair, my only knowledge on anything like this came from television – basically *Criminal Minds* and *Dateline* reruns. The only thing I could ascertain is that there were no set rules for this sort of thing.

Essentially, two types of people conduct ritualistic murders: Those who thought the devil was making them do those things and those who thought they were doing horrific things because they were actually the devil. Both sounded insane to me.

Surprisingly, when I widened my search, I found that there were a disturbing number of ritual murders throughout the country that involved removing hearts. Apparently, the heart was the most common organ to be removed. Nice.

Despite surfing through several websites, I couldn't find one commonality for why people would take the heart. Some did it as a way to appease certain Pagan gods. Others did it as a trophy – putting it in a jar or on display in their homes. The truly disturbed, I found, actually ate them. And I thought liver was gross.

I was so engrossed in my work that I didn't see Edith float through the wall and join me in my research.

"Why are you looking like that?"

"A boy was found in the Harrow Bluff corn maze this morning," I explained. "He had his heart cut out."

"That's awful," Edith intoned. "Was it done with a chainsaw?"

"I don't think so. I think it was done with a simple knife," I replied. I didn't know if that was better or worse, though.

"Was he from town?"

"They don't think so," I said. "No one recognized him. The state police are trying to find out who he is through dental records."

Edith's gaze was focused on my computer screen. "And the police think it was ritualistic? Like a cult?"

"They don't know. They think it's a possibility, though. I was just doing my own research."

"Well, I hope that it's not devil worshippers," Edith said. "The last thing this town needs is devil worshippers – what with all the witches and everything."

I tried not to let her comments hurt me – but it wasn't an easy endeavor. I knew she didn't mean me specifically, but since I was the only one in town who could see and talk to her, I thought she would show a little restraint. If only for my benefit.

Edith didn't seem to notice my sudden discomfort. Or, maybe she did, and she chose instead to ignore it. "This won't be good for the town," she said.

"It's not good for anybody."

I left the office after another twenty minutes of research and decided to go to Hypnotic to tell Clove and Thistle what had happened. I knew they would never forgive me if I didn't give them the details myself. Plus, I wanted to get their thoughts on ritualistic murders. I didn't think they knew any more than I did – but it never hurts to check.

When I entered the shop, I was surprised to see them anxiously waiting for me. Thistle was even pacing, not even pretending to do work. They both greeted me excitedly.

"Is what everyone says true?" Clove asked breathlessly. "Was there a body in the new corn maze?"

I nodded stiffly and sank down on the couch. Thistle brought me a cup of tea, pushing it into my hand. I accepted it absentmindedly.

"Who was it?"

"They don't know. Chief Terry didn't recognize him. He doesn't think he's from Hemlock Cove."

"Why would someone kill an outsider and then bring them here?" Clove asked. "Or maybe he came to the corn maze and was killed here instead?"

"That's a good question," I hesitated. I wasn't sure how much I should tell them. Chief Terry hadn't told me to keep my mouth shut – and he knew I essentially told them everything.

"How did he die?" Clove asked. She was understandably curious, which I understood, but she was almost excited by the day's events. I found that disturbing. This was the biggest thing to happen in Hemlock Cove in, well, forever, though. She wasn't going to be dissuaded from getting the answers she sought.

"He was stabbed to death," I finally said. I still wasn't sure they needed to hear everything. I knew everything – and I knew I would never be able to forget the details, or the sight of that horrible scarecrow.

"Someone said his heart was cut out," Thistle offered.

"Who told you that?" I guess I didn't have to worry about shocking them with the gruesome story – they already knew most of it.

"Mrs. Gunderson. She told me when I went to get donuts." Of course.

"How did she know?"

"Everyone in town knows." Thistle seemed surprised that I would think this would be able to be kept quiet – even for an afternoon. Nothing in this town ever stayed a true secret.

"How?"

Thistle shrugged. "I have no idea. It's a small town, though. They probably all hooked their tin cans together and spread the word."

She was probably right. If I had to guess, Mrs. Little was the source of the leak. She never met a piece of gossip that she didn't like to spread. This would be like Christmas to her – and she would be the center of attention for curious townspeople.

"Someone said you discovered the body," Clove said. She was far too into this story. It had become macabre.

"Technically, it was Emily."

"Who is Emily?"

"That girl from the inn last night."

"The one with all the questions? The one who just got married to that annoying guy who wouldn't stop talking about himself at dinner?"

"Yeah."

Clove and Thistle realized I was still digesting everything I'd seen, so they wisely backed off for a few minutes. They let me sit with my thoughts as long as they could, but Clove just couldn't contain herself.

"Was there a lot of blood?"

I blew out a sigh. "I didn't see a lot of blood. I just saw his hand and it had a little blood on it. He had a mask on, though, so I couldn't see his face. He had overalls on, too, so any damage done to the body was hidden."

"What kind of mask?"

"It was one of those Mardi Gras masks."

"That's weird."

This whole thing was weird. The mask was the least of my worries.

"Did you see a ghost?" Thistle asked.

I stopped at the question and pondered it for a second. "I don't think so. I wasn't really looking for one." I mentally kicked myself. Why hadn't I been looking? The boy had obviously died a violent death. If anyone was going to come back as a ghost, it would be him.

"Maybe all the cops scared him away?" Thistle suggested.

"Or maybe he wasn't killed there," Clove offered. This was the second time she had brought up that scenario. I couldn't tell if she was hoping that was the case or not. I wasn't sure if the boy dying in Hemlock Cove would ultimately make much of a difference – but it obviously was important to her.

I nodded my head silently. "That's possible. Or maybe there's no ghost at all? They don't all come back as ghosts."

"Do most ghosts hang out where they're killed? Or do they follow their bodies?" Thistle was genuinely curious.

"How would I know?" They were starting to irritate me.

"You're the one who talks to ghosts," Clove said rationally.

"It's not like I do it on a daily basis."

Thistle raised her eyebrows suggestively.

"Well, except for Edith," I amended. "And she died in the same place her body was found."

"What about in Detroit? You must have seen a lot of ghosts there?"

I quirked my head as I considered the question. "There's so many people around there, though, that I probably was seeing ghosts without realizing it."

"You didn't talk to a ghost the whole time you were down there?"

"No, I did."

"Well, where were they hanging out?"

I pondered the question for a few seconds before answering. "I saw most of them in cemeteries," I finally said. "At least the ones I knew were ghosts."

"So, that means they follow their bodies," Thistle deduced.

"I don't think there are any hard and fast rules when you're a ghost," I said, my contempt obvious. "It's not like they get a handbook, like in *Beetlejuice*. They pretty much do whatever they want."

"She's probably right," Clove said ruefully.

Of course I was right. I'm always right. When will they realize that?

"I think it probably varies from ghost to ghost," I added, trying to keep my irritation in check. Why are we discussing this again?

"I have an idea," Thistle finally said.

Oh great. "No, you don't."

"Yes, I do."

"No, you don't."

"Don't you even want to hear what it is?" Thistle knew I didn't want to hear what it was, but that wasn't going to stop her from telling me. I honestly don't even know why I'm putting up a fight. I'm going to lose.

"Not really." I sipped my tea and pretended to look around the store. I refused to meet her gaze. I knew exactly what her idea was going to be – and it was not something I was looking forward to – or something I wanted to entertain at all frankly.

"I want to hear what it is?" Clove said innocently. Sometimes, when she slips into naïve ignorance mostly, she drives me crazy.

"No, you don't," I admonished her.

Clove must have finally caught on to what Thistle was insinuating. "Oh, that's a great idea!"

"It is not," I grumbled.

"You don't want to know? You don't want to help him?" *Oh, sure, guilt me. That's a great way to approach the problem.*

I didn't answer.

"You won't be able to sleep if you don't know," Thistle admonished me. She knew she had already won, though.

I knew they were right. I blew out another sigh – I seemed to be doing that a lot today. "Fine, but I'm not going alone."

"We'll go tonight," Thistle said, rubbing her hands excitedly. She did love a good adventure. We had all tried to find a pirate ship in Lake Michigan after seeing *The Goonies* as kids. We were almost charged with trespassing, if I remember correctly. I doubted this would be a fun excursion, though. Since we'd been grounded for a month, *The Goonies* adventure hadn't turned out all to be that fun either.

"Why are we going after dark?" Clove protested. Her bravado was slipping.

"So no one sees us," Thistle responded sharply. "If someone sees us going there during daylight hours they'll think it's suspicious."

"And if they catch us there at night? You don't think they'll find that suspicious?"

She had a point.

"Of course," Thistle said calmly. "But hopefully no one will see us in the dark." *Yeah, because we'll suddenly become invisible and able to fly.*

Great. We were going to explore a corn maze, in the dark, in the hopes of finding the ghost of a murdered teenage boy who had his heart cut out. What could go wrong with this scenario? How about everything?

SEVEN

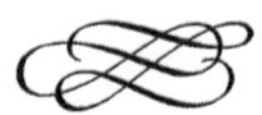

You might think going on a secret mission with your cousins sounds like fun. If that's the case, then I'm telling the story wrong. It's never fun. The fact that I let Thistle and Clove talk me into it was a commentary on how weak I am – I can never tell them no – or how great their powers of persuasion are.

I knew all of this going in. Yet, at midnight, I found myself dressed in black and ready to break about three different local laws and ordinances.

I had to stifle an actual groan when I saw Clove wander out of her bedroom. We'd all agreed to dress in black – although Thistle's idea of black included a disco sequined tank top – but Clove had actually painted her face like we were about to go hunt and kill something in the woods.

"What's with the paint?" I grumbled.

"We're all very pale. You should put some on, too. Otherwise, we'll stand out in the dark and it will be more likely that we get caught."

Thistle, usually the voice of reason in a situation like this, grabbed the canister of paint from Clove and immediately started lathering it on her face. When she was done, she handed it to me.

"I'm not wearing that," I argued.

"If you don't and we get caught, we're blaming you," Thistle warned ominously.

Crap.

I reluctantly took the canister from Thistle and dabbed a little bit on my face. When Thistle was still staring at me reprovingly, I sighed and followed the pattern the two of them had used. When I glanced at myself in the mirror afterward, I wanted to laugh at how ridiculous we all looked.

Clove smiled at our reflection in the mirror as she stepped up between the two of us. "We look really cute. We should take a picture."

Cute wasn't the word I was thinking about using – but I didn't bother voicing that concern. I knew it would get me nowhere. I also wasn't going to take a picture so the cops could use it at our trial at a later date.

Clove started digging through her purse and pulled out a black knit hat and handed it to me.

"Why do I have to wear a knit hat?" I sounded whiny – even to myself.

"You have blonde hair," Clove pointed out, like I hadn't noticed.

"So?"

"My hair is dark and Thistle's is blue. They won't stand out. Yours will stand out. You have to wear it."

"I don't want to wear a hat," I muttered.

"Just put it on and stop being a baby," Thistle admonished.

"I'm not being a baby," I grumbled, pulling the hat on. Clove came over to me and shoved the rest of my hair up under the hat. The look she gave me was daring me to complain. I wisely decided against it.

"There," she said when she was finished.

We had decided that the best way to get to the corn maze was to walk. All of our vehicles were too easily recognizable. It would take us about forty-five minutes to get to the field – but we all agreed that sounded like the safest bet in the long run.

"Chief Terry may have a crush on all of our moms, but that wouldn't stop him from throwing us in jail if the state police are there," Thistle had argued.

I couldn't deny that she had a point. Still, I wasn't looking forward to a 45-minute walk in the middle of the night. Crazy, I know.

We left the guesthouse and made our way along the cobblestone path at the back of the property. If we avoided the roads, not only would we shorten our trip – but we would also have less of a chance of being captured.

Most of the residents in the area avoided the back of our property like the plague. The property was gorgeous, mind you, but years ago our ancestors had set up a special clearing in the forest for Pagan festivals. Through the years, our moms and aunts had started throwing solstice celebrations and equinox engagements in the clearing. Depending on how much liquor was imbibed at these celebrations, they often ended up in nude dances under the moonlight. People didn't risk cutting through our woods anymore. Once you've seen middle-aged boobs that big flopping around – you wouldn't risk it either.

After leaving our woods, we followed the main road toward the corn maze. Clove wanted to cut across the county's park – but Thistle and I quickly vetoed that suggestion.

"We'll get lost," I argued.

"It will be too creepy," Thistle offered.

"You guys are no fun," Clove grumbled.

In truth, I don't think any of us really wanted to chance cutting across the land. It wasn't exactly flat. And if one of us fell and required medical attention, we would have a bitch of a time explaining why we were there.

During our trek, we chatted amiably with one another. We were always comfortable when we were together – even if we were about to commit a felony. Briefly, I wondered what anyone would think if they saw us dressed like this.

Once, we saw a pair of headlights heading our way and dived into the ditch to hide. The truck had passed by us quickly, though, and we remained unnoticed.

"Whew, that was close," Clove was brushing the dirt off her outfit.

"It wasn't that close. We were in the ditch for a full two minutes before the truck passed us by," I argued. I get crabby late at night – and early in the morning – especially when I'm doing something that I expressly don't want to do.

"Still, it could have been dangerous," Clove said conspiratorially. "What if that was the killer?"

"That was old Mr. Browden," Thistle argued. "I recognized his truck. He's probably going down to the pond to go frogging."

Clove wasn't going to be deterred from her excitement. "We don't actually know that's what he was doing. Have any of us actually seen him catch a frog?"

She had a point. Of course, I didn't point out that none of us would have the patience to actually sit there and watch him try to catch a frog either. His frog-catching abilities were legendary around town, though.

When we finally got to the corn maze, we approached the area carefully. We could see the yellow police tape glinting under the moonlight – but everything else was dark and quiet. I scanned the area briefly – looking to see if I could see a hidden police car.

"Do you see anything?" Thistle asked, clearly doubtful.

"No. Do you?"

"No."

"Let's take a quick look around the back of the maze to be sure," I whispered.

Thistle nodded silently. We all moved together as a unit. It probably took an extra fifteen minutes to check out the back of the maze, but I think we all felt better once the deed was done. When we were back at the entrance to the maze, Thistle and Clove looked to me expectantly.

"What?"

"You go first," Thistle licked her lips nervously.

"Why do I have to go first? This was your idea."

"You know where you're going," Thistle argued, although I could tell, now that we were here, she didn't think it was such a great idea anymore.

"She's right," Clove said, moving in between the two of us warily.

"You know where you're going. I'll be in the middle. Thistle, you take the rear."

"You always take her side," I muttered as I reluctantly moved into the corn maze.

I pulled out the flashlight I had tucked into the waistband of my black stretchy pants and flicked it on.

"Should we risk having that on?" Thistle hissed.

"How do you suggest we find our way otherwise? The hay is so tall in there, it will block out the moon and we don't want any of the hay bales tumbling on top of us. Do you really want to feel your way around – especially knowing someone left a dead body in here less than twenty-four hours ago?"

"She has a point," Clove said nervously.

"Oh, *now* you're on my side," I shot back sarcastically.

We entered the maze. I could feel Clove's hand at my back. I had no doubt Thistle's hand was similarly placed at Clove's back.

"How long?" I could tell Clove didn't think this was such a fun adventure anymore.

"I don't know. Like ten minutes," I said.

We made the trek to the center of the maze in relative silence. The only time that the quiet was shattered was when we inadvertently stepped on someone else's foot.

"Ouch, that was my foot," Clove complained.

"You stepped on my foot."

"I did not."

I was relieved when we finally made it to the center of the maze. Even Clove and Thistle breathed a sigh of relief when we were free of the closed in walls of the oppressive corn and could take a step away from one another. Of course, given the fact that we were sneaking into a murder scene in the dead of the night – none of us stepped too far away from the other.

"Do you see anything?" Thistle finally asked.

"No."

"Well, we tried," Clove interjected hurriedly. "Let's go."

I glared at her over my flashlight. "We're here now. We might as well look around."

Clove looked like she wanted to argue – or bolt. Instead, she sighed heavily. "Fine, but I want it put on the record that I think this is a bad idea."

"You thought this was a great idea an hour ago," I teased her.

"That's before we started wandering around a haunted corn maze," she shot back.

"We don't know it's haunted – yet."

"Anyone remember watching *Children of the Corn*?" Thistle asked.

"Why would you bring that up?" Clove practically shrieked.

I smiled to myself. I had forgotten how much that movie freaked Clove out.

"Malachai! Malachai!" I hissed, in my best impression of the creepy kid from the movie's voice.

"You stop that right now!" Clove stomped her small foot indignantly.

"He who walks behind the rows," Thistle whispered evilly. "He's coming for you."

"I'm telling if you don't stop it," Clove whimpered. Who was she going to tell?

I was swinging my flashlight around the area, trying to remember another line from the movie when the beam landed on a pair of Converse sneakers. I felt my heart lodge in my throat and I froze.

While Thistle and Clove are often oblivious to certain life cues, they both stopped what they were doing when they saw my rigid posture. Thistle was at my side in a second.

"What do you see?"

My throat was dry and I could barely form words. Thistle put her hand on my shoulder reassuringly. "What do you see?"

"C-c-converse," I finally squeaked out. "Gray ones."

"Where?"

"In the flashlight," I said.

Thistle followed the flashlight beam with her eyes. "I don't see anything," she said finally. She turned to Clove. "Do you?"

Clove looked like the last thing she wanted to do was see if there was someone – or something – wearing Converse in the corn maze. She knew she wasn't going to get out of here, though, until she looked.

After a full minute of staring at the area where I had the flashlight pointed, she finally shook her head. "There's nothing there."

Thistle turned back to me. "Do you still see them?"

"Yeah."

"It's probably him," Thistle said eagerly. "You said it was a teenage boy. Teenage boys wear Converse."

"So do we," I snapped back.

"They're good shoes," Thistle said comfortingly.

The figure standing behind the maze wall – the one that clearly belonged to the shoes – finally peeked around the corner to look at the spot we were standing. His gaze met mine, and he appeared uncertain.

"We won't hurt you," I promised.

"Do you see him?" Thistle was the one enjoying our predicament now.

The boy swallowed hard and then took a bold step out into the center of the maze. Once he was clear of the maze wall, I could get a good look at him. He had a slight build and shoulder-length brown hair. I couldn't tell what color his eyes were – but they looked brown under the pale moonlight. He was dressed in over-sized jeans, an AC/DC shirt – everything old is new again, after all – and the gray converse shoes. He also had a black hoodie on. He looked like a typical teenager.

"You can see me?" The boy asked cautiously.

I nodded. "I can." I pointed to Clove and Thistle. "They can't, though."

"They know you're talking to me, though," he said. He seemed scared, which made me sad. He was already dead, what did he have to be scared about?

"They do."

"How?"

"They're my cousins."

"But how do they know you're talking to me if they can't see me?"

Now, here's a tricky situation. I wasn't sure if the boy realized he was dead. If he didn't, I had to break the news to him as carefully as possible. Even if he did, though, I didn't know if I should fess up to being a witch. Even ghosts get a little freaked out about stuff like that. I decided to go for a mixture of the truth.

"I've been able to see things that other people can't since I was a kid," I finally said.

"Like ghosts?"

Whew. He knew he was dead. "You know you're a ghost?" I asked, not trying to hide my sympathy.

The boy looked shocked. "I'm a ghost? You're saying I'm a ghost?"

"Why did you ask if I could see ghosts if you didn't know you were a ghost?" I asked, suddenly panicked.

I could see Thistle and Clove taking the conversation in beside me – but neither one said a word.

"I was just asking a question," the boy said indignantly. "You don't just blurt out that you're a ghost to someone, you know?"

"I'm sorry," I said simply. "I thought you knew."

The boy blew out a sigh – or at least the approximation of a sigh. He didn't have breath anymore, after all.

"I had a suspicion that I was dead," he admitted.

I figured that. "Why?"

"Because I tried to talk to all the police who were here earlier and none of them could hear me. Plus, there was that whole body thing."

Yep, that would do it.

I decided to approach the next question delicately. "What do you remember?"

"What do you mean?" The boy furrowed his eyebrows in a confused expression.

"She means, who killed you?"

I swung to Thistle in surprise. "You can see him?"

She shook her head. "No. But I can hear him. It was hard to hear him at first, but now I hear him like he's standing right beside us."

I turned to Clove. "Can you hear him, too?"

"Yeah," she bit her lower lip. "It's creepy."

"I'm not creepy!" The boy was starting to lose it.

"No, you're not," I soothed him calmly. "What's your name?"

"Shane," the boy answered.

"Shane what?"

"Shane Haskell."

"How old are you?"

"I'm seventeen," he said bitterly.

"Where are you from?"

"Beulah," he said.

"Where's Beulah?" Clove looked confused.

"It's on the other side of Traverse City," Thistle interjected. "At least I think. I've never actually been there."

The boy was nodding at their conversation.

"How did you get here?" I asked.

Shane raised his hands in a palms-up motion. "I don't remember."

"You don't remember who killed you?" Clove looked doubtful. At least she wasn't terrified anymore.

"No," Shane glared in her direction.

"Is that normal?" Clove turned to me.

"Sometimes it takes them awhile," I said.

"Will I eventually remember?" Shane asked.

"I don't know. I hope so." Actually, given the way that he died, I wasn't hopeful that Shane would remember his final moments. Maybe they were too horrible for him to process – and that was why he had forgotten them.

"Do you think my mom knows I'm dead?" He looked like he was going to cry.

"I don't know," I said. "They didn't know who you were this afternoon."

"She's going to be all alone now," Shane said bitterly.

"I'll make sure I tell them who you are tomorrow," I promised Shane. How I was going to explain my knowledge of his identity was a conundrum I would tackle then.

"Thanks," he said.

"Until then, why don't you come with us," I offered.

"That's a good idea," Thistle said. "If he does remember, we don't want to have to come back here."

"You want me to go home with you?" He seemed almost relieved.

I paused for a second. I really didn't want him hanging around our house. If the aunts saw him, or heard him for that matter, it would raise a lot of difficult questions I wasn't ready to answer.

"For tonight," I said. "Then you can go and hang around at Thistle and Clove's magic shop tomorrow with them."

Seemed like a good solution to me.

Thistle gave me a dirty look. "Why the magic shop?"

I turned to her and smiled sweetly. "This was your idea. I figured you'd want to help – especially since I know you can hear him. Just think of yourself as his guardian angel."

Shane seemed to be coming out of his funk because he was smiling when he got a better look at Thistle under the moonlight.

"My guardian angel is hot!"

Thistle turned to me. The fake smile on her face looked like it was carved out of granite. When I didn't budge on my earlier proclamation, though, she sighed reluctantly. "Fine, he can come to the magic store."

She turned on her heel and started to head out of the corn maze. I smiled as Shane readily followed us.

"Aw, man, you all have asses like super models! Can I watch you in the shower?"

Clove turned to me as I paused to let her enter the maze in front of me. "Now I can see why he was killed."

EIGHT

The next morning, I was surprised to wake up with a pronounced ache in my back. Last night's activities were coming back to haunt me – in more ways than one. Shane had been a chatterbox the entire way home. Once he came out of his shell, we couldn't shut him up. And, like most teenage boys, he was a vulgar little sex monster.

"Do you guys have boyfriends?"

I heard Shane asking the question as I exited my bedroom the next morning. I smiled when I saw Thistle and Clove sitting at the kitchen table drinking coffee. They both looked as tired as I felt.

"No," Thistle said shortly.

"Thistle is hoping to have one soon, though," Clove supplied. After last night's scare, she was back to her favorite activity: Irritating Thistle.

Thistle shot her a death glare.

"I bet he's hot," Shane said.

"He is," Clove agreed.

"My mom said that I would grow into my looks one day," Shane said sadly. "I guess that will never happen. I'll never get the chance to get a hot girl."

"I'm sure you're cute," Clove said.

I regarded Shane's baby face – and the smattering of acne across his cheeks that was now readily apparent in the daylight – and sighed internally. I felt bad for Shane. Not only had he died a horrible death, but if he did remain a ghost for any extended period of time, he was going to be a teenage ghost with zits.

"Good morning," I said brightly, announcing my presence when I entered the room.

"What's good about it?" Thistle grumbled.

"Didn't you sleep?"

"Who can sleep with Captain Can't-Stop-Talking in the house?"

I turned to Shane, who was studying his shoes sheepishly. "I didn't mean to keep her up," he said. "I just couldn't sleep – do ghosts even sleep? – and I guess I got carried away."

I smirked at Thistle when I saw the dark circles under her eyes and the grim expression on her face. "I'm sure Thistle didn't really mind," I lied. "She's just grumpy until she has at least three cups of coffee in her system every morning."

Shane brightened considerably at my statement. "My mom is like that, too."

"See, Thistle," I teased. "You're just like his mom."

Despite the fact that Shane had proved to be a tenacious little horn dog, I couldn't help but like him. Plus, the reminder of the way he died was weighing heavily on me – so I had more sympathy for Shane than I would a normal teenager.

"I need to take a shower," Clove announced.

"So? Do it. You want us to give you an award or something?" Thistle really was grumpy this morning.

Clove bit her bottom lip. "I can't until .... "

"Until what?" I prodded.

"I can't until I'm sure he won't come in and watch me," she admitted, pointing in the direction she had last heard Shane's voice emanate from.

I turned to Shane, who couldn't take his eyes off Thistle. I didn't think Clove had anything to worry about. Still, I felt the need to placate her. "Shane?"

He turned his attention to me reluctantly. "You won't watch Clove in the shower, will you?"

"No," Shane promised.

"Just take a shower, Clove," Thistle grumbled. "Don't be a baby."

Clove reluctantly got up and headed into the bathroom. I don't think she believed Shane entirely – but I didn't want to crush her ego and tell her he'd barely noticed she was in the room thanks to his infatuation with Thistle.

When Clove was gone, Thistle turned to me expectantly. "So, what happens now?"

"I'm going to get ready for work and stop at the police department on my way in," I said.

"Are you going to tell him who I am? I mean, who I was? I mean, who the body was in the corn maze?" Shane turned his full attention to me for the first time that morning. He didn't seem put off by my out-of-control bedhead.

"I'm going to try and figure out if he knows who you are first," I said. "If he doesn't, then I'll figure something out. I can't just tell him a ghost told me."

Shane nodded, his sympathy obvious. "I guess not. They'd probably lock you up in a mental institution or something."

"Probably."

"I'll find out what else they know on the case, too. If he knows anything new, I'll call Thistle. Since you'll be at the shop with her all day, she'll be able to tell you what I find out."

"Thanks," Shane said sincerely. "You've all been really nice to me."

After Clove showered, I left Thistle and Shane so I could be the next one in the bathroom. Despite her grumpy attitude, Thistle was listening to whatever Shane told her with legitimate interest.

"You can't haunt the popular girl at school," she admonished him after a few minutes. "No matter how much of a crush you have on her."

"Why not?"

"She probably won't be able to see you – or hear you, for that matter – so it would be a waste of time."

"You can hear me . . . and Bay can see me."

"We're ... different."

"Different how?"

Thistle avoided the question. "Plus, haunting a girl just because she didn't notice you when you were alive is petty and mean."

"She wasn't that nice," Shane offered. "She used to make fun of everyone who wasn't popular."

"Well, in that case, haunt the shit out of her."

I snickered to myself as I closed the bathroom door behind me.

Thistle was still in the bathroom getting ready when I left for work. Clove had taken advantage of Shane's fascination with our cousin to get dressed and was now waiting impatiently in the living room.

"We need another bathroom," she complained.

We did. "Tell the aunts."

"They'll turn it into a big thing," she argued.

"Well, we can't magically make one appear – no matter what the townspeople think."

Clove rolled her eyes dramatically. "Why do you care what the townspeople think?"

"I don't," I shot back quickly.

"You're such a liar. You've always been so worried about what they think. It doesn't matter. They're going to think what they want to think. Stop being so insecure."

I left the house without answering Clove. She had a point – but I didn't want to acknowledge that. I hate it when she or Thistle is right and I'm wrong. That doesn't happen very often, mind you. When it does, though, it tilts my whole world sideways.

When I made it downtown, I stopped at the police station before I made my way to the newspaper offices for the day. I went in through the backdoor, like I usually did, and paused in the municipal parking lot when I saw an expensive motorcycle parked at the back door.

I wonder who that belongs to.

I shook my head and pulled away from the bike, entering the building. It still wasn't 9 a.m. yet, so I knew the office wasn't open for regular business. I was surprised when I saw Landon exit Chief Terry's office. I couldn't hear what his parting words to the chief had been, but when he saw me he looked surprised.

"Someone is up early," he said with a warm smile. I noticed he was wearing the exact same outfit he'd been clad in the day before.

"What are you doing here?" *And why hadn't he gone home to change his clothes?*

Landon didn't miss a beat. "The chief had a few questions for me."

I looked down at my watch for a second and then met his eyes again. "At 8:30 a.m.?"

"That's when I was free, so we made a special appointment," Landon said.

He was lying. I could tell. I just couldn't figure out why he was lying – or about what.

"That makes perfect sense," I told him sarcastically.

"You still don't trust me?"

"Nope."

I moved away from him. I was eager to put as much distance between him and the feelings he was roiling up inside of me as possible. I could not have a crush on the new town thug. My mother would have an absolute fit.

Landon watched me as I angled past him and toward the chief's office door. "You'll grow to appreciate me," he said.

I turned to him and saw the knowing look on his face. I found it infuriating, not cute. Okay, maybe it was both. "You have a pretty high opinion of yourself."

"You will, too. I promise."

With those words, Landon turned and left the building. I watched him leave. A few seconds after the door closed, I heard the motorcycle outside fire up and take off out of the parking lot. The bike clearly belonged to him.

Great. Hot man. Hot ride. This wasn't going to end well. I could just feel it.

I sighed as I pushed into Chief Terry's office and tried to force thoughts of Landon and his ridiculously shiny motorcycle out of my head. He didn't seem surprised to see me.

"I figured you would stop here on your way to work," he said.

"I ran into Landon in the hallway."

Chief Terry dismissed the statement with a wave of his hand. "I just needed him to clarify something from yesterday."

Under normal circumstances, I would never suspect Chief Terry of lying. The fact that he averted his gaze from mine, though, made me suspicious.

"What did you need him to clarify?"

"Nothing important."

"Why are you being evasive?"

"Why are you butting your nose into things that don't involve you?"

We were in a stand-off. I decided to move on from the Landon debate and broach the Shane subject.

"Have you identified the boy in the field?"

"Yeah. His name is Shane Haskell. He's from Beulah."

Good. I wouldn't have to try and lead Chief Terry to the truth. "How did you find out?"

"Dental records."

"How did he get here? Beulah is like an hour away."

"We don't know. The state police are interviewing his mom right now."

I paused, unsure how to ask the next question. "How did she take the news?"

If Chief Terry was suspicious of my motivations for asking the question, he didn't acknowledge it. "Not well. The boy was her only child. Her husband died a few years ago. She's devastated."

"Did you tell her how he died?"

"We had to."

Well, that had to be ten kinds of awful. "Do you have any other leads?"

"Not yet. The crime lab is still testing results. The problem we have is that fifty people were probably legitimately in that area of the corn maze – and we have no idea what is evidence and what is incidental."

"So, what's the next step?"

"The state boys have practically taken over the investigation," Chief Terry said bitterly. "They're not letting me do much. They're keeping me in the loop as much as they can, I think, but I don't think they're telling me everything."

"What makes you say that?"

"I don't know, just a gut feeling."

My mind flashed to Landon for a second, but I quickly returned to the conversation at hand. "Do you think it's someone from the town?"

"God, I hope not," Chief Terry replied truthfully. "The problem is, how would a tourist know the area well enough to do what he did?"

That was a good point.

"Maybe they scouted the area beforehand?"

"Maybe. That still doesn't explain why they picked this kid – and why he went missing from Traverse City two days ago and was taken over here to dump the body yesterday. We have more questions than answers."

I sat quietly for a few moments, unsure of what to say next. Finally, I got to my feet and moved to leave the office.

"Keep me informed with anything you find out."

"I'm not exactly at the center of the investigation," Chief Terry said. "But I'll do what I can. I always do."

I thanked Chief Terry and exited his office. My thoughts were decidedly dark as I made my way outside. So Shane had been in Traverse City when he'd gone missing. Somehow, he ended up forty-five minutes away and dumped in a corn maze. That didn't make any sense. Of course, he was also missing his heart when he was dumped. Maybe finding rational answers in an irrational crime was something that simply wasn't possible. Maybe I would drive myself crazy before all of this was said and done.

I called Thistle quickly on my cell phone and told her what I'd found out. I could hear her relaying the story to Shane, who seemed relieved that his mother had been notified of his death.

"At least she's not worried about me being late coming home now," I heard him say sadly. "She knows now that I'm never coming home. Never. That's got to be better than worrying, right?"

"Right," I heard Thistle respond to him. There wasn't much conviction in her voice, though. I figured she was thinking the exact same thing as I was. At least when he was missing there was still hope. What hope did this woman have now? And where was Shane's heart?

NINE

After I left the chief's office, I headed to the newspaper. I knew I would have to write something up on Shane's death, but since the deadline for the next edition was still five days away I figured I had time before I had to file a story.

Instead, I logged on my computer and sat down at my desk. I pulled up my Internet browser and Googled Shane's name.

I was surprised to find that the first link that came up was an online memorial for him on Facebook. I clicked on the link and entered the site. I was stunned to see there were already fifty memorial messages. That was quick.

I scanned the messages with vague interest. Somehow, I doubted that whoever had killed Shane was now posting on Facebook about it. It never hurt to look, though.

Most of the messages were the generic ruminations of empty-headed teenagers.

"I didn't know Shane all that well, but he'll be really missed at school."

"I wish I'd gotten to know him better."

"He was a really sweet guy."

"He was a really smart guy."

"He was a really funny guy."

After sifting through all of the messages, I realized that not one person who actually knew Shane really well had posted. That actually didn't surprise me. In the dramatic world of teenagers, they often create high profile ways to make themselves feel more important when tragedy strikes those amongst them. Teenagers are an example of narcissism at its finest.

Edith had wandered into the office and was now looking over my shoulder as I read.

"Doesn't seem very genuine, does it?" I looked to her expectantly.

She was enthralled by the page, though. "It's really wonderful that all these people are mourning that poor boy."

I guess she didn't see what I saw. "You don't think it seems a little fake? None of these people actually seem to know Shane."

"I think that maybe you're a little too cynical," she pointed out.

She had a point. I reread some of the messages. No. I was right, after all. "Not one of these messages actually conveys a genuine feeling for the person Shane was – or the mother he left behind."

"These people have the right to grieve, too," Edith said. "They're teenagers. When something like this happens it makes them question their own mortality. This is how they do it."

"I think they're just looking for attention."

"That's your cynicism again."

After leaving the Facebook page again, I checked out a few other links that had come up when I'd typed in Shane's name. None of them were of interest, though. One was from a small paper in Beulah that had a picture of Shane from a robotics tournament. The other had nothing to do with Shane at all. When I was done, I closed out of the Internet browser and ran the case through my head.

We knew that Shane went missing from Traverse City two days ago. We knew that he had been found in Hemlock Cove yesterday. Even though we didn't have an exact time of death yet, he probably hadn't been in the field all that long. That meant that whoever had killed Shane had kept him alive – for at least several hours. What had they done to him during that time? Why had they cut out his heart? And where was his heart?

I was jarred from my thoughts when my cell phone rang. I dug it out of my purse and grimaced when I recognized the number from The Overlook on the screen. Great. I knew better than not answering it, though. My mom would take that as a personal affront and either start calling me non-stop or actually show up at the office. Neither of those alternatives was acceptable to me, so I braced myself and answered the phone.

"You have to come over here right now!" It was my mom – and she sounded excited.

"Why? What's going on?" I was naturally suspicious. What my mom considered an emergency was often just an inconvenience in my world.

"There's about to be a catastrophe here." I couldn't quite make out the ruckus in the background, but I could hear my Aunt Marnie yelling at someone.

"What's the catastrophe?"

"Just get over here, young lady," my mother snapped.

"I'm a little busy right now. Maybe … ?" The phone had gone dead. She'd hung up on me. "I hate it when she does that."

I'd walked to work again, so it took me almost a half an hour to get back out to the inn. When I entered through the back door, I found the living quarters empty. It also didn't look as if anything was on fire and there wasn't a police presence – so it couldn't be a real catastrophe, at least not where my family was concerned.

I heard raised voices in the dining room and followed them to see what was going on.

Twila and mom were standing defiantly in front of Aunt Tillie – who was making little jumping movements in the direction of Emily, the girl who had discovered Shane's body with me. She looked like a hacked off – and deranged – rabbit. She was the *Monty Python* rabbit, I thought to myself. The thought made me smile.

I noticed that Marnie was trying to grab Aunt Tillie from behind, but Aunt Tillie kept slipping away from her.

"Grab a hold of her," my mom ordered.

"She's slippery," Marnie shot back.

"She's eighty-five years old. How slippery can she be?"

I noticed that my mom and Marnie were doing all the work. Twila was merely feigning interest in the situation.

"What's going on?" I stepped into the room and regarded the four of them suspiciously. Emily, who kept moving around the dining room table and pulling chairs out to put between her and Aunt Tillie, looked relieved to see me.

"Your Aunt Tillie is a little ... disgruntled," my mom finally said.

"What else is new?"

Aunt Tillie glared at me. "No one needs you here little miss-know-it-all. You can just go back to work. I don't know why they called you."

Neither did I. Aunt Tillie listened to me about as much as she did the doctor – which is to say she didn't listen to me at all.

"She's crazy," Emily shrieked.

"I'll show you crazy," Aunt Tillie promised, escaping from Marnie's clutches again and launching herself on top of the dining room table. She only made it about halfway. I guess – no matter how she liked to spin it – you can only jump so far when you get to be a certain age.

"What is going on?" I asked the question again.

"Your Aunt Tillie is just out of sorts."

"She's always out of sorts. What set her off this time?"

"Set me off? I'm not a bomb." Aunt Tillie looked indignant.

"You're more dangerous than a bomb," I told Aunt Tillie. "A bomb can't be irrational – or vindictive."

Aunt Tillie extended her index finger at me threateningly. "Do not get involved in this, girl," she warned. "You won't like it if I have to curse you."

I paused for a second. She had a point.

Mom saw my hesitation. "I may not curse you, but I will nag you until you want to be cursed if you don't help us," she threatened.

Mom was scary in her own way. "What do you want me to do?"

"Calm her down!" How could she be mad at me about this situation? I still didn't know what was going on.

"Tell me what happened."

Marnie had moved to my side to pause and get her breath. She looked tired. Chasing an eighty-five-year-old woman can do that to you. "She thinks that Emily stole her necklace."

"What necklace?"

"That mini-urn one. The one where she keeps your Uncle Calvin's ashes."

I turned to Aunt Tillie in disbelief. "Why would she steal that? It's not even valuable."

"She knows that it's powerful," Aunt Tillie said through gritted teeth. She was trying to climb on the top of the table again.

"How is it powerful?"

"It's full of magic," Aunt Tillie replied.

I regarded her suspiciously. "What magic?"

"Don't you worry about that," Aunt Tillie replied. "I just want it back."

"What makes you think she has it?" I looked over at Emily, who was crouching in the corner by the grandfather clock. She was annoying, yes, but a thief? I had my doubts.

"I was wearing it earlier and then it disappeared. She's been the only one around."

"Are you sure you just didn't take it off and leave it somewhere?" I was trying to speak to her in a tone that didn't reflect my irritation with this whole situation. If she thought I was irritated, that would just make her more anxious.

"Are you calling me senile?" So not where I wanted to go – even if I did, in fact, think she was senile.

"Of course not," I lied. "I think, maybe, you just took the necklace off and put it on a table or something and forgot about it."

"What's the difference between that and being senile?" Aunt Tillie's green eyes were narrowed dangerously. If I wasn't careful, she'd turn her wrath from Emily to me. As much as I didn't think Emily was a thief, I also didn't want to end up on Aunt Tillie's bad side. If Emily had to be the sacrificial lamb, so be it.

"I just want to make sure that the necklace has actually been stolen before I call Chief Terry – and alert the National Guard."

My mom and my aunts swung on me suspiciously. "You're not calling Chief Terry," Marnie warned me.

Aha! I knew it. They thought she'd lost the necklace, too. They had just called me out here to be the sacrificial lamb for them.

"Theft is a serious offense," I said carefully.

"Do you really think this girl stole it?" Twila looked doubtful.

Emily looked at me desperately. Could I really sell her out? I turned to Aunt Tillie. I saw her rubbing her fingers together anxiously. She was desperate to curse someone. Screw it. Better Emily than me. "I think we should let Chief Terry sort this out," I said finally. "He is a professional, after all."

My mom glared at me openly now. She knew I'd figured out her plan. "We are not calling Terry."

"Then I don't know what to tell you," I said simply.

"You're dead to me," she snapped.

I tried to hide my smirk, but it didn't entirely work. This was a regular occurrence in my family. We were all dead to one another at least once a week. I sat down at the dining room table and poured myself a cup of tea as I watched my mom and her sisters return to their task of trying to wrangle Aunt Tillie into submission.

At a certain point, Emily took advantage of Aunt Tillie's distraction and bolted upstairs. It took Aunt Tillie a full twenty minutes to realize she was gone.

"Where did she go?"

"She left."

"Where?"

"I don't know. Probably to her room."

Aunt Tillie sat down in the chair next to me. I was surprised to see the look of calm that was on her face. I poured another cup of tea and pushed it in front of her. Aunt Tillie drank it down gratefully.

My mom and aunts were watching Aunt Tillie warily, but they

each took a seat at the table and started sipping from their own cups of tea. No one could figure out why the storm had suddenly passed.

"Have you talked to the dead boy's ghost?" Aunt Tillie asked me suddenly.

"Yes." I didn't see any reason to lie to her, especially when she wasn't being judgmental or temperamental.

"Does he know how he died?"

"No."

"He'll remember eventually," she admonished me.

"I know."

I took another sip of my tea and watched Aunt Tillie skeptically. "You never lost the necklace. Did you?"

Aunt Tillie didn't answer. She couldn't entirely hide her small smile, though.

"Why did you make such a fuss?"

"I didn't make a fuss," she argued.

My mom was suddenly suspicious, too. "Was that all an act?" She was glaring at Aunt Tillie dangerously.

"I don't know why you'd think that." Aunt Tillie was averting her gaze from everyone at the table.

I finally pushed my chair back and got up. "She just wanted attention."

"That's not true … ." Twila regarded Aunt Tillie, her concern evident, for a second. "Is it?"

"Of course not," Aunt Tillie scoffed. "I'm not an attention seeker." All evidence to the contrary.

I moved to leave the room. Whatever the catastrophe had been, it was now over. My mom and aunts were now steadfastly studying their Aunt Tillie, though. They realized I was right about her motivations - -and they'd been played.

"Keep the boy close to you," Aunt Tillie offered. I could see she was basking in the outcome of her afternoon performance.

"I will."

"It's important," she warned me.

"I know."

"He'll remember. And when he does, you need to be there to help him."

I turned back to Aunt Tillie with an important question on my lips. "Why would they take his heart?"

"That's a black magic thing," she said honestly.

"Could they want it for any other reason?"

Aunt Tillie cocked her head as she considered my question. "Maybe," she finally answered. "But I honestly don't think so."

"Why do you think that?"

"Whoever did this, they're bad people."

"You think more than one person was involved?"

"Don't you?"

The truth was, I did. I'd felt that from the minute I saw Shane's body. "What do I do?"

Aunt Tillie met my gaze solemnly. "Keep the ghost close, and you're cousins closer. They'll come for you at a certain point. You have to be ready."

I smiled at her gratefully. "Next time you want to warn me, just call me on the phone. Don't cause a scene."

I didn't look back as I left the room, but I heard my mom and aunts explode at Aunt Tillie as I left.

"Is that why you did this?"

TEN

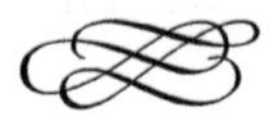

On my way back to the paper, I formed a plan.

Aunt Tillie may be crazy, but she was right about one thing – Shane had to remember how he died. If he didn't, not only could someone else fall victim to his killer, but his murder may go unsolved for good, as well.

I stopped at the guesthouse long enough to pick up my car. I didn't want to risk getting caught without transportation again.

Aunt Tillie may be a dramatic old biddy, but she wouldn't have warned me of impending danger if she really didn't believe it. She didn't mess around when it came to stuff like that.

I had to find a way to get Shane to remember.

Instead of going to Hypnotic to talk to Shane, though, I decided to return to the office and talk to Edith instead. I found her in the records room watching Dr. Oz. She looked up briefly when I entered.

"Can you believe he did an entire show about poo?"

"Poo?"

"You know, poop."

"No, I can't," I said honestly. "What's even worse is that people probably watched it."

"I only watched because I can't change the channel," she said indignantly.

"I wasn't talking about you," I soothed.

"You better not have been," Edith grumbled.

I didn't know how to broach ghost things with Edith. She had never exactly been forthcoming with me. I decided I had better just do it. Otherwise, I'd keep coming up with excuses to delay it – and that would help no one.

"Edith, I have a question for you."

"What?"

"It's about ... it's about being a ghost."

Edith turned to me in surprise. "You've never asked me about being a ghost before."

"I didn't feel it was any of my business."

"And you do now?"

"No, I still don't," I said hurriedly. "But the boy who died in the corn maze, he's a ghost now. He doesn't remember what happened to him, though."

Edith looked surprised. "You went back to the corn maze and found him?"

I didn't want to tell the whole embarrassing tale of my late night trek with Thistle and Clove, so I merely nodded. I figured she didn't need to know how we found him – just *that* we had found him.

"What's the last thing he remembers?" Edith seemed interested, despite herself.

"I don't know. I haven't asked him yet. We just found him last night."

"Why don't you ask him?"

"I'm going to. I just wanted to know if you had any tips to make him remember."

"Why would I have tips?"

I bit my lower lip, lifting my eyes to Edith's and regarding her seriously. "A lot of people think you were murdered, Edith."

Edith pursed her lips unhappily. It was an expression I had become familiar with. "I was found at my desk. Why do people think I was murdered?"

"I don't know," I answered honestly. "I just know a lot of people find it suspicious. You were only in your forties. It would be weird to just drop dead at your desk at that age – even in the 1960s."

Edith turned from me and trained her gaze back at the television. I couldn't figure out if she didn't want to answer me or didn't know how to answer me.

"Were you murdered, Edith?"

Edith surprised me when she shrugged. "I don't know."

"You don't know how you died?"

"I know how I died," she said testily.

I swallowed hard. "How did you die?"

"I was eating lunch at my desk," she said softly. "It tasted funny."

I wanted to ask what it tasted like, but I didn't want to interrupt her. I was afraid if I did I would never get the answers I was looking for.

"I knew something wasn't right about it," she admitted. "It was too late, though. I tried to get up. I tried to reach for the phone. My hands felt numb, though. I couldn't push away from the desk. It felt like I was drowning from inside."

Sympathy bubbled up from inside of me. Poor Edith.

"I died right there, with my face in my spaghetti. My hair was even dripping in it."

The lurid picture she wove almost made me laugh. I realized that wasn't appropriate, so I screwed my face up in the most sympathetic way I could. "How long did it take you to come back as a ghost?"

Edith seemed to consider the question. "Just a few minutes, I think."

"Did you realize you were a ghost right away?"

"No. It took me a few minutes. I kept looking down at my body. I thought I was just having an out-of-body experience," she said. "Like you see on television. I think I hoped I was having an out-of-body experience actually."

"When did you know for sure?"

"One of my co-workers, Debbie was her name, she found me at my desk. She tried to shake me awake. I started yelling at her that I was right here. I was standing right here. She never even looked up at me, though. That's when I knew."

"Do you think you were poisoned?"

Edith nodded stiffly.

"Do you know who did it?"

"No. And I don't want to talk about that anymore," she said forcefully.

I held up my hands in submission. "We won't talk about it anymore," I promised.

Edith nodded mutely. "So what do you want me to do?"

"Will you come with me to Hypnotic? Talk to Shane?"

Edith seemed to consider the question seriously. She didn't look convinced, though. "I don't ever leave the office," she said finally.

"I know. The store is just down the road, though. We can walk there together and then you can come right back to the office."

Edith still didn't look convinced.

"You would be my hero if you could get him to talk." Manipulative, I know. I didn't know what else to do, though.

Edith steeled her shoulders and turned to me. "I'll go," she said.

I smiled to myself. Edith may be a pain in the ass – but she did always try to do the right thing. As we left the office to walk down the street, I couldn't help but notice how nervous she looked. I found it surreal that a ghost was scared to walk down the streets of Hemlock Cove – but I didn't want to scare her off so I kept my thoughts to myself.

Even though she was initially nervous, I saw that Edith had relaxed a few minutes into our short journey.

"I can't believe they've turned this place into a tourist trap."

"I don't think they had a lot of choice," I admitted. "It was either a tourist trap or let the town die. There was no other way to sustain it – especially since there was no manufacturing base anymore."

"Still," Edith paused and looked in the window of Mrs. Little's unicorn store. "It's so tacky."

I opened my mouth to answer her, but saw Mrs. Little staring at me suspiciously from inside of her store. I knew I couldn't explain talking to thin air in front of her business, so I quickly shut my mouth.

"Is that Margaret Riddle?" Edith asked.

I shifted so Mrs. Little couldn't see my mouth before I answered. "I think Riddle was her maiden name. Now she's Margaret Little."

"Did she marry John Little?"

"Yeah."

"I used to have a crush on him," Edith admitted. "How did he turn out?"

"I think he died – like a decade ago," I answered.

Edith didn't look happy with the news, but she continued to follow me down the street, kibitzing about the tacky businesses as she went.

"The bakery is still the same. That's good."

A few minutes later: "Why is all that horrible stuff in the front window of the hardware store?"

I let her keep up her own running commentary. I didn't get the feeling she wanted my input anyway.

When we got to Hypnotic, I held the door open until Edith entered. I could tell she was really disgusted by Thistle and Clove's store. "This is a hocus pocus shop," she hissed.

"It's not hocus pocus," I argued. "It's just a nature store ... essentially."

"They're threatening to curse people," she shot back.

"That's just a joke." Or, at least I hoped it was.

Thistle and Clove were busy behind the counter when we entered. They looked up expectantly. They didn't seem surprised to see me.

"Who were you talking to?" Clove asked.

"Edith," I said tightly. I was hoping they wouldn't scare her off by asking too many questions.

"Edith from the paper?"

"Yes."

"Hi, Edith," Clove said breezily. She was apparently over her discomfort of being around ghosts.

"She looks just like Tillie," Edith said distrustfully.

"She looks just like her mother," I corrected Edith.

"She's Marnie's girl?"

"You knew Marnie?" I was essentially just trying to keep her talking at this point. I didn't want her to clam up.

"I knew them all."

I glanced around the store quickly, but I didn't see Shane. "Where is Shane?"

"He's in the backroom," Thistle said through gritted teeth. "He doesn't believe we don't smoke the herbs back there."

I smiled despite myself. I often wondered that, too.

Edith had turned her attention to Thistle. "Her hair is blue."

"Yes."

"She must be Twila's."

"Yes, she is Twila's."

"What is she saying?" Thistle asked suspiciously.

"She said you look like your mom."

"Did she mean it as an insult?"

"I don't think so." Probably, though.

"Go get Shane," I told Clove.

"Do I have to? He's been driving us crazy all morning."

"Just do it."

Clove grumbled as she disappeared behind the curtain. I could hear her talking for a few minutes and then she came back out into the main area of the store. "He'll be here in a minute," she said.

"What's he doing?"

"I told him you brought another ghost to talk to him and he's scared."

"He's a ghost," I protested.

"*You* tell him that! I'm not your go-between," she grumbled.

I threw myself on the couch to wait. I watched as Edith walked around the store. "I knew your family was into some hinky stuff, but this is ridiculous."

"We're not hinky," Thistle said testily.

"You can hear her?"

"I can now. I think if you're talking to them in our presence, eventually we can hear them. I have no idea why."

I didn't either. "We'll ask the aunts later," I suggested.

Shane was peeking his head out from the curtain. He smiled at me, but frowned when he caught sight of Edith.

"She doesn't look like a ghost," he said.

"Neither do you," I assured him.

Shane took a step out into the room. He didn't make a move toward Edith, though. She turned and regarded him distastefully. "Are you a hobo?"

"What's a hobo?"

"A vagrant. A tramp."

"I'm not a tramp!"

"You're dressed like a hobo," Edith said. "Your pants are too big and that jacket looks like it belongs in a dumpster."

Shane looked down at his coat in confusion. "It's just a hoodie."

"That's just how people dress today," I interrupted. I didn't want the conversation to devolve any further.

"Well, it's stupid," Edith said.

I turned back to Shane. "What's the last thing you remember?"

Shane looked confused again. I had a feeling he looked that way a lot in life. "I was in the backroom."

"I mean before you died."

"Oh," Shane furrowed his brow in concentration. "I was at the mall."

"What were you doing?"

"Shopping. I bought some new shoes."

"Those shoes?" I pointed to his gray Converse.

"No. They were black."

"Black Converse?"

"Yeah."

Well, that at least was something. If we found the shoes, maybe we would find the killer.

"Did you leave the mall?"

"Yeah. I was out in the parking lot, loading stuff in my car," he said.

"Then what?"

Shane thought hard before shaking his head. "I don't know."

"Did someone come up behind you?"

"I told you, I don't know." He was getting snippy now.

Edith stared him down for a few minutes. "I think he doesn't want to remember," she said.

She was probably right. I couldn't force him to remember, though. "He will when he's ready," I said finally.

"I hope so," Shane said. "I want to know who killed me so I can haunt them."

"You want to haunt everyone," Clove grumbled.

"Hey! If I'm going to be a ghost I might as well have some fun with it."

You really couldn't argue with that.

ELEVEN

I spent the rest of the afternoon at Hypnotic quizzing Shane about his final day. My questions increasingly irritated him, so I convinced Thistle to start asking them for me. As much as Shane didn't want to answer the questions, he did want to please Thistle. I figured I might as well use his crush to my advantage.

Despite steady hours of questioning, though, we didn't learn anything else of any interest. Until he remembered on his own, we were at a standstill.

Edith lost interest in the conversation pretty early on and decided to leave.

"Are you going back to the newspaper?"

"No," she said.

That surprised me.

"I'm going to take a look around town."

Now that she had gotten the courage to leave the office, I wondered if she would ever go back. The world had just grown exponentially for her.

"Well, have fun."

"I don't have fun, missy," she chastised me. "I just want to see if anyone I know is still around."

"Aunt Tillie is out at the inn," Thistle offered evilly.

"Why would I want to see her?" Edith looked insulted.

"She can see ghosts, too. You could irritate the crap out of her."

Edith looked intrigued by the prospect. After she left, I turned on Thistle. "I'm telling Aunt Tillie you're the one who sent her."

"I'll tell her it was you – and she'll believe me. She thinks you're out to get her anyway."

I told Clove and Thistle about my visit out to the inn earlier in the afternoon. They both seemed surprised by my story.

"So, you're saying that she faked a 'freak out' just to get you out to the inn?" Clove looked like she didn't believe me.

"That doesn't surprise me," Thistle offered. "She cares. She just doesn't want us to know that she cares."

"Still," Clove sniffed. "That seems like a lot of wasted energy."

"You know she likes to irritate our moms. It was probably her afternoon entertainment."

I decided to stay at the store and help Clove and Thistle bag herbs and stock their shelves. The weekend was coming up, and like any other weekend in Hemlock Cove in the fall, the store would be slammed.

At about 3 p.m., the store phone rang. Thistle answered it. I could tell by the shift in her body language, though, that she wasn't happy to hear the voice on the other end. "We just had dinner out there the other night," she complained.

Crap.

Clove and I both stopped what we were doing to listen to Thistle's end of the conversation.

"No, I'm not saying that I don't want to see you," Thistle argued. "We were just out there, though."

Thistle was quiet as she listened for a few moments. I figured it was her mom. Thistle only got twitchy when she was talking to her own mother. We all found our aunts more entertaining than our own mothers. I think that's just a biological rule or something.

"No, there's no rule that you can only see your mother once a week."

Thistle was rolling her eyes.

"Yes, I know you won't be here forever."

Thistle glared at Clove and I openly when she caught us smiling at her.

"Yes, Clove and Bay are here right now, as a matter of fact. They already know and they can't wait for dinner."

Clove and I weren't smiling anymore.

"Yes, we'll be there at seven sharp," Thistle grumbled. "I said yes!"

Clove shot a look in my direction. There was no way out of this for us either.

"I'm not crabby! Why do you always think that?"

Clove moved around the counter and stood beside me. "Why do you think they want to have another dinner so soon?"

"I don't know," I admitted. "I don't like it, though. It means they're up to something."

"They're always up to something," Clove countered.

"Then they're up to something especially irritating," I suggested.

Thistle was still arguing with her mom. "Of course I didn't forget the equinox celebration."

Clove and I both froze as we looked up at Thistle. We had all forgotten the autumnal equinox celebration. Shit.

"Of course, we're all looking forward to it," Thistle lied.

We all looked at each other resignedly. It was going to be a long night. After Thistle hung up, Shane looked at us expectantly. "What's the equinox celebration?"

"An excuse for our moms to get naked in the woods," Clove said bitterly.

Shane seemed to consider her response for a second. "Are they hot?"

"They're in their fifties," Clove said disgustedly.

"Are you guys going to get naked?" He was looking at Thistle with renewed interest.

"No," Thistle said determinedly. "Absolutely not." That almost never happened – at least since we'd hit our teens.

We all shared a dubious glance with one another. "This isn't good," I said finally.

"That's the understatement of the year," Thistle sighed.

The three of us dragged our feet for the rest of the afternoon. We were all dreading the evening's upcoming activities. There was no way to get out of them, though. We had all tried in the past – and we had all failed miserably.

Thistle and Clove closed up the shop at six, and we all climbed into my car. Shane even got in the backseat with Thistle – much to her chagrin.

He kept up a steady stream of chatter during the drive out to the inn. He seemed interested in what was going to happen tonight. I didn't blame him. It's always more interesting in theory than in practice.

"So why do they get naked in the woods?"

"They dance around a fire," Thistle said grumpily.

"Why?"

"To drive me crazy."

"But why?"

"It's a Pagan practice," Thistle said shortly.

"Pagan? Like witches?"

Thistle rolled her eyes. "Yes, like witches."

"Are you guys witches?" Shane looked suddenly scared.

"Yes."

"Do you cast spells on people?"

"No."

"Then what do you do?"

"We don't really do anything. We were just born into a family of witches." Thistle didn't feel like explaining – and I didn't know how to help her – so I kept my mouth shut.

"Then why do they dance naked in the woods?"

"It's just tradition."

Shane wasn't happy with her answer. "I still don't understand."

"Just watch what happens tonight and you'll understand."

"I get to come?"

"Could we stop you?"

"No."

I parked at the gatehouse. We all went into our rooms and quickly changed for dinner and then made our way up to the inn.

"This place is so cool," Shane said when he saw The Overlook. "It looks like a haunted house."

"Technically, since you're staying there, the guesthouse is haunted," I pointed out.

Shane shrugged off my statement. He was much more interested in The Overlook now than anything else. He seemed to have temporarily forgotten about the promise of naked dancing in the woods – which was a blessing.

When we entered the family living quarters, Aunt Tillie was sitting in front of the television watching *Jeopardy*. It was the only television show she cared about.

"Hey, Aunt Tillie," Clove greeted her.

Aunt Tillie grunted in response. We knew better than interrupting her show, so we started to move through the house. "She's not what I expected," Shane said when we walked into the kitchen.

"What did you expect?"

"I don't know, a little old lady with a wart on her nose," Shane said innocently.

"Do not say that to her," Thistle warned.

"Why? Can she curse a ghost?"

Thistle merely shrugged. "I don't know. If anyone can, she can, though. Besides that, she'll curse us for bringing you here."

"She'd curse her own family?" Shane didn't look like he believed us.

"It wouldn't be the first time."

Twila and Marnie were staring at us all when we entered the room. "Whom are you talking to?"

"Shane," I answered simply.

"The boy who died?"

"Yes."

Aunt Twila clucked. "Oh, that poor boy. How is he doing?"

"Ask him yourself."

"I can't talk to ghosts," she chided me.

"Neither could Clove and Thistle. They can now."

Both Twila and Marnie looked surprised. "They can?"

"Who can what?" My mom entered the room, making her way to the stove to stir whatever she had simmering in a big pot.

"Clove and Thistle can see ghosts now."

"We can't see them," Thistle corrected. "We can just hear them."

"Them? More than one?"

"We met Edith today, too," Clove answered.

"Well, that must have been a thrill," Aunt Tillie harrumphed as she entered the room. I noticed her gaze rested on Shane for a long moment before she turned to me.

"Is this him?"

"That's Shane," I acknowledged.

"Hi," Shane greeted her shyly.

"Bet you wish you'd picked a different outfit to die in," Aunt Tillie said.

Twila, Marnie and my mom all sucked in disapproving breaths. "Don't you be mean to that boy," Mom warned. "He's been through enough."

Shane smiled at Aunt Tillie. "I like her," he said finally.

"That will change," I said under my breath.

"What did you say?" Aunt Tillie looked at me suspiciously.

"I said I was glad he liked you," I lied.

I knew Aunt Tillie didn't believe me, but she apparently wasn't going to pursue the matter any further right now. "Is he coming to the equinox celebration tonight?"

"Yep, and he's very excited," Thistle said. I think I was the only one to pick up on her exaggerated sarcasm.

"Good."

"Why good?"

"It will just be good for him to be there," Aunt Tillie said.

She was up to something.

"Let's eat," my mom said brightly, exchanging quick looks with Marnie and Twila as she tried to distract us.

Oh, great. They were all up to something.

TWELVE

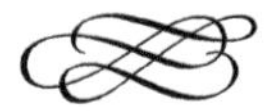

Dinner was surprisingly entertaining – especially when Aunt Tillie and Shane got in a snarky argument about whether or not smoking herbs or grinding them up into a poultice was more efficient for pain management.

"You don't fool me," Aunt Tillie shook her head at Shane. "You think I'm an old lady, but I know what herbs you're talking about smoking."

Clove and Thistle smirked at each other – an exchange that wasn't missed by the ever eagle-eyed Aunt Tillie.

"You two aren't funny either," she warned them.

I thought they were funny. I wasn't going to tell Aunt Tillie that, though. "Aunt Tillie is right," I admonished them. "Pot jokes are never funny."

Thistle glowered at me. "Since you're the one who taught us to smoke pot when we were teenagers, that's rich."

My mom swiveled in her chair and regarded me suspiciously. "You never smoked pot, did you?"

"Of course not," I lied.

My mom looked momentarily placated.

"She's lying," Clove said.

Whoops. She was looking tense again. "Are you lying?"

"Of course I'm lying," I admitted.

"I'm really disappointed in you," she sniffed.

"Yeah, let's get worked up about something that happened more than a decade ago," I said sarcastically. "That seems like a great way to waste a couple hours."

"There are some great rehabs out there these days. I've seen them on television," Twila said gently.

I glared over at Thistle. "Are you happy now?"

"I'm not unhappy," Thistle smiled.

"Well, I'm not going to rehab alone. I'll make you two go with me."

"They're not the potheads," Marnie argued. "You're the one who apparently has the problem."

"I haven't smoked pot since I was in college," I shot back. "Thistle and Clove smoked before the last solstice celebration."

"Hey!" Clove protested. "You said you wouldn't tell."

"Is that true?" Marnie's eyes were narrowed dangerously as she regarded her daughter.

"I ... I ...I can't remember," Clove said lamely.

"They say that's the first sign of a problem," I said. "Blackouts."

"You are so hateful," Clove gritted her teeth.

"You started it."

"It was funny when it was about you."

"Maybe we can get a group rate," Twila fretted.

I turned to her in disbelief. "Please. You have a bag of weed in your nightstand. I saw it there a few weeks ago when I was looking for candles."

"That is not weed," she said. "That is just a satchel to make my socks smell better."

"You want your socks to smell like hemp? Oh, and there were no socks in that drawer."

"Why were you going through my drawers?" Twila's voice had climbed an octave.

"It was the night the power went out. I was looking for extra candles."

Now my mom and Marnie were staring at Twila suspiciously. "You don't keep pot in your drawer, do you?"

"It's medicinal," Twila argued. "I have a lot of back pain."

Clove was right. It was a lot more fun when the onus was on someone else.

The argument continued for another twenty minutes before Aunt Tillie put an end to it. "No one is going to rehab," she said finally. "This is just ridiculous. If you want to spend your time in a haze, then that's your business."

"Says the woman who empties an entire bottle of wine by herself at dinner every night," I muttered.

Aunt Tillie glowered at me. "You want to start something with me now?"

Did I? Not particularly.

Everyone started clearing the table in relative silence. From time to time, we all cast sideways glances at one another. I was hoping that the conversation had derailed their planned equinox celebration. I doubted I would be that lucky, though. I never was.

"Your family is all kinds of awesome," Shane said as he sidled up to me while I was loading the dishwasher.

"If you say so."

"No, really. They're great. You guys talk about everything."

"We talk about too much, if you ask me."

"But you're all so close."

"There's close and there's co-dependent. I used to think we straddled the line to co-dependency. I think we crossed that line a long time ago, though."

"Yeah, but everyone is always there for you."

I looked at him contemplatively a second. "I'm sure your mom was always there for you."

"She was. It was just the two of us, though. You have a big family and everyone is always into everyone else's business. I think it's fun."

"It's only fun when it's not you."

"I don't think you'd trade them for another family, though, would you?"

I considered his question for a moment. "I wouldn't trade them," I finally said. "I'd just send them on extended vacations from time to time."

After dinner, we all settled around the fire in the den for a cup of tea. Shane was back on the question train about the equinox celebration. I couldn't blame him. It always sounds more interesting than it actually is.

"I asked them, but they wouldn't tell me," Shane said, jerking a thumb at Thistle, Clove and I. "What exactly is an equinox celebration?"

"The equinox and the solstice are when our powers are at their most powerful," Aunt Tillie explained. I think she was warming up to Shane – despite his outfit. "Some days have special power. There are four each year. Two equinoxes and two solstices. This is technically a fall equinox. The solstices fall in the winter and summer."

"Then why do you call it an equinox celebration?"

Aunt Tillie shrugged noncommittally. "I don't know. It's just something we started doing every year."

"Do you have a celebration for each solstice?"

"We usually skip the winter one," Aunt Tillie said truthfully.

"Why?"

"Because no one wants to dance naked in a foot of snow," I offered.

Shane snickered.

"That's not why," Aunt Tillie disagreed.

"Than why?"

Aunt Tillie pursed her lips. "Don't be smart."

No matter what she said, that was the reason. The summer solstice was our biggest celebration, but we always played up the autumnal equinox, too. The spring equinox and the winter solstice got short shrift in the Winchester house.

Shane wasn't going to be deterred from his questions. "But why do you dance naked?"

"To be closer to our gods."

"Pagan gods?"

"Yes."

"We don't really believe in Pagan gods," I argued.

"You don't?"

"No. It's more a symbolic thing."

"For you, maybe," Aunt Tillie said disdainfully. "I believe in the old ways."

"You do not."

"I do, too."

"Really? What are their names?"

Aunt Tillie huffed. "That's hardly important."

"Knock it off," my mother warned me. "Don't wind her up."

After our tea, we all put on our coats and headed out to the woods surrounding the property. We walked in order of age, like we always did, with Aunt Tillie leading the way with a kerosene lamp. She was wearing her traditional sparkly cape as she moved spryly in front of us. Occasionally you could see the moonlight glint off the sewn sequins in the cape.

"Why is she wearing a cape?" Shane asked.

"She thinks she's a superhero," Thistle whispered.

"She's Witch Woman, able to leap tall nieces in a single bound," Clove chuckled.

It took us about five minutes to make our way to the ceremonial clearing. We were all used to the trip, so even in the dark it wasn't much of a difficulty for us.

Once we got there, Twila lit a bonfire – which Marnie had stacked earlier in the day in anticipation of the celebration. The circle was empty except for the fire pit. We all took turns maintaining in the spring, summer and fall. We all separated an equal distance from one another, extending our hands so they almost touched – but not quite – and looking up to the moon. We all knew our part in the dramatic play that was about to be performed.

"I thought you were going to be naked," Shane complained.

"That comes later," I hissed. "And not everyone gets naked. Just the four of them."

"Yeah, Clove, Thistle and Bay don't do it because they're worried they won't stack up compared to us," Marnie teased.

Yeah, that was it.

"Mother Earth, we call to the four points," Aunt Tillie started, invoking her most serious incantation voice.

"What are the four points?" Shane didn't seem to grasp how seriously the elder generations of our family took this.

Aunt Tillie shot him a death glare. Shane shut his mouth when he caught sight of the look. It may just have been a trick of the light, but I swear I saw him gulp.

"From the earth, we look to the air. From the fire, we look to the sea."

I had heard this so many times I could practically recite it myself. Soon she would call to the night. Then she would drop her clothes and dance for an hour with a bottle of wine in her hand.

As Aunt Tillie called to the earth a few minutes later, I saw Thistle go rigid in the circle. I had seen this before – never in the circle – but on the rare occasion when she got a vision of the future. I could feel the prickle of magic as it washed over all of us – but settled on Thistle.

I heard her gasp and started to move toward her.

"Don't break the circle," Aunt Tillie snapped.

I thought about disobeying her but remained in my spot. My eyes never left Thistle, though.

"They're coming," she said in a hauntingly empty voice.

"Who is coming?" Twila asked.

"The two faces of death."

"The killers?" I knew there were two of them. I just knew it.

"They'll come before the next full moon." Thistle was saying the words, but I wasn't sure she was conscious of them.

"The next full moon is in a couple of days," I said, more to myself than anyone else.

"Before they come, they will take another."

"Another? Another murder?"

"When they come, they will try to take us."

"They'll try to kill us?" I wish she would answer me.

"When they go, they will take something from us."

"What does that mean?" Shane was as white as a ghost – which was ironically fitting – under the pale moonlight. His gaze was focused on Thistle. It was like he was frozen in time along with her.

"Can you see who they are?"

"They're shrouded in dark," Thistle furrowed her brow. At least it seemed like she could hear what we were saying.

"All I can see is that it's a boy and a girl who will die."

"Why are they killing people?"

"They think it will bring them forever."

"Forever? Like they'll never die?"

"Yes."

"Is that even possible?" I turned to Aunt Tillie.

"There are many dark magicks that have been long since forgotten," she said. "Maybe they think they've discovered one."

"In other words, they're probably just crazy."

"There is that."

I could see the clouds shifting in the sky above us. They were drifting in front of the moon. I knew Thistle would lose her connection when they did.

"Can you see a name? Anything?"

"I only see the sky – and the stars are going black." With those words, Thistle fell to her knees in the circle.

This time, I did make my way over to her side. Aunt Tillie didn't argue. She stayed in her spot, though, and watched the two of us.

"Are you all right?" I asked Thistle.

"Yeah," she rasped. "I wasn't expecting that, though. I thought we would just get drunk to the point where we blacked out so we hopefully wouldn't dream about the dancing."

"That would have been nice."

"What do you think?"

"I think there are two killers – although I think I already knew that," I admitted. "I also think someone else is going to die, and we're helpless to stop it."

Thistle bit her lower lip. "I think someone else has already died. We just haven't found them yet."

"Why do you think that?"

"I saw ... I don't know what I saw. I saw a knife. I saw blood. And I heard a scream."

"Could you see a face? Could you see where?"

"No, it was dark. I think it's a girl, though. And I think she's already gone."

Aunt Tillie had appeared at my side. I hadn't even heard her approach. "We must reflect on what we've learned," she said gravely.

"Let me guess? That involves wine and dancing around a fire? That hardly seems appropriate now."

One guess who won the following argument?

THIRTEEN

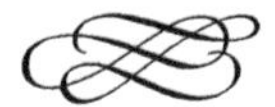

"It gets worse every time."

I looked up from my spot on the couch, where I was laying with my legs draped over the edge and a cold compress on my forehead, and regarded Thistle seriously. "I can't believe they still did it, especially after your vision. You'd think they'd be more worried about the fact that another body is about to be dropped on us – not that the rhythm is going to get them."

"It's not like they could stop it," Clove said.

"It shouldn't be celebrated either," I shot back.

"I thought it was cool." Shane was perched on the arm of the chair where Thistle was sitting. He'd barely left her side since her vision. She couldn't see his proximity, but she knew he was near.

"You thought it was cool? Bras and Spanx were invented for a reason." I shuddered involuntarily.

"That was a little weird," Shane acknowledged. "They had a strange sense of rhythm, though."

"How can they have rhythm when there's no music?"

"I heard music. In my head. Didn't you?"

"All I heard was the pounding of an impending migraine," I said bitterly.

"Don't be so dramatic. I think it's kind of fun when they do it," Clove admonished me. She always was the one who talked big and then backtracked.

"Then why don't you join in?"

Clove looked decidedly uncomfortable. "It's more fun to watch than participate," she said finally.

"You just have a complex about your thighs," Thistle laughed.

"I do not."

"It's fine," Thistle said. "We all have big thighs. It's a family thing."

"My thighs aren't big," I argued. "They're just not little."

"We should work out more," Thistle suggested.

"We always say that."

"Then we always get distracted by the fresh cookies at the inn," Clove giggled. "And the pies. And the cakes."

We all went to bed after that. I knew what we would all be dreaming about – and it wouldn't be pleasant.

When I woke the next morning, I wiped the sleep out of my eyes and stretched languidly. It took a full minute before the previous night's events rushed me. Another body!

I jumped out of bed and made my way into the kitchen. Clove was making coffee at the counter. She was still in her flannel pajama bottoms and tank top. There was no sign of Thistle.

"She's still asleep," Clove said to my unasked question. "Last night took a lot out of her, I think."

"I don't doubt it." I climbed up onto one of the stools that we had placed on the other side of the kitchen counter and watched Clove as she filled the coffee machine mechanically.

"You're up early," she said. "You think they'll find a body today, don't you?"

I shrugged. "I don't know if I should be hoping for that or not. On one hand, I want to believe that no one else died. On the other hand, I doubt that Thistle is wrong, so it would be better if they find the body sooner – rather than later."

"For her family?"

"For all of us."

Clove nodded understandingly. We both looked up when we heard Thistle's bedroom door open. She staggered out into the living room – looking like I'm sure Clove and I both felt.

"I didn't sleep for shit," she announced, running a hand through her tangled blue hair haphazardly.

"I slept, but it wasn't exactly well," I said.

"I only slept a few hours," Clove said as she handed me a cup of coffee.

Thistle perched on the stool next to me and accepted the cup of steaming liquid that Clove slid toward her.

"Where's Shane?" I looked around the guesthouse but didn't see him.

"We can only hear him, remember," Thistle said grumpily. None of us were morning people. "How should we know?"

"Don't get snippy with me."

"I'm not getting snippy," she said harshly, but then her expression softened. "I'm just tired."

"I think we're all on edge ... waiting," Clove said.

That was definitely the truth.

We lapsed into silence, the only sound occurring when one of us sipped from our cups. The silence was comfortable but strained. We all jumped when there was a loud rap on the door.

Thistle glanced up at the clock on the wall. It was only 8:30 a.m. "This can't be good."

I think we all knew what it was.

I climbed off the stool, leaving my coffee on the counter, and moved to the door. I didn't bother looking to see who it was. I knew, without being told, who stood on the other side of the aged oak.

"Good morning, Chief Terry." I greeted him somberly.

The chief looked like he hadn't slept in days. His gray hair was tangled and dirty. He entered the guesthouse, glancing around to see who was present. He greeted Thistle and Clove with a short nod. "Girls."

"Good morning, Chief Terry," Clove greeted him. "Would you like a cup of coffee?"

Chief Terry nodded blankly. "That sounds good." He took the freshly poured cup that Clove offered him and sat down heavily at the kitchen table. He looked to us all expectantly.

"You're probably wondering why I'm here?"

Not really.

"There was another body found this morning," he continued.

"Where?"

"The Johnson maze, just outside of town."

"Was it ... was it another teenager?" I knew the answer. I still had to ask the question.

"Yes. It was a girl this time. Her name was Sophie Maxwell."

"You identified her already?"

"The killer left her purse next to the body this time."

"Where is she from?"

"Traverse City."

"Why are they taking kids from Traverse City and bringing them here?" Clove asked.

If Chief Terry noticed that Clove said *they* instead of *him,* he didn't acknowledge it. "I don't know. That's just one of a hundred questions that have to be answered, isn't it?"

"Was she ...?" I broke off. I didn't know how to phrase the next question.

"She was stabbed, just like the other boy. And, yes, her heart was removed, too." Chief Terry looked out the front window from his spot at the table. He had a clear view of the inn. Usually, he would have asked about my mom or one of my aunts early in the conversation. I didn't think he had the energy. "The state boys say there are no signs of sexual assault, though, so at least that's something."

Yes, a very small something. "Has her family been told?"

"They're doing that right now."

"Was she reported missing?"

"Not to my knowledge. We don't have any information on her movements yesterday, though."

"When did she die?"

"We don't have a time of death yet, but sometime last night seems to be the general consensus."

"They're obviously putting the bodies in public places," I said. "They want the bodies found right away."

"The state boys said they might call in federal help."

"Like profilers?"

"Yeah."

"That might not be a bad idea."

"I'll take any help I can get right now, not that I have any real control over the case." Chief Terry sounded more tired than bitter, but I knew that having the case taken from him was probably driving him crazy.

"They still don't have any ideas why this is happening – and why it's happening here?"

"They have some ideas," Chief Terry said grimly.

"Like what?" Thistle asked.

"They think that it's happening because of how we rebranded the town," he said quietly.

"You mean, because we made it a witch town?" Clove looked incredulous. "Like we asked for it?"

"More like someone here is trying to expand the brand of the town – in a real life way," Chief Terry said.

"That's crazy! Why would we want to do that? This will kill the tourism trade for the entire season, not increase it." Not that tourism really mattered in this situation.

"That's what I told them," Chief Terry said. "I'm just one step up from Barney Fife to them, though, so they pretty much just disregard everything I say. They're only keeping me in the loop because they have to."

"They're never going to solve it if they keep looking at the town," Thistle argued. "It's not someone from the town."

"Are you sure of that?" Chief Terry looked at her probingly.

"Aren't you?"

"No one wants to think of their neighbor as a murderer," he said. "We can't rule people out, though, just on a feeling."

Thistle didn't look convinced.

"I don't believe it's anyone from the town either," he said. "But we have to look at everyone."

Chief Terry turned to me expectantly. "I was hoping you would come out to the maze with me?"

"Me? Why?"

Chief Terry hedged. "We all know your family is ... different. I just thought you might be able to see something that we didn't."

Like a ghost?

"Let me get dressed." Chief Terry didn't ask for help from outsiders very often. I couldn't say no to him – not that I wanted to.

I moved toward my bedroom. Clove was close on my heels. "Don't talk to a ghost in front of them," she warned in a low voice. "That will just cast suspicion on you. That may be what they're fishing for."

"I don't think Chief Terry would do that," I argued.

"I don't think that Chief Terry has a clue what the state police are up to. Just be careful."

I'm always careful. Okay, I at least consider being careful before I jump into the deep end headfirst.

FOURTEEN

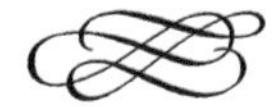

The ride to the maze was short – only about fifteen minutes – and it was spent mostly in silence. There really wasn't a lot to say. If we talked about magic, Chief Terry would be uncomfortable. If we talked about the murders, I would be uncomfortable.

When we turned onto the road that led to the Johnson farm, I could see the kaleidoscope of flashing lights that were illuminating the early morning sky about a mile down the road – at the entrance to the corn maze.

The Johnson corn maze was the oldest in town – the first, so to speak. There were now a total of five, and most of the others were fancier, but there was something refreshing in the simplicity of the original.

"There's a lot of police here," I breathed.

"Double what we had the other day," Chief Terry acknowledged. "This has made the national news. They say Nancy Grace is sending someone out."

Great. That was exactly what we didn't need, a media frenzy.

Chief Terry parked his cruiser next to the other vehicles. We both exited the vehicle in unison. I still wasn't sure what he expected of me. I was just glad he'd thought to bring me out here. At least I wouldn't have to sneak into this corn maze in the dark this time. Or, at least I hoped.

Most of the chatter that greeted us was typical police talk. I saw a handful of people being questioned to the left side of the maze. They all looked understandably nervous. I turned to Chief Terry questioningly.

"Workers," he said simply. "They found the body. At least this time only one or two people had been in the maze before the body was found."

Thank the Goddess for small favors.

I noticed another grouping of police officers positioned off to the right of the maze – and I was surprised to see who they were questioning. It was Landon and his cronies. What were they doing here?

Chief Terry seemed surprised to see them, too. "They weren't here when I left to come pick you up."

"I wonder what they're doing here now."

"You think it's suspicious?" Chief Terry was staring at me intently.

"I think it's weird that a bunch of biker guys keep showing up at corn mazes – especially ones that have dead bodies in them."

Chief Terry pursed his lips. "I think focusing on them might be a mistake."

"Why?" I looked at him suspiciously.

"Do they seem like the type of guys who run around cutting people's hearts out? Or the type of guys who would just plug a guy in the head if he crossed them? I think they're bad guys, just not the bad guys we're looking for in this case."

Good point. No sale.

"You know something?"

Chief Terry sighed. "I'm going to tell you something, but I don't want you printing it in the paper – at least not yet."

"What?"

"There's something else going on in town, and I think our new friends are tied up in that, not in the murders."

"What?"

"There's been a new, um, business that's entered Hemlock Cove over the past six months or so."

If I had to say 'what' one more time, I was going to scream.

"It's crystal meth."

"You're kidding!" Never what you expect.

"Drugs are a part of our culture now. You shouldn't be surprised."

"This is Hemlock Cove, though," I protested. "Not Detroit."

"Drugs can be anywhere. They're not just a city thing. Heck, before you were born, your mom and aunts had a small pot field hidden in the woods that they thought no one knew about."

After last night's conversation, I found that hard to swallow. Chief Terry must have read the disbelief on my face.

"It's true. It wasn't big or anything. They tried to hide it behind their herb patch."

"They just busted us last night for smoking pot when we were teenagers," I complained.

"Well, that was a little hypocritical of them."

I couldn't wait to tell Thistle and Clove about this new development. Then I felt a wave of disappointment in myself wash over me when I realized I was gleefully planning an ambush on my family – when we were about to go see the body of a dead teenage girl.

"When did they get rid of it?" I asked despite my now open disgust with myself.

"Before any of you were born. One day it was just gone. Maybe your Aunt Tillie found it?"

Maybe she started it?

I turned my attention back to his meth comments. "Do you think that our new friends are behind the meth trade?"

"I think that's a fair assumption."

Something wasn't adding up to me. "Is that why Landon was in your office the other day?"

"I already told you, I was just asking him some questions," Chief Terry snapped.

Better avoid that line of conversation for the time being, I figured.

"If you know it's them, why aren't you arresting them?"

"I don't know it's them," he said finally. "It's an ongoing investigation. I just suspect it may be them."

Chief Terry now turned to me with a new warning on his lips. "Don't get involved in this. It's too dangerous."

"Why would I get involved?"

"Just ... just stay away from Landon. He's bad news."

"Why would I be hanging around with Landon?"

Chief Terry looked at me knowingly. I felt myself blushing under his gaze. "I'm not into Landon," I said hurriedly.

"See it stays that way."

Chief Terry flashed his badge and led me into the corn maze. I cast a look back in Landon's direction and found him watching me. The gaze he cast on me was reflective and thoughtful. Could he really be dealing meth? Something told me there was more to this story. Either Chief Terry didn't know everything, or he was holding something back. It could be both of those scenarios, too. If I had to guess, that was the most likely option.

I followed Chief Terry into the maze. He seemed to know where he was going. About five minutes in, he took a hard left and led me to a central clearing. There were about ten more police officers steadily working here.

I had to catch my breath when I saw the body strung up on another cross in the center of the clearing.

"Another cross," I murmured.

"Yeah."

The girl had long blonde hair, but the ends of it seemed to be dyed another color. I realized, all too quickly, that they weren't dyed another color. They were stained with blood.

I couldn't see her face because there was another garish mask on the body. I turned to Chief Terry in surprise. "I thought they would have taken the body by now."

"They're still getting photos," he said. "They'll cut her down shortly."

I looked around the clearing doubtfully. I still wasn't sure exactly why I was here. Chief Terry watched me scan the area.

"Do you see anything?"

I was surprised by the question. "Like what?"

"I don't know, something that maybe we missed." Chief Terry was being evasive again.

"Like what?" I prodded him again.

"I don't know," Chief Terry sighed. "Just look around."

I didn't know what he expected me to find, but I took a couple of tentative steps into the clearing. It had been a few years since I'd visited the Johnson maze, but it looked exactly like I remembered it.

Unlike the other mazes in the area, the Johnson maze wasn't designed to scare, just to entertain. It was billed as a family maze and not a haunted maze. I didn't know if it would ever be able to recover the innocence it used to boast. It would probably be forever stained – like poor Sophie Maxwell's golden hair.

As I carefully edged around the clearing – making sure to avoid getting in the way of any of the officers – I couldn't help but feel like I was being suffocated. The fact that I was out in the open air made the sensation all the more baffling.

Suddenly, I felt a pair of eyes on me. I swung around, expecting to find a police officer standing behind me. Instead, a few feet away, I saw a teenage girl standing in the corner and watching the police busily hurrying from place to place.

No one else noticed her. Not her long blonde hair. Not her timid blue eyes. Not her pink fuzzy sweater – which made her stand out like a rose in a field of daisies. They didn't notice her, of course, because I was the only one that could see her.

It was Sophie Maxwell. Well, her ghost, at least.

I stood stock still as I watched Sophie. She didn't look confused, just resigned. Her gaze followed different officers as they buzzed about – but it always returned to her body. Her broken and bloody body. Her body, which had been erected as a garish monument to hate, and would never be whole again. She would never feel the warmth of the sun. Or laugh with her friends. Or flirt with whatever boy caught her attention.

She was lost, but not gone.

Sophie lifted her sad eyes up and saw me staring at her. She swung around, to see if someone was standing behind her, but found only empty space.

"Can you see me?" She asked tentatively.

I didn't answer her. I only nodded.

"I'm dead, aren't I?"

I nodded again.

"Why won't you talk to me?"

How could I explain that I couldn't? How do you tell a dead girl that saving face is more important than helping her?

I glanced around the corn maze and found Chief Terry watching me speculatively.

"There's nothing here," I said to him hollowly.

He nodded. I knew he didn't believe me, though. He started to head back out of the maze and I followed. I turned back to Sophie for a second and surreptitiously motioned for her to follow. Thankfully, she recognized the gesture and did just that.

"I'll take you back home," Chief Terry sighed heavily. Luckily he didn't see me smile warmly – and encouragingly – at Sophie. She followed us mutely.

Landon was still waiting outside of the corn maze when we exited. He made a step toward me, but Chief Terry draped a protective arm around my shoulders and glared at Landon. I couldn't really deal with him now, anyway. I had to get Sophie back to the guesthouse so I could talk to her.

I climbed into Chief Terry's cruiser. Sophie was already in the backseat. Chief Terry had paused long enough to say something to one of the officers who approached him.

"I can't talk to you here," I whispered to Sophie. "Just ride with us back to my place, and when he's gone, we'll talk."

Sophie nodded mutely. I think she was just glad she would have a chance to talk to someone – to anyone.

The ride back home was as quiet as the ride to the corn maze had been. I felt a desperate need to break the silence.

"I'm sorry I couldn't be more help," I finally said.

Chief Terry shrugged. "I don't know what I expected you to do. Maybe you'll be able to figure something out later ... after some time."

"Maybe," I agreed.

"Just do what you can."

When we got to the guesthouse, Chief Terry didn't get out of the car. I opened the door but paused before climbing out. Sophie was already waiting for me on the lawn.

"You should go up to the inn," I said gently. "I know a gaggle of women who would be willing to feed you."

Chief Terry smiled, despite himself. "Maybe I will."

"It's blueberry pancakes day," I said as I climbed out of the car. One final enticement couldn't hurt.

"Well, I wouldn't want to miss blueberry pancakes," Chief Terry said heavily.

I left him knowing that he would end up at the inn. I was thankful they would take care of him. He needed a little pampering. I didn't know how much pampering three women fighting over him would be, but at least it would be a distraction.

When he was gone, I turned to Sophie. "Come inside. I have some people I want you to meet."

FIFTEEN

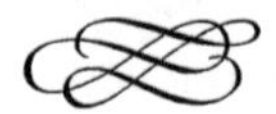

I led Sophie into the guesthouse. She was understandably nervous – what with the brutal death and being strung up in a cornfield and all.

"It will be all right," I promised her.

"What else could go wrong, right?" The laugh Sophie let loose was hollow. At least she wasn't dwelling on her predicament, though. If I came back as a ghost, I'd be bitching like nobody's business.

Clove and Thistle were waiting for me anxiously in the living room. "Well?"

I nodded grimly. "Another murder, another ghost."

"Can they see me, too?" Sophie seemed intrigued.

"They can't see you. We've found that, if I'm talking to you for a few minutes, they'll eventually be able to hear you."

"You talk to a lot of ghosts?"

"I've met my fair share," I admitted ruefully.

"Why can you see me and no one else can?"

I wasn't sure how to answer the question. I wouldn't have to, though. Shane did the honors for me.

"They're witches," he said simply.

Sophie seemed surprised when she saw him. "He's a ghost, too." Thankfully she wasn't focusing on the witch admission.

"He is."

Thistle and Clove were still sitting quietly. Apparently the supernatural hearing aid hadn't kicked in yet. I hoped it happened soon.

"This is Shane," I introduced the duo. "Shane, this is Sophie."

"Did the same people who killed me kill her?" Shane asked.

"Yes."

Sophie looked surprised. "You're the dead boy the police were talking about?"

"Yeah, that's me, Saint Shane of the Corn Stalks."

Teenage humor baffles me sometimes. Other times, the levity can be welcome. I laughed, despite the surreal nature of the situation.

"You're not a saint," Thistle grumbled. "You're far from a saint."

I couldn't help but smile as I saw Shane and Sophie swap shy grins nervously. Maybe the urge to flirt doesn't die when your body does? At least they had each other now.

I brought Clove and Thistle up to speed, including a brief detour about the meth trade in the area. They seemed as surprised as I was when I first heard about it.

"You're kidding? That's unbelievable."

"Drugs aren't just a city thing," I chided Thistle, using Chief Terry's line to my benefit.

"I know that," she said. "I just can't see how it would be profitable here. There are not enough people. Plus, this is a closed community. How do they expect to get away with it?"

"Maybe that's how Chief Terry knows?" Clove said helpfully.

She could have a point. "That's not something you're going to be able to hide very long," I agreed.

"They probably just think we're a bunch of hicks who are too stupid to figure it out," Thistle said.

"Probably," I agreed. Suddenly I remembered the other part of the conversation Chief Terry and I had shared. "Hey, by the way, did you know that our moms used to have a pot field behind the herb garden?"

"No way!"

"Get out!"

"Chief Terry told me. He said he saw it."

"And he never busted them?"

"That's probably when they started feeding him three times a week."

"I thought that was because of the Aunt Tillie situation," Thistle mused. "It makes sense, though. They always did like to dote on him."

"I sent him up to the inn for breakfast," I admitted. "I figured it couldn't hurt his ego to have them fighting over him. He's feeling pretty low about the state taking over the investigation."

"I hope he doesn't tell them he told you," Clove said mischievously. "I can't wait to ask them about their little side endeavor – and I don't want them to have time to think up a lie."

"This is all fascinating," Sophie broke in. "I'm sure the fate of the world rests on whether or not your family used to grow pot in the middle of the woods. If you haven't forgotten, though, you've got two dead people in your living room."

I turned to Sophie in surprise. She'd seemed so meek at first. I guess she was getting more comfortable in her current situation. Her real personality was coming out to play.

I noticed that Shane was mirroring her disdainful stance – hands on hips – a few feet behind her. I think his crush on Thistle was a thing of memory. She'd probably be relieved.

"Sorry," I apologized quickly. "I just wanted to tell them before I forgot."

"Yes, well, your family hijinks are clearly more important than my recent death." There it was, the typical teenage narcissism. One of the many reasons I was wary about ever having children.

"Hey! Just try to calm down," Thistle ordered the voices that were invading the guesthouse. "We're here to help you. We're not your slaves, though."

That's a good way to approach the situation, I thought sarcastically. *Shame the ghosts. This should turn out well.*

I saw Sophie's bottom lip start to quiver. Could ghosts cry? I couldn't see any tears. I got the feeling this was a move she had perfected through life to manipulate her parents. "They can't see you," I reminded her.

Sophie's face immediately went back to the way it had been before. I'd been right. "I forgot," she said finally. "That doesn't change the fact that we're the important thing here, not your family's drug problems."

"We don't have drug problems," Clove grumbled.

"I say we threaten to put them in rehab," Thistle suggested. She was as enamored with the new information as I was.

I could see that both Shane and Sophie were starting to get irritated, though, so I shifted my attention back to them.

"What's the last thing you remember, Sophie?"

Sophie considered the question for a second. "I was shopping."

"At the mall in Traverse City?"

"Yes."

"That's the same place I was taken from," Shane said suddenly.

Sophie looked surprised. "You lived in Traverse City?" She seemed interested.

"No, Beulah."

Sophie wrinkled her nose delicately. "Oh. That's all farms, right?"

"So, what's wrong with a farm?" Now Shane was looking offended.

"Nothing is wrong with farms. They're just so ... country."

"What's wrong with the country?"

"Well, it's boring," Sophie answered honestly.

"You were from Traverse City, not Chicago," Shane scoffed.

"It's still better than Beulah."

"Let's not focus on the merits of the country versus the city right now," Thistle interrupted them. We were masters at breaking up petty arguments, after all. "Let's focus on what you remember."

Sophie looked properly chastised – but Shane was still shooting small glares in her direction when he thought I wasn't looking. Maybe his crush on Thistle would be returning, after all?

"Did you make it out to the parking lot?" I turned back to Sophie.

"Yeah. I think I was putting stuff in the trunk of the car."

"Then what happened?"

Sophie looked like she was really concentrating for a few minutes. Whatever thought she was trying to grab on to, though, seemed to be eluding her.

"I don't know," she said finally.

"Did you get in the front of the car?"

"I don't think so. I don't remember it anyway."

"Was this yesterday?" Clove asked.

"I don't know. What day is it today?"

"It's Tuesday."

Sophie thought again. "Yeah. Yeah. It was Monday. I remember I went to the mall right after school. I wanted to get a new sweater."

I looked at the pink, fuzzy monstrosity she was now wearing. I hoped that wasn't it.

"I guess I'll never get to wear it now," she said sadly.

Yeah, that was the real tragedy of this situation, an abandoned sweater.

"So, you're putting stuff in your trunk. Do you sense someone moving up behind you?"

Sophie shook her head doubtfully. "I honestly don't know. Everything just gets hazy."

"Hazy? Or goes black?"

"Why does that matter?"

"Because, if it goes black, maybe you were knocked out from behind?" I was thinking aloud, but everyone seemed to take my musings in and roll them around their minds for a few minutes.

"Don't they have cameras in the parking lot of the mall?" Clove asked finally.

"I don't think so," I said. "I'm sure the cops have already checked into that, though. If there was video of the parking lot, I think we would have heard about it after Shane."

"They probably went back to the same place because they got away with it the first time," Thistle said.

"That would be my guess," Clove agreed.

"Either that or they don't know the area and they didn't want to risk getting lost," I said. "I mean, if they're tourists, or if they're just visiting the area, they wouldn't know all the hot spots. The mall is an easy hunting ground. Teenagers live there. And the mall in Traverse City is marked really well."

"That's a good point," Clove said.

"I don't care what Chief Terry said," Thistle said vehemently. "I don't think it's someone from the town. It has to be an outsider."

"I agree," I said. "I understand why they can't rule anyone out, though."

"If it was anyone in this town we'd already know who it is," Clove argued. "We all spy on each other like we're in the CIA. If someone in town's vehicle was seen out by one of the corn mazes, someone would have seen it and even if they didn't tell the cops, with the gossip mill in Hemlock Cove we'd all already know about it."

"That means that it has to be a vehicle that doesn't stand out."

"And one that's big enough to hide a body in," Clove said.

"They could have just put the body in the trunk of a car," I reminded her.

"Yeah, but that would look suspicious in a parking lot – even if it was after dark. I doubt someone would risk that."

"So you think that they knocked them out and then carried them to a vehicle and just put them in the backseat?" That seemed risky, too.

"It's less suspicious than shoving a body in the trunk."

"Yeah, but what if they woke up? How could they be sure they could control them in the backseat of a car?"

"Maybe they knew they wouldn't wake up?" I suggested.

"How could they be sure of that?"

"Chloroform." It was Shane's voice.

"Huh?"

I had practically forgotten that Shane and Sophie were still in the room with us. They seemed to have forgotten their earlier argument – at least for the time being.

"It was chloroform," Shane said finally.

"You remember?"

"Not who did it. I just remember someone coming up behind me and pressing a cloth to my mouth. It smelled like medicine. I passed out right away. I tried to fight it, but I couldn't."

Well, that was something new. He was starting to remember. The question was, would he remember enough to identify the killers before it was too late? Would someone else die before his memory completely returned?

SIXTEEN

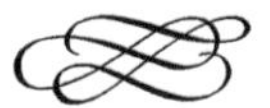

I left Thistle and Clove to entertain our ghostly guests while I showered and got changed for work. It felt like an empty gesture – but there wasn't much more I could do at this point. Shane was slowly starting to remember. Until he fully remembered, or something sparked Sophie's memory, we were kind of stuck.

When I went back out in the living room, I noticed Clove had disappeared and Thistle was alone with Sophie and Shane. The two teenage spirits were chattering away about the new season of *American Idol* – I guess they'd made up and realized pop culture stretched through farmland and urban sprawl to unite them all. Thistle looked like she was ready to throttle them both – even though she couldn't see them, or touch them. She looked up when I entered the room. "They are not coming to work with us today."

I sighed. Usually, I would argue with her. Given how rough her night was the previous evening, though, I didn't want to put any undue stress on her. "They can come to work with me. It's Tuesday. No one will be there."

Shane and Sophie seemed oblivious to our conversation. They looked over, though, when they sensed that I was staring at them.

"What?"

"You guys are coming to work with me today," I told them with false brightness. I didn't want them to think it was a punishment – even though it essentially was just that.

"Why?" Shane whined. "I like the magic shop."

"Thistle has stuff she needs to get done," I started with the truth and then swiftly changed tactics. "And I want you guys close to me in case you remember something." I figured that, if I told them Thistle would rather choke them than chatter with them, I'd get a teenage meltdown of epic proportions. This way, I was placating their egos – and soothing Thistle's frazzled nerves at the same time.

"Oh," Sophie said sagely. "That's probably a good idea." Like a typical teenager, she was trying to appear older than she actually was.

I led Sophie and Shane out to my car and ushered them both toward the backseat. As I was driving up the cobblestone driveway, I noticed that Chief Terry's car was still parked at the inn and smiled to myself. I could just picture the three little dope fiends fawning all over him.

When we got to the office, I led Shane and Sophie in through the back door. They both looked around dubiously – with the disdain that only teenagers can muster. There wasn't nearly as much to look at – or as many people to watch – in the newspaper offices as Hypnotic. I could already tell it was going to be a long day.

"Do you guys want me to turn the television on for you?"

"Yeah," Sophie said. "I want to see if I'm on the news."

Of course she did. I led them into the records room, which was empty, and flicked on the television. I turned it to one of the local news stations and sat down on the couch to watch it with them for a few minutes.

The slim newscaster – with her perfect brown pageboy and flawless Chanel suit – had a fake look of concern plastered on her face when she came back from the commercial break. "Now for the story that seems to be all everyone across the region is talking about."

"See, I knew everyone would be talking about me," Sophie said brightly.

"The small hamlet of Hemlock Cove has been shocked not once, but twice this week with the gruesome discovery of two teenagers in different corn mazes within the confines of the small town. The bodies of Shane Haskell and Sophie Maxwell were found less than ten miles from one another – but the two teenagers were much farther apart in life than they were in death.

"Shane Haskell was a seventeen-year-old who came from Beulah, a small farming community. He and his mother lived a comfortable, but quiet life.

"Sophie Maxwell, though, she came from an upper-middle-class home. The daughter of a city councilman, Maxwell was actively involved with her church and community."

I turned to Sophie in surprise. "Your father is a councilman?"

"Shhh." She waved me off. She was engrossed with watching the steady stream of pictures flashing across the television. Apparently she was voted queen of a few dances.

"No one can know what these two young people went through in their final minutes, the terror they must have felt. Police aren't releasing a lot of details. Shane Haskell's autopsy is expected to be released this afternoon. Sophie Maxwell's autopsy might not be available for days.

"The only thing we do know is that the hearts of both teens were removed – and they weren't found at the scene of the crimes. We also know that they both disappeared from the same mall – just a few days apart.

"Many people in the area are pointing a finger at Hemlock Cove – a town that has been known for absolutely nothing in decades – which turned itself into a haunted town years ago as a way to brand itself as a tourist destination.

"I know I'm not alone when I wonder: Did Hemlock Cove want something like this to happen? Is that why they embraced the occult?"

I jumped to my feet in angry determination and switched the television off. "That is just ridiculous."

"Hey! I was watching that!" Sophie's whine was going to get old pretty quickly.

"You'll get over it," I grumbled.

"They got me on television quick," Sophie said proudly.

"You had your identification with you," I said. "Shane didn't."

"My dad probably sent out a press release, too," Sophie said bitterly. She was back to being petulant and pouty. Man, she could turn it on when she wanted to.

"Why would he do that?"

"He sends out a press release when he crosses the road and looks both ways."

I looked at her, sympathy welling. I kept reminding myself that she was just a teenage girl. She didn't mean to be annoying. It is just part of the teenage DNA makeup. They can't help it. "He likes attention, huh?"

"I'm sure that this just sealed his re-election."

"I'm sure he misses you, Sophie."

"Oh, I'm sure he does, too. I was his biggest tax write-off."

I didn't know what to say to Sophie. Not only had she been brutally murdered, but she apparently had parental issues, as well. And these aren't the normal parental issues people have – you know, like when your mom drops you off for kindergarten without putting on a bra – but actual, serious issues.

"Well, your Aunt Tillie has totally let herself go." Another voice just joined the conversation.

I turned to see Edith had entered the building. I was actually relieved to see her. I was worried she would disappear forever once I helped her rediscover the town. "You went and saw Aunt Tillie?"

"I did. She wasn't very happy to see me."

"I bet."

"She started accusing me of trying to sleep with your Uncle Calvin."

"I know. She thinks you were hot for him."

"Do you remember your Uncle Calvin?" Edith had a dubious look on her pinched white face.

"No, he died before I was born."

"Well, he was no prize."

"From all the stories I heard, he was a great man." I actually had heard that. No one I had ever met had a bad thing to say about Uncle Calvin. Most people actually used the term "angel" when referring to him, in fact.

"Oh, he was very nice, but you have to question the sanity of anyone who would marry your Aunt Tillie."

She had a point.

"So, what did you and Aunt Tillie talk about?" I was guessing it wasn't warm memories from the past.

"Not much. She wasn't in a very good mood, like I said. You were right, though, haunting her is fun."

Uh-oh. "You didn't tell her that I sent you up there did you?" I heard a slight hitch in my voice when I asked the question. Was that fear?

Edith looked uncomfortable. "I might have mentioned you thought it would be a good idea."

Crap. "She's going to curse me now, I just know it." Yup, that was fear coursing through my veins.

"Curse you?" Edith looked confused. I couldn't blame her.

"It wouldn't be the first time. When I was ten, she made it so my shoes were incapable of staying tied. I spent three straight days tripping. I ruined two pairs of jeans and three pairs of tights. I had to wear sandals for a month straight – even when it snowed. It was terrible ... and cold."

"Maybe you just didn't know how to tie your shoes right?" Shane offered helpfully. "I didn't learn until I was seven."

"I learned how to tie my shoes when I was five," I protested. "Plus, she made me weed the garden every weekend – for free – to lift the curse."

"She always was a mean old witch." Edith was back on the Aunt Tillie hate train. I was glad I wasn't traveling alone.

"I don't think being a witch has anything to do with it," I said breezily. "I think it's more that she's a bitch."

"I can't wait to meet her," Sophie said excitedly. Her blues eyes were sparkling with undisguised anticipation.

I turned to her and looked her up and down. "She's going to hate that sweater."

"She would make fun of a dead person because of what they were wearing? I doubt that." Sophie obviously thought I was exaggerating. Aunt Tillie needed no exaggeration, though.

"Ask Shane."

Sophie turned to Shane expectantly. He looked her up and down a second. "She'll make fun of your outfit," he said finally. "I don't think she means for it to be hurtful. It is, though. Just prepare yourself."

Edith seemed to have suddenly noticed Sophie, who was helplessly trying to smooth a sweater she couldn't physically touch. "Who is this?"

"This is Sophie. She was found in the Johnson corn maze this morning. I mean her body was found."

Edith didn't seem surprised at the news. "I heard Chief Terry telling your aunts about that this morning when he stopped by for breakfast. He obviously didn't know you found a ghost."

"Of course not. I can't tell him that. He'll think I'm crazy."

"I think he already knows, he just doesn't know how to bring it up," Edith said knowingly.

"Knows that I see ghosts? Why do you think that?"

Edith shrugged. "It's just the way he was acting. He knows you're all abnormal. He just seems to find it attractive instead of repulsive."

"We're not abnormal – that makes it sound like we belong in that asylum on *American Horror Story*," I countered.

"Honey, there's no shame in not being normal," Edith said, surprising me with her tone. "The shame is fighting what you are. You know what you are and what you do. Why do you care what other people think about you?"

"She's right," Shane said, smiling at Edith for the first time since he'd met her. "I'm starting to like you. You're old school."

Edith pursed her lips. I could tell she was trying to decide if she had been insulted or not.

"That was a compliment," I supplied.

Edith smiled at Shane. It was still a little forced, but she was definitely warming up to him too.

I couldn't help but smile at Edith in turn. Getting out of the office was having a positive effect on her. If I knew that she was capable of softening, I would have forced her out of the office years ago.

Edith seemed uncomfortable by the sudden warmth being directed toward her. "Have they remembered how they died?" She swiftly changed the subject, gesturing toward Shane and Sophie.

"No," I said, my mind returning to the problem at hand. "You still don't have any ideas on how to jog their memories do you? We're kind of stuck until they start remembering stuff."

"If I knew that, I'd be using it on myself," Edith chided me.

"We'll remember when we remember," Sophie said haphazardly. "There's no hurry. It's not like we can die again."

"No hurry? What if they kill someone else?" I met her gaze solidly.

"They don't want to kill anyone else," Sophie said simply. "They only wanted two. One boy and one girl."

"How do you know that?"

Sophie paused. "I don't know," she said slowly. "It just ... it just came to me."

"Do you remember anything else?"

"It's like a dream at the edge of my memory more than anything else," she admitted. "I can't see faces, but I'm starting to remember feelings. There were two people there. A man and a woman."

"Were they old? Young?"

"I can't be sure," Sophie bit her lower lip. "I don't think they're old. Younger than forty for sure. I just don't have a clear picture."

"You will," I encouraged her.

"I hope so," she said. "It had better be soon, though. Whatever they have planned, it's going to happen in the next few days."

"You're sure?"

"I remember the man saying that it has to happen the night of the next full moon," Sophie said. "That's like two days away, isn't it?"

The full moon. I had forgotten. If it was ritualistic, then of course they would try and tie it to the full moon. Even novices knew that.

Thistle had said something about the full moon when she'd been in her trance, too. We should have paid more attention to that little detail.

"So, if we don't catch them then what happens?" Shane asked.

"I think, if we don't catch them soon, then we'll never catch them," I admitted truthfully. This was a feeling I couldn't shake. We were running out of time.

"Well, that's just not acceptable," Sophie huffed. "I refuse to die for nothing. Someone has to pay for killing me – especially before I got to wear my new sweater."

SEVENTEEN

I remained at the office – Googling similar cases throughout the United States until lunch – and then excused myself to go down to Hypnotic to eat with Thistle and Clove. While I had found numerous cases that involved killing teenagers and cutting out their hearts – sick, I know – I could only find a handful that involved killing both a boy and a girl. Either the cases involved a lot more victims or the killer picked one gender and stuck with it.

I expected Shane to put up a fight to come with me. He hardly noticed, though. He was deep in conversation with Sophie and Edith, with the latter imparting her ghostly wisdom on her younger students.

When I got to Hypnotic, Thistle looked around wildly for a second. "You didn't bring them here, did you?"

"I left them at the newspaper office," I answered. "They're bonding with Edith. She's giving some sort of ghost lesson."

"That sounds like a fun afternoon," Clove said sarcastically.

"I don't know. Edith seems to have loosened up since I introduced her to the world she was missing."

"Yeah, we heard."

"You heard what?"

"Your mom called and asked us if we knew anything about Edith paying a visit to Aunt Tillie." Clove delivered the statement in her typical absent-minded nature, but that didn't stop the pang of fear from rushing through me. *Uh-oh.*

"What did you tell her?"

Thistle must have caught on to my panic because I saw a sly grin track across her face. "Why? Are you worried she knows that you encouraged Edith to go up there and haunt her?"

"No." Yes, absolutely. "Besides, you were the one who told Edith to go up there. It wasn't me."

"She's going to come after you. You know that, don't you?" Clove cautioned. She ignored the part about Thistle actually being the guilty party in this particular situation.

"I'm not scared of her." *What? I'm not. I'm terrified of her.*

Clove smiled at me knowingly. "This will at least be entertaining for us. You're not going to have a good night. We will, though."

Crap, crap, crap.

I ate lunch with Clove and Thistle – but my heart wasn't really in it. I was worried this would be my last meal – and it wasn't very good.

After lunch, I made my way over to the police department. Shane's autopsy results were supposed to be in and I wanted to see if they revealed anything that we didn't already know. I also needed a distraction. Obsessing about whatever punishment Aunt Tillie was going to mete out to me wasn't going to lead to a very productive afternoon.

Chief Terry looked up when he saw me come in. He didn't look surprised to see me. "I figured you would show up."

"How was your breakfast?"

"How did you know I went up for breakfast?"

"I saw your car there when I left for work."

"I just figured a solid breakfast couldn't hurt," Chief Terry explained.

"You don't have to make excuses," I countered. "I'm the one who sent you up there, remember?"

I could see Chief Terry redden slightly. I figured the ego boost he received while he had been up there had done him a world of good. "I'm sure they were happy to see you," I added.

"They seemed to be." He seemed a little too pleased with himself. "Well, all except your Aunt Tillie," he amended.

"I wouldn't take it personally," I said. "She's never happy to see me either."

"Yeah, but she was persnickety – even for her."

"What do you mean?"

"She kept running around and yelling that she was being haunted by an angry stick figure from hell."

Edith.

"Did she seem angry about it?" I tried to act nonchalant, but I don't think it was working.

Chief Terry looked puzzled. "No, more perplexed than anything else. Your mom kept trying to force her to sit down and have a cup of tea. I think they put a shot of bourbon in it to finally convince her. She calmed down some after that."

My guess would be three shots.

"You didn't hear her mention my name, did you?"

"Why would she mention your name?"

"No reason."

"I only heard her mention you once," Chief Terry said. I think he thought he was placating me, but my heart clenched up in fear when he said the words.

"What did she say? What did she say exactly?"

"Just that she was looking forward to seeing you." *I doubt that.* "And that she couldn't wait until the next family dinner." That was probably the truth.

I could feel the blood drain from my face. *God, what hell had she dreamt up for me this time?*

"Your mom told her you would be there for dinner tonight, not to worry."

"Family dinner night," I gritted out through clenched teeth.

"There's something I'm missing here," Chief Terry said.

"It's nothing important," I swallowed hard. "Just the normal family drama." *With a hint of vindictive old lady mixed in for good measure.*

"Sounds fun." Chief Terry was angling for an invitation. I guess he hadn't gotten enough Winchester attention to satiate him today. He might make a good buffer.

"Why don't you come with me?"

"Oh, I don't know, it's a family thing."

It wouldn't take much cajoling to convince him. "All the inn guests will be there, too. I'm sure, given what's going on, everyone would be thrilled to have someone from law enforcement in attendance," I lied. "It will be comforting." She couldn't openly curse me in front of him. Even she wouldn't go that far. Would she?

"Well, if you're sure …. "

"I'm sure."

"Well, okay then." He looked genuinely happy. "I guess you're here to find out what the autopsy results said?"

"Yeah."

"Well, they were interesting and yet not surprising."

"What do you mean?"

"We were right about the hearts being removed."

"We already knew that."

"It looks like someone tried to sew the bodies back up afterward, though."

"What? It didn't work?"

"It's not as easy as it sounds, especially when you're using sewing thread." Chief Terry grimaced, despite himself.

"Sewing thread? Gross."

"Yeah."

"Why would someone use sewing thread?"

"I don't know. Maybe it's all they had access to." Chief Terry looked as confused by the new tidbit of information as I felt.

"Why sew them up to begin with?"

"That's an even better question. All I can think is that maybe they thought it would make the bodies easier to transport if they didn't have huge gaping wounds. Maybe it was simply an attempt to cut down on the amount of blood they left behind when they were dragging the body through the maze."

Hmm. "Anything else?"

"As best as we can put it together, Shane Haskell was kept alive for about seven hours before he was killed."

"Did he have defensive wounds? Did he fight them?"

"There was some wear on the body, but the pathologist believes that was from dragging him through the corn maze after he was dead."

"So he was killed someplace else?"

"That's what it looks like."

"Well, that makes sense. There wasn't a lot of blood at the scene. Either scene, for that matter."

"No."

"Do you think they did it in their vehicle?"

"Probably not. That would be a big risk if they were pulled over," Chief Terry said.

True.

"Plus, that's not a lot of room to work with when you're trying to cut someone's heart out," he expounded. "I have never done it personally, but I would imagine that you need a little more room to maneuver when you're cutting through that much bone."

"That means we're looking for a secondary location entirely."

"And if we don't know what we're looking for, it makes it that much harder to find," Chief Terry admitted.

"It's probably closer to here than Traverse City, though." I don't know why I believed that, I had no actual proof, but the minute I said it something in my mind clicked. It felt like the truth.

"That would be my guess, too," Chief Terry agreed.

"Anything else?"

"We're still waiting for the toxicology results," he said. "Those won't be in for at least another day, maybe two. They're putting a rush on them, but they still take time. We'll probably know more after that."

I got up from the chair. "Well, keep me in the loop."

"I will."

As I exited his office, I turned back. "Don't forget dinner. It starts at 7 p.m."

"I'll be there."

I went back to Hypnotic after I was done at Chief Terry's office. Clove was busy doing a Tarot reading for a young couple when I entered, so I sat down on the couch and kept what I'd just learned to myself. I didn't want to freak anyone out.

Thistle was behind the counter. She met my gaze but didn't say anything.

Clove finished up the reading about fifteen minutes later, but the tourists didn't immediately leave. Instead, they started perusing the store. They looked like they were going to be awhile. Clove joined me on the couch.

"I invited Chief Terry to dinner," I said finally.

"Why?"

"No reason. I just thought he could use a good meal."

"I know why," Thistle practically sang from behind the counter.

I glared in her general direction.

"Why?" Clove asked.

"Because she thinks Aunt Tillie is less likely to exact revenge with a member of law enforcement in attendance."

"That's not why," I protested. "I like Chief Terry. I thought he deserved a home cooked meal."

"You're the worst liar ever," Clove laughed.

The couple was now up at the register and checking out with a variety of trinkets and power crystals. Thistle conversationally chatted with them. "Are you guys staying locally?"

"Yes, we just checked into The Overlook this afternoon," the woman said enthusiastically.

"Oh, really, that's my mom's place … well, all of our moms own it together," Thistle gestured to Clove and me.

"Oh, it's so cool," the woman enthused. "We had lunch there today, too, and it was amazing. We're looking forward to dinner there tonight."

"We'll all be there, too," Thistle said warmly. "It should be an entertaining evening." Her gaze met mine. I wanted to flip her off, but I knew better than doing it in front of customers.

"Do you eat dinner there every night?" The woman seemed genuinely curious.

"Not every night," Thistle said. "We go up there a couple of times a week, though. It's a way for us to all be together as a family."

"That's sounds really nice," the woman said sincerely.

"Oh, it is," Clove stifled a laugh. "It's going to be really fun tonight. A lot of precious family time."

I just hoped my mom had hidden the meat cleaver.

"Why?" The woman asked.

Clove looked like she wasn't quite sure what she wanted to say. A family joke is only funny to the actual family at the center of it. Any way she tried to explain it, things were going to look odd to strangers.

"We just think people are going to be excited because all of the town activity," Thistle said smoothly.

"Oh, you mean the murders?" The woman said sagely.

"Yes, the murders."

"Yeah, we heard about them on the news. That's terrible. Do you think the corn mazes will be open this week? That's one of the reasons we came."

That was a little morbid. "I don't know," I said carefully. "Maybe."

After the couple left, I filled Clove and Thistle in on the autopsy results. I was still bothered by the couple's curiosity about the corn mazes. It didn't sit right with me. Were people coming to town just because of the murders? Had the television reporter been right?

EIGHTEEN

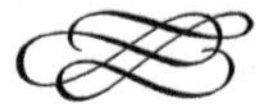

I rode back to the inn with Thistle and Clove – and my panic continued to grow exponentially during the drive. We stopped at the guesthouse long enough to drop off our purses and then headed for The Overlook. I was understandably nervous.

"Don't let her see you're scared," Thistle warned me. "She can smell fear. She's like a dog that way."

"Maybe Bay should act like a dog," Clove suggested.

"What do you mean?"

"You know, roll over on the floor and expose your belly. Show her you're subservient." Clove's dimple came out to play.

I slapped Clove's hand away when she reached out and tried to pet me. "You're so not funny."

"I think we're funny," Clove giggled.

"I think we're downright hilarious," Thistle agreed.

Clove opened the door into the back living quarters and stepped into the room first. I let Thistle follow her – but I remained on the front stoop, frozen in fear.

Clove tilted her head back out the door and regarded me. "Why don't you just come in and get it over with. Your fear is bound to be worse than any punishment she'll actually think up."

"That's not true," I argued. "Remember when we were kids and we all cut each other's hair and she cursed us for six months so our hair wouldn't grow and we were stuck looking like that for what seemed like forever?"

"Well, we never cut our own hair again, did we?" Thistle said reasonably.

"I didn't touch scissors for ten years," Clove admitted.

"I'm not comfortable with my hairdresser coming at me with scissors even now," I countered ruefully.

"She's getting old," Thistle chided. "She probably already forgot what she was mad at you about. Maybe she'll just swear at you a couple of times, kick you in the shins and move on?"

That would be nice – but I knew I wouldn't be that lucky.

I finally swallowed as much fear as I could – shoving it down into an uncomfortable mass in the pit of my stomach – and wandered into the den. I wanted to sigh out loud when I saw that the room was happily vacant. "Why didn't you tell me no one was in here?" I hissed at Thistle.

"Because that would have been the nice thing to do," she said simply. "I'm feeling anything but nice tonight."

What makes tonight different than any other night? She really is my least favorite cousin.

"I agree with Thistle," Clove said with an uneven smile. "Watching you get terrorized by Aunt Tillie is pretty much going to be the highlight of my evening."

And yet I liked Thistle better than Clove.

I stiffened when I heard a pair of heels clacking on the hardwood floor coming from the kitchen. I didn't release the breath I'd been holding hostage until I caught sight of Twila. She smiled warmly when she saw us all. When her gaze met mine, though, I swear I saw a hint of sympathy flash across her face.

"Hi, Mom," Thistle greeted her. "Is Aunt Tillie on a rampage after Bay, or what?" Thistle never met a thought she didn't immediately utter.

"Whatever do you mean, dear," Twila feigned ignorance. She never met a lie she didn't immediately bungle.

"Yeah, that doesn't work on us, Mom," Thistle admonished her. "We know when you're lying – and you're telling a big old whopper right now. Besides, we already heard Aunt Tillie is gunning for Bay."

"Who told you that?" she asked suspiciously.

"Well, Edith herself told Bay. Then Chief Terry might have mentioned something to her when she stopped by his office this afternoon. Oh, and let's not forget that you told me that very thing over the phone when you talked to me this afternoon," Thistle's voice was practically dripping with sarcasm by the time she was done with her diatribe.

"No one likes a bitch, dear," Twila said in a saccharine voice as she patted Thistle a little too harshly on the cheek. "You'll never find a man if you talk down to him like that. Of course, any man you find right now would have to look past your hair and try to find the warmth inside you, anyway. That might be too much of a task for most men."

"Yep, I walked right into that one, didn't I?" Thistle chastised herself.

"It could be worse," Twila countered. "At least your Aunt Tillie isn't looking to exact revenge on *you*."

Great. Now I felt much better.

I puttered around the den while Thistle and Clove moved to the kitchen door. Clove cast a long glance back at me and smiled. "Are you coming?"

"In a minute."

"Just suck it up and get it over with. Maybe if you beg, she'll give you a shorter sentence."

"You're my least favorite cousin," I informed her angrily.

"That will only last until Thistle pisses you off and we both know it," Clove said absently. "You've been dead to me three times this month and she's been dead to me two times this month – which I guess means that she's due."

My family has some pretty faulty logic in the grand scheme of things.

Despite my rampant misgivings, I reluctantly followed Thistle and Clove into the kitchen. I glanced around the room nervously. My mom was at the stove stirring what looked like gravy. Marnie was at the counter mashing potatoes. Twila was at the other counter transferring stuffing from the skillet to a big serving bowl.

"Mm, something smells good," Clove murmured, inhaling excitedly. "Is that meatloaf I smell?"

"Yes," Marnie said. "We thought, given all that's going on in the town, people would feel better if we had some nice, old-fashioned comfort food."

You can't argue with food logic – especially when it's spot on. Who doesn't love mashed potatoes?

I saw Thistle lean over the pan of meatloaf and wrinkle her nose distastefully. "I don't like meatloaf," she complained.

"Then eat the mashed potatoes, stuffing, creamed spinach, salad and the peach cobbler we made for dessert," Twila frowned at her. "You'll hardly starve."

Thistle looked appropriately abashed. I thought now might be a good time to distract everyone by making them look at something else – like Thistle.

"Didn't you say you were thinking of becoming a vegetarian?" I said the comment innocently enough, but Thistle knew exactly what I was doing.

"No," she said through gritted teeth.

Marnie had practically dropped the handheld masher into the bowl when I'd uttered the words. "A vegetarian?" The horror in her voice was evident. She was reacting like I said Thistle had decided to become a pedophile or something. This was a good start.

"That's not true, is it?" Twila looked equally upset.

"Bay is just trying to distract everyone because of Aunt Tillie," Thistle shot back.

"I bet Aunt Tillie won't want to hear the news about you becoming a vegetarian." I winked at Thistle cheekily.

Thistle narrowed her eyes at me dangerously.

"I think she'll be more upset when she finds out that it was your idea for Edith to come up here and bug her," Thistle shot back.

"I already know that," a cranky voice grumbled. Crap! Aunt Tillie had just swung into the room like a tiny little Energizer Bunny on a mission.

"Thistle's becoming a vegetarian," I boldly announced.

Aunt Tillie froze, despite herself. "A vegetarian? Meaning you're only going to eat rabbit food? Like you're going to walk around munching on carrots?"

Point for me.

"No," Thistle said harshly. "I just said that I don't like meatloaf. I never said I was going to become a vegetarian. Bay is just trying to distract you."

"Not true. Didn't you say that the venison stew they made last week tasted like feet? And it made you want to not eat meat for an entire week, didn't it?"

Thistle froze. She had said that.

Thistle glared at me harshly. It was all out war now. "Bay told Edith the best way to get you was to sing when you're trying to sleep."

That was a blatant lie. "Thistle said that eating a burger is like murdering a child."

Okay, that was a blatant lie, too.

"Bay told me that you guys used to have a pot field behind the herb garden!"

Whoa, where did that come from?

Mom, Marnie and Twila all reared back in shock. I turned to see Chief Terry standing behind all three of them. He had obviously walked in at the tail end of the conversation. His face had turned bright red.

"Who told you that?" Marnie hissed, turning on me aggressively.

"Apparently it's common knowledge," I lied. I refused to even look in Chief Terry's direction. They would know if I did.

Aunt Tillie had narrowed her eyes to dangerous slits. Thankfully, though, they weren't resting on me.

"You told me that was oregano!"

I saw my mom swallow hard in the shadow of Aunt Tillie's fury. I couldn't help but feel a momentary shot of relief – but it was short-lived. Thistle had sold out our mothers to save her own ass. Well, to save both our asses, actually. Well, on second thought, maybe it wasn't so bad. It's not like they hadn't done the same thing to the three of us on previous occasions.

"We never told you that was oregano," Marnie countered. "You asked us if that was oregano. We just didn't correct you."

"No, I asked you if it was pot. I said I hoped it was oregano," Aunt Tillie was practically seething.

"Well, we gave you your wish," Twila twittered. "You should be happy. We made you very happy that day."

Now I see where Clove, Thistle and I get it from. It's really scary what things get passed from one generation to the next – like lying.

"I knew it," Aunt Tillie blew out her rage in an exaggerated sigh. "I knew the minute you uprooted it that something was going on. Then I saw that it sprouted up again last spring behind the creek, off in the corner by weeping willow, and I knew you'd been lying to me all along."

Thistle turned her eyes and met my gaze with a look of incredulity on her face. They hadn't destroyed the field. They had just moved it. We both turned our eyes to Chief Terry. He obviously was having an internal debate about what he had and had not just heard. I still didn't think my mom, Marnie and Twila had any idea he was in the room. If Aunt Tillie knew, she certainly didn't care. I couldn't help but wonder if the guests were out in the dining room listening to us rip each other to shreds.

"What field? We didn't move the field." My mom is the worst liar of the seven of us.

"Really? Did it sprout wings and move itself?"

"Magic is a wondrous and mystical thing. Maybe it did?" Twila was desperately grasping at straws. Okay, maybe she was the worst liar.

"And why would the pot be so desperate to save itself?" Aunt Tillie was about to throw down on all of us. I just knew it.

"It has medicinal purposes. It knew we might need it," Twila said sincerely.

Oh, very nice.

Thistle had apparently decided she'd had enough of the conversation. "Oh, who cares if they have a pot field? As long as they're not selling it to the kids in town, it's really not a big deal."

"Pot is a gateway drug, young lady," Aunt Tillie pointed her gnarled finger in Thistle's direction. "They'll get addicted and then they'll try harder drugs."

"They're in their fifties," Clove shrugged. "If they haven't experimented further at this point, they're not going to do it now. It's not like they're all going to pack up in the Scooby van and go on the never-ending search for 'shrooms – or acid."

Aunt Tillie turned her evil eye on Clove. "You seem to know an awful lot about drugs, young lady."

Clove's face drained of color when she realized Aunt Tillie was now focused on her. "I saw it on television," she said hastily.

"Quite frankly, I'm relieved," Thistle added. "At least now I know that it was the pot that led to all that naked dancing in the woods. Otherwise, it was just weird."

Aunt Tillie shushed her with a single look. Then she turned her gaze to me, a look of frank consternation on her face. Uh-oh. "You've been awfully quiet," she said.

"I'm just appalled at the lack of judgment this family has shown," I said. "I mean, drugs, how terrible – and unexpected – how terribly unexpected." Okay, maybe I'm the worst liar in the family.

Clove and Thistle shot me death glares. I did feel a little bit like a hypocrite.

"Oh, stuff it," she muttered. "You're only saying this because you know I'm pissed about the Edith situation - -and I will exact revenge for that at a later date – don't think I won't. You sent that stick thin ghost out here to haunt me because you knew it would upset me and you're only happy when you're upsetting me."

I had begun slashing my hand across my chest to cut her off the second I realized the road the conversation was going to take us down. She obviously didn't get the gesture, though. "And don't think I don't know that's some newfangled way to tell me to go fuck myself. I know what the kids today are doing." Obviously.

I turned to Chief Terry, fear was written all over my face. What would he say? How would he react? Maybe he'd just think she was a crazy old lady.

My mom, Twila and Marnie seemed to notice that I was looking in the other direction. They were stunned when they saw Chief Terry at the door.

"Did I mention I invited Chief Terry to dinner?" I asked lamely.

Aunt Tillie turned and met Chief Terry's steady gaze. "It's not like he didn't know we were weird already. Stop crapping yourselves," she admonished. "Bay talks to ghosts. So do I. Edith Harper is a ghost who haunts the paper. Bay recently convinced her to come up here and start haunting me as a joke – only it's not funny at all."

If Chief Terry was surprised by Aunt Tillie's small speech, he didn't show it. Instead, he smiled at every woman in the room in turn – six of whom were currently drowning in a sea of silent panic – and then he finally spoke in a clipped and even tone. "Is that meatloaf I smell? It smells delicious."

An audible release of pent up breath could be heard amongst all of us. Chief Terry took a bowl of green beans and carried them from the kitchen into the other room. We all made a move to follow suit. Everyone was carrying a separate dish when we paused at the kitchen door and exchanged worried glances.

"Maybe it just hasn't sunk in," my mom said.

"Maybe he's not going to say anything," Twila, the eternal optimist, offered.

"Maybe he just doesn't care," Aunt Tillie practically growled. She gets grumpy when she doesn't get fed at exactly 7 p.m.

We diligently walked into the dining room to find the entire cadre of inn guests already seated at the dining room table. They'd been sitting stock still and watching the kitchen door expectantly. *Uh-oh.*

They all broke into spontaneous applause when they saw us. A couple even got to their feet.

I moved around the table, despite my confusion, and lowered the meatloaf dish to the table before my hands suffered serious burns. The dish was hot. I turned to Emily, the girl who had discovered Shane's body with me, in confusion.

"Why are you clapping?"

She didn't get a chance to answer. The young woman from Hypnotic that afternoon did it for her. "I love dinner theater!"

NINETEEN

Instead of correcting the dinner guests, we all made a tacit agreement to pretend the ugly scene that had just transpired in the kitchen was exactly what they thought it was – entertainment for the masses – and nothing else.

We all managed to make it through dinner without cracking – or cracking up – but there was a decided pall across the table.

The female shopper from Hypnotic – I found out her name was Carrie – wouldn't stop asking me if we'd ever had formal theater training.

"There's not really any formal theater training out here," I said ruefully.

"But you were all so good," she gushed.

"Just a lot of practice, I guess," Thistle laughed. There was true merriment behind Thistle's laugh – but it wasn't for the reason that Carrie thought.

It was obvious that Aunt Tillie wasn't exactly happy about our ruse. She sat at the end of the table, arms crossed obstinately across her chest, and she made periodic snorting sounds when people kept referring to our "marvelous performances."

Chief Terry was sitting in between Marnie and Twila – and across from my mom – and he kept shooting wary glances toward Aunt Tillie, but he didn't say anything. Even when the crowd started questioning him about the murders, he answered their questions in a reassuring manner – but he never did give them the inside tidbits that they truly wanted. I realized that he was better at holding things close to the vest than I ever imagined.

After the main course, I managed to extricate myself from the situation. I said I had to get some sleep because I had to get most of the articles for this week's edition of the paper prepared tomorrow. Everyone knew that Wednesdays were my busy days – so they really didn't put up much of a fuss about it.

"I'll send a slice of cobbler home with Thistle and Clove so you can have a snack later," my mom said as I was leaving.

My reasons for leaving weren't exactly a lie. I was exhausted. I also wanted a little time to myself to think. I made my way back to the guesthouse, changed into my blue flannel sleeping pants and a tank top, and braided my hair quickly so it wouldn't get all snarled during the night. I debated washing my makeup off – but that was one rule I usually followed, out of habit, if nothing else.

I had just settled into bed when a thought occurred to me: I hadn't seen Shane and Sophie since this afternoon.

Huh.

Maybe they were still with Edith? Could something bad happen to ghosts? I didn't think so, but I really couldn't rule it out either. Crap! It's not like I could pick up a phone and call them.

I climbed out of bed tiredly. I would like to forget the whole thing, roll over and get some sleep. I knew that wasn't even remotely possible, though. As long as my mind remained busy with worries about their whereabouts, I wouldn't be able to drift off. Sophie had been too excited to meet Aunt Tillie to purposely miss dinner.

I slipped into a pair of tennis shoes – but I didn't change out of my pajamas. It was after dark. No one would be at the paper except the ghosts – and I wasn't exactly worried about what they would say about my choice in sleeping apparel.

I grabbed a hoodie off the hook on the wall as I exited. I thought briefly about leaving a note on the counter for Thistle and Clove, but I had a feeling I would get back to the guesthouse before they did.

During the drive to the paper, I pondered the day's events. We knew we had two killers – a man and a woman – and if Sophie was right, they didn't plan on killing anyone else. Why kill two kids in the first place then? It didn't make any sense.

The other thing I couldn't quite let go of was Chief Terry's brief comments about the meth trade. Did the new visitors in town really have nothing to do with the murders? Could they only be tied to the drugs? Is it possible they were tied to neither?

Thanks to a quick bout of curiosity, I swung my car right – so I would drive past the Johnson farm – on my way to town. It added about two miles to my trek – but I wanted to make sure that no one was out at the scene – including Sophie and Shane.

When I got close to the maze, I slowed down. I was still almost half a mile away from it. Since I was going so slowly, I couldn't help but notice when my headlights bounced off a metallic object that was halfway obscured in the ditch. A bicycle?

I don't know what possessed me to do it, but I killed the lights on my car. I slowly rolled it to a stop, parking alongside the side of the road, and exiting my vehicle curiously. I know. I've seen enough horror movies to realize that this is exactly how you get yourself killed – and yet I did it anyway. I moved back toward the area where I saw the sudden reflection of light. It wasn't a full moon, but it was close. There was enough illumination for me to get at least a semblance of what was in the ditch.

It was a motorcycle.

My mind immediately jumped to Landon. Why was he in the corn maze? Then my mind went to another place. What if it was Russ? Then my mind went to the worst place. What if it was all of them?

I had a decision to make. The smart thing to do would be to run to my car, drive it into town and use the office phone to call Chief Terry. Like an idiot, my cell phone was sitting on the nightstand in my bedroom. And the office was closer to me – and in a more populated area – than the guesthouse.

Instead, I did the stupid thing. I squared my shoulders and headed toward the corn maze purposefully.

One could argue that self-preservation isn't my strong suit – and they would be right. I should be the lone girl who survives a horror movie. Instead, I'm her dippy friend who gets killed in the opening reel.

I tried to be as quiet as I could as I entered the corn maze. I had to dip low to slip underneath the police tape, but it's not like it was much of a deterrent. I had a small flashlight on my key ring, but I didn't want to risk using it. Truth be told, I had no idea what I was going to do – even if I found someone in the maze.

I had been moving through the maze for about five minutes when I realized I wasn't sure if I could find my way to the center of it without Chief Terry. He had led me the first time. Had I paid attention?

Not only was I trying to make my way through the darkened maze by the power of moonlight alone, but I was also trying to do it as stealthily as possible. If someone was in the maze and they heard me traipsing around, they would undoubtedly try to find out who was here.

I had just about convinced myself to turn around when I felt a presence slip in beside me. I froze in fear. It wasn't a human presence, though. When I looked to my left I saw that Sophie was beside me. "What are you doing here?" She whispered, even though I was the only one who could hear her.

I shook my head. I couldn't bring myself to open my mouth and answer her. Someone would definitely hear us then.

I felt another presence move up to my right side. I didn't have to turn to see that it was Shane. I looked at them questioningly. What were they doing here?

Shane must have read the confusion on my face. "We thought that revisiting this place might jog our memories. We went out to where I was found first, but nothing happened. That's why we came out here."

Sophie had obviously heard a noise in front of us because she quirked her head slightly. "There's someone else here?"

I nodded mutely.

"Do you think it's the person who killed me? Who killed us?"

I could only shrug. Even if I could speak out loud, I wouldn't be able to answer that question.

"Go to the car," Shane ordered. "We'll go see who it is and meet you back at the guesthouse. We can't die twice."

I wanted to listen to him. I honestly did. My feet didn't seem to be working properly, though. I looked up to them both helplessly.

Shane looked perplexed. "I think she's frozen in fear."

"Wouldn't you be?" Sophie admonished him. "We're already dead and I'm terrified."

We could all hear the footsteps getting closer. It was too late at this point. If I did manage to move, he would hear me and give chase. If I didn't move, he would inevitably run into me.

I could hear the slow shuffle of feet just around the corner. I was powerless to do anything but take a deep breath and wait. When the dark figure moved around the corner it froze a couple of feet in front of me.

"Who is that?" The voice was low and clearly male.

"Don't answer him," Sophie urged me. "Maybe he'll run the other way in fear."

"Not if he's the killer," Shane argued.

I couldn't make out the figure in the dark. I could see a couple of furtive movements, but in general it was just a tall blob. The only thing I knew for sure is that it was a man – or a female wrestler. The figure reached behind its back. I held my breath for a second, exhaling sharply when the figure brought the hand back out and snapped a light on my face.

It took my eyes a second to adjust to the light – and the only refrain going through my mind was: Please let it be the cops. Please let it be the cops. Jail is better than death, after all.

I was shocked when the figure openly swore. "Jesus H. Christ! You've got to be kidding me! Bay? Bay Winchester? Just what in the hell are you doing here?"

Despite the fear ripping through me only seconds before, I recognized the voice, and it didn't bring the heart-gripping fear I expected it to. "Landon?"

"Yeah, it's me," he grumbled. He still hadn't lowered the flashlight from my face.

Sophie had moved over to the side of him and was giving him a piercing look. "I don't recognize him," she said finally. "He is really hot, though."

Shane shot her a dirty look. "I don't recognize him either. I think he looks like he's up to no good, regardless."

I wanted to snap at them both to shut up, but I didn't think that now was the right time to give Landon further evidence that I was crazy. Plus, if he did kill me and carry my body away, the two of them would be the only ones capable of telling Thistle and Clove where to find me.

"Are you suddenly deaf?" Landon snapped. "Are you in some sort of shock? Why are you here?"

I managed to recover – if only momentarily – and shot him an evil glare of my own. "I might ask you the same question."

"I asked you first," he muttered.

"I thought I saw someone going into the maze and I thought I should probably check it out." That's not really a lie. Okay, it's not really the truth either, but it's not an overt lie.

"You saw a shadowy figure go into a corn maze, after dark, a corn maze where a body was found less than 24 hours ago, mind you, and you thought it was a good idea to follow that figure?" Landon ran the flashlight up and down my body. "In your pajamas?"

What? That's totally possible. "Yes, I did." If you're going to lie, commit to the act and don't even think about abandoning it.

Landon regarded me for a second. I could tell he didn't believe me, but he didn't look like he particularly wanted to challenge me either. He seemed to be waging an internal battle with himself instead. "That story makes no sense," he said finally.

"Why don't you tell me what you're doing here and I'll tell you if that makes sense?"

Landon looked flustered again. "What?"

"You were obviously the person I saw go into the corn maze. Why are you here?"

Now Landon looked uncomfortable. "I just wanted to look around."

"At a murder scene?"

"I thought the cops said that this was just the body dump?"

Body dump? That was a weird way to put it. "How did you know that? I didn't see that on the news."

Landon ignored the question. "I guess I was just a little morbidly curious." He was trying to act badass. He lacked a certain level of conviction, though.

"You get off on seeing body dump locations?"

"I didn't say that," he protested.

"I still don't understand why you're here," I repeated.

"I just wanted to see the crime scene," he snapped.

"I'm sorry, but that seems weird for a random biker guy."

"That seems judgmental for a random newspaper woman." He challenged.

I narrowed my eyes as I regarded him. "I'm not judgmental."

"You've been obsessed with me since the moment you laid eyes on me." Even under the pale moonlight, I could see the twinkle in his eye.

"I am not obsessed with you," I said hotly.

"I would be," Sophie said from beside me. "He is dreamy."

"He is not dreamy," I muttered.

I saw Landon look around for a second. It was clear I'd said that last statement as part of a conversation – and yet he hadn't heard Sophie's comment. "What did you say?"

"I said, I hope I'm dreaming," I lied.

"You dream about me a lot, do you?" Landon was back to being flirty. At least he wasn't trying to kill me.

"Listen, as much as I would love to sit in the middle of a corn maze and continue to get nowhere with you, I really need to get some sleep."

Landon smiled at me. "You want to go somewhere with me?"

I was confused for a second, and then I realized what I said. "I meant as far as you telling the truth," I said through gritted teeth.

"Oh," he nodded knowingly.

"I don't have time to play games with you," I said harshly. "Some of us have actual jobs."

I turned, mustering as much righteous indignation as I could, and started to flounce out of the corn maze. Instead, I tripped over something on the ground – I think it was the corner of a bale of hay – and sprawled forward.

"Oww!"

"Are you all right?"

"Yeah, I'm great. I just broke my ankle. What couldn't be great about that?"

"You broke your ankle?" Landon sounded genuinely concerned.

He flicked the light around until he saw me sitting on the ground, rubbing my ankle. "It's not broken," I grumbled. "It's just twisted."

I saw that Landon was trying not to laugh. The absurdity of the situation wasn't lost on me, but I didn't think now was the time to start making fun of me either. "Don't you dare laugh! This is not funny."

"I'm not laughing."

"You're laughing inside."

"No, I'm not."

"Don't lie to me; I can see it written across your face."

"It's dark; you can't even see my face."

Landon reached down and helped me to my feet. I could put a little weight on my ankle, but I had a feeling I was going to be in a world of hurt tomorrow. Landon must have realized that, too.

"Are you going to be able to drive home?"

"I'll be fine," I said crossly.

"Is there someone at home who can help you in the morning?" He asked the question innocently enough, but I noticed the slight edge to his voice when he uttered the words. He was hoping for a specific answer.

"Yes, I live with someone."

"Your cousins," Shane scoffed. "That's not what he was asking, and you know it."

I ignored him.

I saw Landon's face fall slightly. He didn't say anything, though. "Well, let me help you to your car anyway."

I wanted to tell him no, but I could feel my ankle starting to balloon. As it stood now, I was going to have to sit in the driveway at home and honk until Thistle and Clove came out to help me into the house. Thankfully, Twila was a master at making healing poultices, and I would probably actually be able to walk tomorrow (even if it was with a limp).

It took Landon about ten minutes to maneuver me to my car. He opened the door and helped me slide in, but he didn't shut the door even after he was sure I was settled inside comfortably.

"Are you sure you're going to be able to get home?"

"I already told you. I'm fine."

"Are you sure the guy you live with will be able to help you?"

I saw him grimace when he said the word guy and couldn't help but smile to myself. "I don't live with a guy," I admitted. "I live with my cousins. It will be fine. They should be home by now."

"I'll follow you to make sure you get there," he said finally, although I did see him perk up when I admitted to living with my cousins.

"I don't need a babysitter," I protested.

"It will make me feel better," he mock pleaded.

"Fine," I relented.

I was surprised when he started moving away from me instead of toward the ditch. In other words, he was moving away from his motorcycle.

"Where are you going?"

"I parked my bike behind the maze," he said. "It will just take a second for me to get it and then I'll follow you home."

"I thought your motorcycle was in the ditch over there," I faltered, pointing in the direction where I had found the motorcycle earlier.

Landon's eyes narrowed. "Why did you think that?"

"That's why I stopped," I finally admitted. "I saw the bike in the ditch."

"Where?" Landon's voice had taken on a hard edge.

I made a move to get out of the car, but Landon stopped me. "Just point."

Landon jogged over to the area I had identified. I watched as he dropped to his knees and peered into the ditch, but I couldn't see what he was looking at. After a few minutes, he jogged back over to me.

"There's nothing there," he said. "It looks like something was there, the grass is flattened, but it's not there anymore."

I bit my lower lip. "So someone else was here?"

Landon nodded grimly. "And I have an idea who."

Neither one of us said it aloud, but we were both thinking the same thing – I could tell. Russ.

TWENTY

There was good news and bad news the next morning. The good news was that I was right, the poultice I had put on my ankle the night before had done wonders. It was still a garish looking purple color – but I could put some weight on it. I would be limping for the next two days, but it was nowhere near as bad as it could have been.

The bad news? I still had no idea who had committed these murders and I was now completely convinced that Landon's friends – if not Landon himself – were tied up in something hinky. He had been out at the corn maze looking for something. I don't know if he found it or not. Of course, he could have killed me. No one knew I was out there, after all. Still, he hadn't even shown the slightest inclination that he was considering that.

I stumbled out into the kitchen. Thistle looked up when she saw my very ungraceful entrance. "How are you feeling?"

"Like I got caught in a corn maze when I shouldn't have been there."

Thistle smirked. "I mean your ankle."

"Oh, it's okay. It doesn't feel great. It doesn't feel like it's going to fall off or anything either, though."

"Well that's good," Thistle said with fake enthusiasm. "It's good to start out every day with something to be thankful for."

Smartass.

I slid into one of the stools, being careful not to jostle my ankle against anything hard, and accepted the cup of coffee Thistle shoved toward me. It smelled like heaven in a cup – with cream.

"So …." Thistle started.

"So what?"

"You want to tell me who the guy on the motorcycle was last night?"

"What guy?"

"You know very well what guy. Long, black hair. Killer blue eyes. If I had to guess, a washboard stomach and some truly impressive shoulders are probably part of that package, too."

"He's just a guy I know," I averted my gaze from her, although I could feel the heat creeping up my neck.

"Who are we talking about?" Clove was coming out of the bathroom and she looked interested in our conversation. "Mr. Hottie on the motorcycle last night? You said you weren't going to ask her about him if I wasn't here," Clove said accusingly.

"Well, you should have been faster. I couldn't hold it in anymore."

"She's been up for like two minutes," Clove countered.

"Well, you know I have zero impulse control. You should have planned accordingly."

Clove frowned. "You're dead to me."

Well, it looked like we were both up to three deaths this month. I wondered who would get the tiebreaker.

If I thought Thistle and Clove had forgotten what they were originally interested in – I was sadly mistaken.

"So, who was he?" Clove asked. She was still shooting angry mental daggers in Thistle's direction.

"I told you, he's a guy I met around town," I said evasively.

"Well, we have a store right on the main drag in town and we've never seen him," Thistle argued. "Where did you meet him again?"

"I met him at the corn maze the day we found Shane's body," I admitted.

Thistle puzzled the answer over in her head for a few minutes. Then I saw a sudden flash of recognition register on her face. "He's one of the people Chief Terry thinks is involved in the meth trade, isn't he? He's the guy Chief Terry warned you to stay away from?"

Who told her that? *Don't freak out,* I cautioned myself internally. *If she smells blood in the water she'll attack. She's like Jaws that way.* I mentally calmed myself and then shrugged calmly. "I have no idea what Chief Terry thinks of him." I just know he hates him.

"If Chief Terry thinks that you should stay away from him, maybe you should." Clove bit her lower lip as she thought about it. "On the other hand, he's really hot. Screw Chief Terry. There's probably nothing wrong with him."

Sometimes I love the way Clove's mind works.

"At least have sex with him before you ask if he's a drug dealer," she added. "If you do it beforehand, that could make the sex really weird."

Sometimes Clove's mind is a frightening place – like a house of mirrors at a carnival, or a bag full of really angry cats.

"I don't think he's a drug dealer," I said finally.

"Why? Because he's cute?" Thistle kept trying to catch Clove's gaze so they could make up – but Clove was resisting the process. She didn't even take the donut that Thistle kept trying to entice her with – and they were pumpkin donuts, Clove's favorite.

"No …." I started. "There's just something about him. If he was doing something illegal out there and he wanted to shut me up, he could have hurt me last night and no one would have known. Instead, he helped me."

"He didn't know that for sure, though," Clove reminded me. "For all he knew, someone else could have been with you."

"No, I don't know. It's just a feeling I have."

If anyone else would have made that statement, Thistle and Clove probably would have scoffed at them. The truth is, though, most of our 'feelings' were usually justified.

"Then why do you think he was out there?"

"I honestly don't know," I said. "He seemed genuinely surprised when I told him about seeing the other motorcycle."

"That could have been an act." Thistle was still reluctant to the idea of Landon – even if he was hot.

"It could have been," I agreed. "It didn't feel like an act, though."

"Most people are better liars than we are," Clove reminded me.

She had a point.

Clove and Thistle offered to help me shower – but that was too weird for any of us to actually contemplate for more than a few seconds. I actually managed to get in and out on my own with very little difficulty.

Instead of driving to the office, I rode with Clove and Thistle and they dropped me off at the front of The Whistler before heading over to Hypnotic. "We'll bring you lunch and pick you up after work," Thistle promised.

I waved them both off. The last thing I needed was two more mother hens pecking at me. The four I already had were more than enough.

When I made it to my office, I heard voices from the records room. Instead of sitting at my desk, I made my way toward the voices. I wasn't surprised to see Edith. I wasn't even surprised to see Sophie and Shane with her. I was surprised to see several files spread out on the countertop by the filing cabinets, though.

"How … did you do this?" I looked at Edith incredulously.

"Do what?"

"Take out the files. You did do this, right?"

"Yes. I remembered something and I couldn't wait for you to come here and do it for me so I did it myself."

"You actually managed to move something … something physically?" I was amazed.

"You act like I cured cancer," Edith said bitterly. "It's not a big deal."

"You've never done it before."

"Of course I have," she countered. "I change the channel on the television all the time."

I thought about this a second and then shook my head. "I don't remember ever seeing you change the television channel."

"That's because I always do it when you're not looking," Edith chided me.

"Why would you do that?"

Edith stopped flipping through the pages of the file she was looking at and fixed me with a cold stare. "Maybe I didn't want you to know what I was watching. I am entitled to a little privacy."

"You weren't watching porn or anything – we don't have any pay channels here – so what was the big deal?"

"She likes *Nick at Nite*," Shane supplied.

Nick at Nite? "You mean she likes reruns of old sitcoms?"

"Basically."

Edith looked momentarily flummoxed. "They help me learn about all the things I've missed throughout the years," she said finally.

"It's not a big deal. I like old sitcoms, too."

I couldn't understand why she was so worked up.

"She's got a crush on the father on 'Everybody Loves Raymond,'" Shane teased.

"I do not. I think he's just very charming."

"Frank?"

"That's his name, yes," Edith said.

"Isn't he the gross one that walks around farting?"

Edith changed the subject. "Anyway, I remembered something last night."

"What?"

"About thirty years ago, there were a couple of similar murders," Edith said triumphantly.

The surprise must have blatantly registered across my face because Edith didn't wait for me to respond before she plowed on.

"I was obviously already a ghost by that point," she explained. "No one could see me then, though, so I basically just sat around the office and listened to everyone. We had five workers at that point. One day I remember them talking about the body of a boy being found – and it was missing its heart."

"Was it in a corn maze?" I had trouble believing that I wouldn't have heard about a brutal slaying like this. I had done research on the Internet, too, and hadn't found anything about these other supposed murders.

"That's the thing. It wasn't in a corn maze. And it technically wasn't here either."

"What do you mean?"

"The body was found in a deserted barn," Edith said. "And the barn was in Barker Creek."

"Barker Creek? That's like forty miles away."

"Yeah. But it was big news at the time. That's really not that far away when you think about it."

She was right. "A few days after the boy was found, a girl was found the same way. Her heart was missing and her body was abandoned in a barn. I think this one was in like Acme, but it was only a few miles away from the first body."

"Did they ever catch who did it?"

"No," Edith shook her head. "It was big news for a long time, but the police ran out of leads and eventually everyone forgot about it."

"I guess, since it didn't happen right here in Hemlock Cove, that explains why I've never heard of it," I said to myself.

Edith nodded. I looked over her shoulder at the articles she was perusing. I asked if I could borrow them and then sat down heavily on the couch to read through them.

I spent the next two hours wading through the extensive coverage. "It looks like they covered it really well," I said when I was done.

"I told you, it was the biggest thing to happen to this area in years," Edith said.

"They sound like similar cases," I broke off, biting my lip.

"What are you thinking?" Edith looked confused.

"If it's the same killer – or the same killers – then they would be kind of old right now," I explained. "If you were that old, would you be confident enough to approach teenagers in a high-risk area? Would you be strong enough to carry their bodies?"

Edith considered my question seriously. "Maybe it's not the same killers. Maybe it's someone who read about the previous killings and wanted to repeat it?"

"Like a copycat?"

Edith nodded.

"Why do it now, though? Why not do it when people still remembered the old case? As far as I know, no one around here even talks about these cases."

"Maybe the killer is just crazy," Edith clucked. "You can't find reason in crazy."

"That's a good point, too."

I gathered up all the articles and shoved them back into the envelope. "Are you done with them?" Edith looked at me quizzically.

"No," I said. "I have to focus on this week's edition. I'm going to take this out to the inn later and see what my mom remembers."

"That's probably a good idea," Edith acknowledged. Then she brightened suddenly. "If I remember right, your Aunt Tillie was called in as a psychic in that first case."

Well, this was definitely the first time I heard of anything like that. As far as I knew, Aunt Tillie had a general disdain of law enforcement. "Who called her in?"

"I can't remember exactly," Edith said. "One of the families hired a private investigator and they came out to talk with Tillie and to see if she could talk to the dead or something, if I remember right. Which I guess she can actually do, so I probably should stop making fun of her for that."

"I don't understand why I've never heard about any of this?"

Edith seemed nonplussed. "I would wager there are a lot of things you don't know about your family."

I'd give even odds that she was right.

TWENTY-ONE

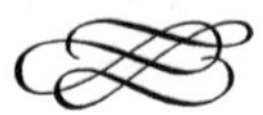

After my discussion with Edith, I couldn't really focus on work. Instead, I did something I rarely do – I delegated. I called the paginator Lynn in early and told her I'd be willing to pay her overtime if she could handle a few of my duties. I explained that I was working on a banner story on the murders that would take up most of the edition – and that was essentially true.

Despite the fact that my ankle was still tender, I managed to hobble downtown to Hypnotic. I had brought the files Edith had unearthed with me.

"What are you doing? You're not supposed to be walking!" Clove chided me when she saw me stumble inside the store.

"It's fine," I waved her off. "Trust me. It could be a lot worse."

"What are you doing here? We were going to bring you lunch."

"I'll just eat here with you guys."

"What about Friday's paper?" Clove was like another mother sometimes, I swear.

"I called Lynn in early."

Thistle and Clove exchanged wary glances.

"What?" I asked in irritation.

"You just seem a little obsessed," Clove said gently.

"Really? I seem obsessed? Why? Because we have ghosts living with us? Because we have murderers dropping bodies in cornfields? Because Aunt Tillie is still figuring out exactly how she's going to get back at me for the Edith situation?" My voiced had taken on a decidedly shrill tone.

Thistle took an involuntary step back. "Fine, you're not obsessed. You're acting totally normal."

I blew out a random sigh as I regarded them. "I know I'm a little …"

"Nuts?"

"Scary?"

"I was going to say intense," I corrected the two of them. "I just can't help it."

"We know," Thistle said. "You're going to get hurt if you don't watch it, though, and that's what we don't want to see. So, just chill."

I flopped onto the couch and watched them both as they continued to pretend they were actually doing work behind the counter. I knew better.

"Now," Clove said primly. "What do you want for lunch?"

"Middle-Eastern."

"We just had that the other day," Thistle complained.

"I'm hobbled. Don't you think I should get the food that I want?"

"Oh, nice. You managed to walk down here fine – I don't think that you deserve special treatment, especially considering how you hurt yourself."

"If she wants Middle-Eastern we can have Middle-Eastern," Clove caved.

"You always take her side," Thistle muttered. "I don't want Middle-Eastern."

"What do you want?"

"Mexican."

"Uh," I groaned. "I don't want Mexican today."

Clove glared at us both. "You're going to have to decide."

"You're the tiebreaker," Thistle said.

"I don't want to be the tiebreaker," she argued.

I stuck my lower lip out and dramatically rubbed my ankle when she glanced over at me. "Fine, Middle-Eastern it is."

Thistle opened her mouth to protest. "We'll get Mexican tomorrow," Clove added.

Thistle didn't look like she was entirely placated, but she also didn't look like she wanted to engage in World War III over lunch – and I was prepared to dig my heels in.

While Clove placed the orders, Thistle came over to see what I had in the file. She looked surprised when she'd sifted through a few of the articles. "Are these what I think they are?"

"You tell me," I answered.

She read through a few more articles and then lifted her eyebrows when she turned back to me. "They sure sound awfully similar. How come we don't know anything about this? Wouldn't this have been big news?"

"That's a very good question."

Clove joined us, grabbing a few of the articles from Thistle. "What are we talking about? The food will be here in twenty minutes, by the way."

"It's two teenagers who were killed and had their hearts ripped out – only it happened thirty years ago, and like forty minutes away," Thistle supplied.

Clove looked momentarily speechless. We both watched as she scanned the article on the top of the stack she'd taken from Thistle. When she was done, she let loose a long – and pointed – whistle. "Well, this can't be a coincidence."

"How can it be the same person, though?"

"What do you mean?"

"I mean that serial killers are usually white males in their thirties," I explained. "If that is the case, this would be a killer – or killers – well into his sixties. How is he controlling young teenagers? "

"How do you know that?" Thistle seemed impressed with my knowledge.

"I watch *Criminal Minds*," I admitted.

"Shemar Moore is so hot," Clove laughed.

"He is. They should make the entire show about him solving cases with his shirt off."

"Is that true, though?" Thistle didn't seem to think our television detour was nearly as cute as we did.

"I think it's pretty close to true," I said.

"Well, Sophie did say she was sure it was a man and a woman," Clove suddenly broke in. "Maybe the woman is younger and that's the reason he had to get a partner?"

"That's possible," I agreed. "Like maybe it's his daughter or something?"

"That's a pretty twisted family," Thistle grimaced.

"Ours isn't much better," I offered.

"True."

Thistle and Clove went back to reading the articles and I went back to watching them anxiously. The store was so quiet at this point that we all practically jumped out of our seats when the wind chimes at the front door sounded.

We all looked up expecting to see Clyde, the delivery boy for Hazel's Chinese Food and Other Stuff (don't ask). He delivered to us at least once a week.

I think we were all surprised to see Landon standing there instead.

Clove jumped to her feet. "Oh, can I help you?"

Thistle and I exchanged knowing looks. It was always fun when Clove got flustered.

Landon seemed surprised by Clove's reaction. "I'm looking for Bay Winchester," he said finally. He hadn't yet noticed Thistle and I sitting on the couch. "I was told that I might be able to find her here."

"Who told you that?" I asked from my comfortable position on the couch.

Landon turned and finally noticed that Thistle and I were in the room, too. Clove was still flittering around him like a nervous little butterfly.

"Sit down, Clove," I ordered.

She automatically did as she was told – although she didn't look very comfortable perched on the edge of the chair she had been sitting on before either. I couldn't decide if it was Landon's good looks – or the fact that she thought he might be a murderer – that was making her more nervous.

Thistle and I were more studied with our agitation. We could at least pretend that his presence didn't unnerve us.

"So, you're the biker dude," Thistle said finally.

"You must be one of the infamous cousins." Landon was trying to be charming, but I could tell he was thrown off by the current situation.

"I'm Thistle," she said finally. She didn't get up to greet him appropriately. Instead, she relaxed back into the couch. I could tell she was trying to retain some control over the situation.

"My name is Landon," he offered. He did extend his hand to her, but Clove batted it away nervously.

"What? He might have poison on it or something," she hissed. Clove was always good in a crisis.

"What can I do for you Mr. … Landon?" I realized I didn't know Landon's last name. That was a little disconcerting.

"I just wanted to make sure you were okay," he said.

"Oh, well that's so nice of you," Clove gushed. Thistle and I shot her sharp glares. She can turn on a dime, I swear.

I could see Landon smirk at her sudden change of attitude. He raised an eyebrow as he turned his head back to me. Thistle was hurriedly shoving the articles we had been looking through back into the envelope they came in. He reached down and picked one up and glanced at it quickly. He seemed surprised when he looked back at us.

"This has happened before?"

"So it would seem," Thistle said nonchalantly.

"Why didn't you tell me this before?" Landon asked the question to the room, but it was clearly pointed at me because his eyes never left my face.

"I didn't realize I was now reporting to you," I said sarcastically.

Thistle snickered, but Clove was looking at both of us disapprovingly. "Would you like a cup of coffee?"

"He's not staying," I interjected quickly.

Landon must have noticed my discomfort because he sat down in Clove's vacated chair, fixed me with a hard look and then turned to Clove with a warm smile. "I would love a cup of coffee."

Clove seemed happy to have something to do with her hands. If she was like me at all, she probably had to constantly remind herself not to run them through his silky black hair. Whoa! Where had that come from?

I turned my steely gaze back to Landon, who was accepting his cup of coffee from Clove in a congenial manner. He even shot her a flirtatious smile – complete with a saucy wink – when she started to walk away from him.

When Clove tried to squeeze herself between Thistle and me, we both balked. "There's no room," Thistle complained.

"Be careful of my ankle!"

"Oh, just stop your whining," Clove countered.

"Hey, I'm injured here," I reminded them.

Landon sipped from his coffee contemplatively for a few minutes. He seemed comfortable just to watch us interact with one another.

"So you all grew up together?" He asked finally.

"Yes," I said.

"Up at the Overlook?" He smiled to himself when he said the name.

It was one thing for us to make fun of the new name of the inn, it was quite another for a stranger. Thistle looked like she wanted to jump out of her chair and throttle him. "Do you have a problem with that?" She asked icily.

Landon seemed surprised by her sudden vehemence. "Sorry, did I say something wrong? I didn't mean to offend anyone."

As much as I loved watching Thistle get under Landon's skin, he still hadn't told us what he was doing here. "Did you find out who the bike belonged to?"

Landon feigned ignorance. "What bike?"

"The motorcycle in the ditch," I said shortly.

"Oh, *that* bike," Landon said smoothly. "I have no idea. I had almost forgotten about it until you reminded me."

Liar.

Landon turned his attention back to the article in his hand. "Where did you find out about this?"

"Edith," Clove answered before she thought.

"Who is Edith?"

"You're unbelievable," Thistle grumbled, kicking Clove viciously.

"Sorry, I forgot," Clove whined. "You know how I get when I get nervous."

If Landon wasn't confused before, he definitely was now. "Who is Edith?"

"She didn't mean Edith," I lied smoothly. "She meant Lynn. She just got her confused with the woman who used to work at the paper." What? That's not entirely a lie.

"Lynn remembered the case?"

"She remembered something similar, yes. We pulled out the file to get all the details, though."

"So you found the stories and brought them down here to your cousins instead of taking them to Chief Terry?" Landon seemed flabbergasted – and yet I couldn't figure out why. He may have just met me, but this was nowhere near out of my realm of usual behavior.

"Why do you care?"

"I would think this is information that would benefit Chief Terry," Landon said hotly.

"Well, when we're done reading them, we'll take them to him," I lied again. *Hey, we'll at least call him. I promise.*

Landon surveyed the three of us suspiciously. Thistle and I reflected the glares right back in his direction while Clove was steadfastly studying her nails. No one was going to break – even Clove. We wouldn't let her.

Landon got up slowly. "I actually did stop by here for a reason," he said reluctantly.

"And what reason is that?"

"I just wanted to warn you that running around corn mazes in the middle of the night probably wasn't a good idea."

"Thanks. I would never have figured that out without your valuable input," I seethed.

Landon tensed up when he heard the front door open and I swear I saw his hand hover under his coat – like he had a weapon – for just a second. He visibly relaxed when he saw Clyde wandering in with a big box of food. "Got your food ladies," he said with a simple smile. He wasn't exactly slow, but he was pretty far from quick. Still, the whole town loved him.

Thistle got up and paid for the food, including giving Clyde a $10 tip. He smiled when she handed it to him and ran out the door excitedly. He didn't even say goodbye to us. He never did. We always gave him a big tip, which he proceeded to take right down to Mr. Culverson's bookstore and buy comic books.

"You gave him a $10 tip for walking food three buildings down?" Landon looked incredulous.

"So?"

"Well, that's just stupid," he sputtered. "Why couldn't you just walk down the street to get the food?"

"We were busy looking through the file," I said with mock innocence.

"This place ..." Landon started.

"This place what?" I narrowed my eyes at him dangerously. I just dared him to say something about Hemlock Cove.

"This place would make a compelling psych experiment," he said finally.

"Says the guy I found creeping around the corn maze in the middle of the night," I shot back.

Landon stared at me hard for a few moments. He seemed unsure of what to say. When he did finally speak, it wasn't at all what I was expecting. "Are you this unpleasant with everyone? Or do I just bring out the worst in you?"

"Oh, she's always like this when she likes a guy," Clove answered indifferently. "At least at first. She'll calm down in a few days."

I slid a sideways glance at Clove. If I could have grown an invisible hand to smack her with – I would have.

Clove immediately realized what she'd done. "Not that she likes you," she amended lamely. She shifted slightly as she tried to take a step away from me. "In fact, if I had to guess, she really hates you."

Thistle met her gaze with a disappointed look and clucked softly. "Now I think you're dead to her," she offered.

Landon looked pretty pleased with himself when he left a few minutes later – despite my attempts to pretend that Clove was on some serious medications that made her mentally unbalanced.

When he was gone, I realized he had managed to squeeze information from us but he hadn't given us anything in return. Again.

"He really is hot," Clove said after a few minutes, when we'd doled out all the food.

I pretended I didn't hear her.

"You're still dead to her," Thistle informed Clove. "It's probably going to take homemade cookies to get her to talk to you again."

Clove looked genuinely sad.

"If I were you, I'd steal some of my mom's pot to put in them," Thistle laughed. "It really couldn't hurt at this point."

TWENTY-TWO

I was stuck at Hypnotic for the rest of the afternoon, so I made a few calls and emailed my story back to the office. Since The Whistler was a weekly, everything would be old news for the readers by the time it printed, but there was no way I could print an edition without at least mentioning the murders. I would never hear the end of it.

By mid-afternoon, though, I was starting to go stir crazy. "I should have driven to work myself."

"Stop your whining," Thistle said, not looking up from the handmade candles she was dipping at the table in the corner. She's the craftiest of the three of us. Her candles were actually really big sellers – especially the ones she infused with herbs for scent and glitter for decoration.

"I'm bored, and I want to go out to the inn and ask if they remember these other cases." Although why they wouldn't have mentioned them was beyond me.

"Call them," Clove offered, tossing the black cordless phone onto the couch next to me.

"No, I'd rather do it in person."

"Walk out there," Thistle said evilly.

I shot her a dirty look. "Bite me."

"I'm a little busy, why don't you see what Landon is doing," she shot back. "He looked like he wanted to sample you for lunch."

Clove giggled from behind the counter. When she caught my dark look, though, she immediately stifled it. She knew she was still in the doghouse from earlier.

I tried to get comfortable on the couch – but without anything to distract me, that was a losing proposition.

"Doesn't someone want to drive me out to the inn?" I figured if I badgered them long enough, one of them would cave. Probably Clove, if I had to guess.

"Not particularly," Thistle answered dryly.

Clove tried to look busy for a second and then sighed heavily. "I'll take you." I knew it would be her.

"You're only taking her because you're hoping she won't be mad at you anymore," Thistle scoffed.

"I am not," Clove said indignantly. "She's injured. She needs help."

"She's fine," Thistle countered. "She can sit there for another two hours until we close and then we can all go up to the inn together. They'll be thrilled to see us. Another dinner to torture us over."

Clove was caught. "Can you wait?"

I sighed dramatically. "Not really."

Thistle gritted out what sounded like a growl. She stalked into the back room and came out with a huge box, which she proceeded to drag over to me and drop at my feet.

"We just got a new shipment of incense," she announced. "Why don't you sort it? Make sure that you only put like scents together."

"You want me to do actual work?"

"Rather than sitting there and bitching? Yeah."

I grumbled a few choice words under my breath, but I proceeded to tackle the task put before me. If I was stuck here, I might as well do something. Anything was better than sitting here and staring at the walls. They really needed a television in here or something.

Surprisingly, the next two hours went relatively quickly. Even Thistle was impressed with my work ethic. "Good job," she patted me on the head when she took the last stack of incense from me and placed it on the shelves.

"I'm not a dog," I mumbled.

"No, a dog is easier to take care of."

"And friendlier," Clove said under her breath.

"I heard that."

"I think she meant for you to."

When we got out to the inn, Thistle parked in guest parking at the front of the inn so it would be easier for me to be able to maneuver through the main door. When we got inside, Marnie was checking a middle-aged couple in at the front desk. She seemed surprised when she saw us.

"Why are you limping?"

"I fell." I didn't think telling her how I sustained the injury would be a good way to start out this visit. Damn. I should have thought of a lie ahead of time. They were bound to sniff out the truth.

"She was trying to make Clove eat dirt again and things got out of hand." Thistle had obviously done my thinking for me. I shot her a grateful look.

Marnie seemed to accept the explanation without complaint. I had made Clove eat more dirt than was probably healthy. In return, Clove had ripped more chunks of hair out of my head than was necessary to fill a full wig.

We left Marnie to finish checking the couple in and made our way through the formal dining room and into the communal kitchen. My mom and Twila were both chopping vegetables at the center island. They had been engrossed in a conversation that stilled the moment we walked through the door.

"Wow, what a nice surprise," Twila enthused.

"We can hardly believe it ourselves," Thistle deadpanned.

Twila paused what she was doing and took in her daughter's appearance for a second. She shook her head slightly but didn't say anything.

"What?" Thistle already sounded exasperated, and her mother hadn't even insulted her yet.

"Nothing, dear, it's just that ... it's nothing."

"You might as well say it."

"It's just that, well, makeup is meant to enhance, not cake on. You shouldn't look like a human coloring book."

"This is the style," Thistle argued.

"You look like a rainbow raccoon."

"Yeah, well you look like …"

"You're working hard," I cut Thistle off. I didn't need things to evolve into World War III before I had some answers. After I had my answers, they could verbally smack the shit out of each other to their hearts content.

"Yes, vegetable soup and sandwiches," Twila said obliviously.

They did make good soup. I guess we could stay for dinner.

I shuffled over to the small desk in the corner of the kitchen, trying to hide my hobble as much as possible. I saw my mom eyeing me suspiciously. Nothing got past her.

"What happened to you?"

"She was trying to make me eat dirt and I tripped her and she sprained her ankle," Clove lied smoothly. I saw the lie was now growing.

"Really? I thought maybe you tripped when you were out in the corn maze last night."

"How could you possibly know that?" I protested.

"Chief Terry was out here for lunch." My mom was keeping her hands busy. I had a sneaking suspicion it was so she wouldn't reach over and smack me.

"How could he possibly know that?" Thistle asked dryly.

That was a good question.

"He didn't say." I could tell by my mom's tone of voice that a righteous rant was heading my way. "He just thought that maybe we should give you a good talking to about walking around crime scenes in the dead of night. I told him that was common sense, and we shouldn't have to tell you things like that, but he seemed to think you might be lacking common sense."

And here we go.

"What were you thinking?" My mom practically exploded.

Best just to lie and get it over with at this point. "I wasn't."

"And it will never happen again," Thistle supplied for me.

"She'll never be that stupid ever again in her life," Clove chimed in.

I shot a pained smile at my cousins. What a great help they were being.

"You may have a general disdain for life, young lady, but this is just ridiculous." She was apparently still wound up – and since she was wrapped pretty tight on a normal day – this was going to last for a while. I sighed as I sat back to listen to what I was sure was going to be a ridiculously long diatribe.

After about twenty minutes of being told how lucky I was that I wasn't raped, murdered, and robbed blind – and what if someone had seen me in my pajamas – she finally began to taper off. Throughout her lengthy speech, she never once paused from cutting up vegetables and shifting them over to Twila. They were like a well-oiled kitchen machine. It was fairly impressive.

Marnie had come in halfway through. When my mom was done yelling, she turned to Thistle. "And you need to stop lying," she added.

"She lied?" Twila asked in disbelief.

"She said Bay got hurt wrestling with Clove."

"They tried that on us when they first came in," Twila clucked.

"They lie to us all the time," my mom said. "I don't see why you guys act like this is such a big surprise."

Cripes.

"We actually came out here for a reason," Thistle prodded me.

Oh, right. "Yeah, we …"

"Just seeing your poor mothers isn't enough?"

"Well, as much of a bonus as that is, we do have something we want to ask you," I said sweetly.

"Fine, what is it?"

I pulled the file of newspaper clippings out of my purse and handed them to Thistle. She pushed them across the counter toward my mom and Twila.

"What's this?" My mom opened the envelope. We watched her read for a few minutes, but she didn't belie what she was feeling as she did so. Finally, she looked up at us expectantly.

"So?"

"So? Don't you think that's a little, I don't know, coincidental?"

Twila and Marnie were looking at the clippings now, too.

"Oh, I remember this," Marnie said. "This was a big deal when it happened."

'I don't really remember it," Twila said.

I was dumbfounded. "Two teenagers, a boy and girl, who had their hearts ripped out and were left in area barns? You don't think that bears mentioning given what has happened here?"

My mom shrugged. "I didn't really think about it. You could have a point, though."

"About what?"

Great, Aunt Tillie was here.

Marnie showed her the articles. Aunt Tillie wasn't impressed either. "That's from like thirty years ago."

"Yes, but it's the same thing that's happening now."

"But it happened like forty miles away," she countered.

"That's really not that far."

Thistle and Clove seemed surprised by their reactions, too. "You don't think those murders have a lot in common with the murders of Shane and Sophie?"

"I guess," Marnie hedged. "Isn't it unheard of for a serial killer to have such a long cooling off period, though?"

"How do you know about cooling off periods," Clove asked incredulously.

"She watches all those *Dateline* shows whenever they're on," my mom answered for her. "She's quite knowledgeable about serial killers."

What a great expertise to have.

"They never caught the killer, right?" Clove asked.

"No, I don't think so. I just think people forgot about it after a little while," Marnie said.

"You don't find that weird? That would have been one of the biggest things to ever happen around here."

"Eh, it wasn't happening here so people really didn't care," Aunt Tillie said, absently waving her hand.

"You didn't care that teenagers were getting their hearts ripped out?"

Aunt Tillie turned toward me. "Don't you use that tone of voice with me, young lady! I've had just about enough of you lately."

"Enough of me? What did I do?"

"All three of you are so full of yourselves," she said. "You act like you're so much smarter than us. Where do you think you got those brains you're so proud of, missy?"

"Um, college."

Aunt Tillie made a move to smack me, but even with an injured ankle I managed to get out of her way. "Hey!"

"You need to learn to respect your elders."

"I do respect my elders. I just don't understand how they don't see how this is relevant!"

"I didn't say it wasn't relevant," she seethed. "I said that it wasn't that big of a deal at the time. "

I turned to Marnie for help. She seemed to be the only one who understood the importance of the previous case. She obviously wasn't willing to take a stand against Aunt Tillie, though.

She handed the envelope with the articles in it back to me and smiled brightly. "I hope they find the killer."

This was really unbelievable.

TWENTY-THREE

I woke up the next morning with what felt like an alcohol hangover – which was impossible, since I hadn't had anything to drink the night before, besides about a quart of mom-and- aunt-instilled guilt, that is.

I rolled out of bed and found Thistle and Clove both standing at the kitchen counter. They were both already dressed and showered. Had I slept in?

"We have a tour group coming in at 8 a.m.," Thistle answered the question before I even uttered it.

"How many people?"

"Like a hundred," Clove said. "They're coming from the Bay City and Saginaw area. They're all staying at area inns for the entire week-end. We expect to be busy for the next four days."

"Well, that's good for you guys," I said.

They both watched me walk to the counter. "What?"

"You can drive yourself today, right?" Clove asked.

"Yeah."

"Good, because neither of us wanted to drive you," Thistle said.

"I love you, too."

Clove was peering a little too closely at my face from across the counter. I was starting to get a little uncomfortable. "What? Do I have dried drool on me or something?" I made a motion to wipe the corner of my mouth.

Thistle was suddenly staring, too.

"Seriously, what are you guys looking at?"

"That is just one monster of a zit," Thistle laughed, pointing at my lip.

My hand flew up and felt around the area they were staring. I groaned inwardly when I felt what could have been a small village popping up on my upper lip. "But I washed my face," I protested.

"Seriously, that thing looks like it could be an extra in a monster movie," Clove said disgustedly.

I stood up and made my way over to the ornate mirror hanging on the wall. They were right. It was really big.

Thistle and Clove had followed me. They seem entranced with my new zit. It was big enough to need its own room, after all.

"It's one of those really hard underground ones," Thistle finally said. "You can't even pop it."

"You should never pop them," Clove supplied. "That just makes things worse. It could leave you with a scar."

"It actually kind of hurts," I muttered.

"Don't touch it," Thistle slapped my hand away.

Clove tilted her head. "You could tell people it's a cold sore."

"Yeah, because having lip herpes is better than having a zit."

It isn't, right?

I was still studying it when something occurred to me. "Aunt Tillie."

"It's not as big as her," Thistle countered.

"Not that! I mean Aunt Tillie did this to me."

"It's just a zit."

I glared at Clove. I noticed she had her own situation popping up dead center on her chin. "Oh, really? Then why are you getting one, too?"

"I am not!" Clove looked panicked as she pushed me from the front of the mirror. "That was not there when I got up!"

We both turned to Thistle. I couldn't stifle my snicker when I saw the protuberance growing from the center of her forehead.

"No," Thistle whined. She turned and stared at herself in the mirror for a second and then swore under her breath. "I'm going to make that old lady pay."

"That's not a good idea," Clove argued. "Whatever you do to someone comes back on you threefold. Don't forget."

"Then how come nothing ever comes back on her?" I grumbled.

"Maybe she's too old."

"Or maybe even karma is scared of her," Thistle suggested.

After Thistle and Clove left, I showered and got ready for work. The more I tried to hide the zit, the more I looked like I had had some sort of seizure while applying my makeup. Finally, I just gave up.

I stopped by the office to check and see how the layout was progressing. It actually looked pretty good. I signed off on it, so they could send it to the printers, and then I set out for Hypnotic.

I saw a large tour bus parked downtown. I figured that must be the group that Thistle and Clove had been talking about. Hemlock Cove got a lot of buses from all over the state – especially this time of year. We had actually started getting groups from as far away as Canada. It was kind of fun to see how people reacted to the town.

When I walked into Hypnotic, I was surprised to see how packed it was. Thistle was busily handling the register while Clove had a line of customers waiting for Tarot readings.

"Do you need help?"

Thistle looked relieved when she saw me. "Yeah, can you just circulate and make sure everyone is finding what they need?"

I spent the next two hours busily shuffling from person to person. All of them were over the age of sixty – and all of them were extremely thrilled to be here. When they found out I worked for the paper, everyone started grilling me about the gruesome murders.

I told them the bare basics, which wasn't easy after Shane and Sophie showed up. "What's with all the old people?" Sophie wrinkled her nose.

"I think they're cool," Shane said. "It's like an entire room full of Aunt Tillies."

"Don't mention her name," I barked.

The elderly woman I was helping as she looked through the pewter jewelry jumped. "I didn't say anything, dear," she said.

"I wasn't talking to you," I apologized. "Thistle asked me something." What? She's old. She doesn't know the difference.

When the store had finally emptied out, Thistle, Clove and I all exchanged exhausted glances. "Well, that was …"

"Lucrative," Thistle supplied, snapping the cash register door shut.

She came over and joined Clove and I on the couch. "A lot of them said they're coming back tomorrow," Clove said. "I couldn't give everyone readings today and there were a lot more who wanted them."

"Well, it's good that people are still coming – despite the murders," I said.

Sophie was looking at my lip intensely. "Is that a zit?"

'Yes," I said shortly.

"It's gross."

"Yes."

"Have you remembered anything else?" Thistle asked Sophie. I think she was hoping that the teenager wouldn't notice she had her own growth to contend with. It didn't work.

"No. And gross, you have one, too."

"Damn, Aunt Tillie," I swore.

"I'm going to make the potion," Clove said finally.

"What potion?" Shane seemed excited.

"The pimple potion," Clove answered simply.

"You have a pimple potion?" Sophie seemed intrigued.

"Yeah," Thistle sighed. "It works like a gem, but it's a bitch to make."

Clove had pulled her compact out of her purse and was studying her chin. "It's worth the effort."

I wasn't particularly adept at making potions, so I remained on the couch while Clove and Thistle started to grind ingredients at the corner table.

"Aren't you going to help?" Sophie asked.

"I'm not good at potions."

"If I were them I wouldn't share with you." I hate teenagers.

"I just helped them calm the mob of the century," I argued.

"If we're going to make it, she can have some," Clove said. "Besides, we're in this together, at this point." She was grim and resolute.

"A united front," Thistle grumbled. "I still say that we should pay her back. We can't just let her keep getting away with stuff."

"She'll probably curse us again just for thinking about that," Clove said.

"How would she know you're thinking about it?" Shane asked.

"She's magic," Sophie said with reverent awe.

"She's evil," Thistle, Clove and I said in unison.

It took Thistle and Clove about an hour to make the potion. They left it sitting on the table and joined me on the couch.

"Aren't you going to use it?" Sophie clearly wanted to see if the magic pimple potion actually worked.

"It has to sit for twenty minutes," Clove explained.

The conversation turned back to Aunt Tillie – which was causing Thistle to grow redder and redder. After a few moments, though, I realized that she had also gone rigid.

"She's having a vision," Clove exploded.

We both moved to Thistle's side to make sure she didn't tumble forward. Then we just waited.

"More death," she mumbled.

"New victims? I thought they only needed two?" Clove shot a glance at me.

"These aren't new, they're old," Thistle said.

"The murders from thirty years ago?"

"Just because it's old, that doesn't mean it's over."

"See, we were right. I can't wait to tell that old witch that we were right," I practically crowed.

"Is now really the time for that?" Clove chastised me.

"Two are here, two were there. One male. One female."

"One of the killers is female?"

"I already told you that," Sophie protested.

"We don't have long," Thistle intoned. "Hours, not days."

"Can you see them?"

Thistle exhaled sharply as she relaxed in the chair. "I hate it when that happens," she grumbled.

"Could you see faces?" I asked. Clove had gotten up and poured a cup of tea for Thistle and brought it back to her.

"No," Thistle said. "It's like ... it's like they're blurry or something."

"Blurry?"

"Like when I get up in the morning, before I put my contacts in. There are no sharp edges to grab on to."

"You said we have hours instead of days," I prodded. "Do you have anything more to go on?"

Thistle shook her head ruefully. "No. I'm sorry."

"It's not your fault," I waved her off. "It's not like these 'gifts' come with a road map."

"They should," she said.

I smiled at her, the expression small and fruitless. Then I turned to Sophie and Shane with a certain amount of trepidation. "You're all we have, guys. Have you remembered anything else? Even something little might be able to help us."

Sophie shook her head helplessly. "There's nothing."

"Isn't there a way to jog our memories?"

"Not that I know of," I admitted.

"I think we have to take them back to the corn mazes," Thistle said.

"They've been back."

"What else do we have?"

Nothing. We had absolutely nothing. And time was running out.

TWENTY-FOUR

Given how busy the store was – members of the tour group continued to circulate in and out – we couldn't go back out to the corn maze until the store was closed. I could have survived without Thistle and Clove, but I wasn't really keen on that idea – especially since my ankle was still tender.

We all managed to find time to apply the potion, though. The minute I felt it touch the world's biggest pimple, I couldn't help but sigh in relief. By morning it would be gone. I had a feeling Thistle's rage would remain long after her face had cleared up, though.

When it was time to close the store, we all agreed to drive together. "We'll just pick up your car tomorrow," Clove said. I could tell she was already nervous.

We decided to go to Harrow Bluff first. This was where Shane's body had been found. He seemed excited at the prospect.

"I'm not sitting in the back with them," I argued when Clove yelled shotgun outside of the store.

"Why not?"

"My ankle is still hurt."

"It's not like they can jostle it," Thistle scoffed.

Crap. "Well, I'm not sitting in the middle."

I slid into the seat behind Clove – she was shorter, after all – and I couldn't hide my frown when the excited Sophie and Shane popped into the car next to me.

"It's like a road trip," Sophie said excitedly.

Yeah, a road trip to hell.

When we got out to Harrow Bluff, I was surprised to find that it was open again. I had expected to find it deserted.

"You've got to be kidding me," Thistle swore.

"It's Hemlock Cove and it's tourist season. What else do you expect?"

"A little respect, maybe?"

"Yeah, I think you're asking for too much."

"Well, at least with the three of us together we can talk to Sophie and Shane without people thinking we're crazy." Clove always finds something to be optimistic about. It's endearing – and annoying.

"They already think we're crazy," I complained.

"Oh, get over it," Thistle grumbled.

We exited the car, greeting a handful of people we recognized at the food table before we positioned ourselves at the front of the maze.

"When did the maze reopen?" I asked Mrs. Little, who was holding court with a couple of biddies from her bridge club.

"Shouldn't the newspaper already know that?"

"I guess I must have missed it," I said brightly.

"Today," she answered.

"Don't you think that's a little rude," Thistle challenged her.

"This is a tourist town," Mrs. Little glared at Thistle. Given the way she was looking at her hair, I guessed she hadn't seen the blue tresses yet. "We don't let bad times get us down."

"Or murders affect the bottom line," Thistle mumbled.

"What did you say?" Mrs. Little was spoiling for a fight.

"She asked if you could pass her a glass of cider," I broke in. Now was not the time to fight with the town's favorite pain in the ass.

Since I'd brought up cider, we were obliged to drink it. It gave me a chance to look around the maze to see who was here. I recognized a couple of the elderly ladies from the tour earlier in the day. I also recognized Emily, the woman from the inn, who had discovered Shane's body with me.

"Why is she here?"

"Who?"

"Emily."

"That woman from the inn?"

"Yeah."

"Wasn't she the one that discovered Shane's body with you?"

I nodded.

"She's a horror fanatic, right?" Clove asked.

"She said she was. She was kind of squeamish, though."

"Maybe Ron wanted to come?" Thistle said.

"Who is Ron?"

"Her husband."

"Oh, I never got his name, I don't think."

"They're from New York," Clove supplied.

"How do you know that?"

"He told me that night at dinner. He was actually kind of chatty."

"What did he say?"

"He said that they were on their honeymoon and they were from New York," Clove answered simply.

"He couldn't have been that chatty," I sniped.

"No, I mean that he kept telling these really long and boring stories about how they met and how it was love at first sight and how he thought he'd found his soul mate. It was actually pretty annoying."

Since Clove was an eternal optimist – and a hopeless romantic – he must have been really annoying.

Emily caught sight of us and ran over to us excitedly. "You guys came for the reopening, too."

"Yes," I lied.

"Her hair looks like a poodle," Sophie complained.

I looked at Emily's tightly wound blonde curls and couldn't help but agree. "Her hair was straight before. Maybe she does this for a special occasion," I whispered. Thankfully Emily's attention was focused on Clove.

"Nothing is that special."

Thistle snickered. She can transform into a snarky teenager when she wants to. Actually, we all can.

"I'm surprised you're here," I said to Emily. "I thought you were kind of … traumatized when you were here before."

"I was," Emily said, her tone blithe. "But, like Ron tells me, the best way to face your fears is to actually face your fears."

"Ron sounds wise," Thistle said sarcastically.

Clove shot her a dirty look. We were never supposed to be mean to the guests at the inn.

Thankfully, Emily seemed oblivious to sarcasm. "Oh, he is," Emily said dreamily. "He's the smartest man I've ever met."

Ah, young love.

"So, have you been in yet?" I felt the need to at least pretend I was interested in Emily – mostly because we'd discovered a body together. What? That's a thing. I swear.

"I'm still working up to it," Emily confided.

"Me, too," I lied.

Emily's husband was motioning for her to join him, so she said her goodbyes and then practically ran to him across the parking lot. They were making out within five seconds flat.

"That's so gross," Thistle complained.

"I think it's sweet," Clove argued.

They both turned to me expectantly. "I think it's a little obnoxious," I said finally.

"I bet if it was you and Landon you wouldn't complain," Clove said.

Thistle snorted.

"Who's Landon?" Sophie asked. "Is he the hot guy from the other night?"

"No."

"Yes," Thistle and Clove countered in unison.

"How is Marcus?" I verbally shot over to Thistle. I saw her redden at the question. "You thought I forgot about him, didn't you?"

Clove was smiling conspiratorially at me. "We haven't seen him again," she said.

"Why not?"

"Well, there *have* been two murders," Clove argued rationally.

She had a point.

"I think you should invite him out to the inn for dinner," I teased. "Once the zit is gone, that is."

"Does it look any better?" Thistle was momentarily distracted from her growing anger.

I narrowed my eyes as I regarded it. "It already looks like it's shrinking," I admitted. "How about me?"

Clove stared at it a second. "You, too."

"That old lady is going to pay, I swear," Thistle grumbled again.

"Back to Marcus," I said.

"What about him?" Thistle was getting increasingly irritated.

"I think you should invite him out to dinner." What? That's a great idea. My mom and the aunts would spend the entire night fawning over him. It would be a stress-free evening for me. And, that's really all that matters.

"I'll invite him the same night you invite Landon," Thistle seethed.

Well, that's never happening.

"Did I hear my name?"

I froze. I recognized the voice. Crap.

I turned around to see Landon standing behind me. What the hell was he doing here?

"She said landing," I lied.

"You're going to invite landing somewhere?" Landon seemed a little too pleased with himself.

"Why are you eavesdropping? That's rude."

"He's hot. Don't scare him off," Sophie warned.

"He's suspicious," Shane chimed in. His dislike of Landon was still apparent.

"You're in public," Landon argued. "You can't eavesdrop in public."

All evidence to the contrary.

"What are you doing here?"

"Probably the same thing you are. I'm just checking it out," Landon explained vapidly.

I glanced around the maze, but I didn't see any of his hooligan friends. "Where are your buddies?"

"Off doing business."

"What kind of business?" Thistle and Clove leaned in closer when I asked the question. They were curious, too. If he was involved in meth trade, no matter their teasing, he was simply unacceptable. Sure, our family was apparently made up of potheads, but there was a big difference between growing it and selling it. What? There is.

"A little of this, a little of that." Landon was being evasive.

"What's this?" Thistle asked.

"What's that?" Clove asked.

They were both appropriating aggressive stances.

Landon took an involuntary step back. "Nothing important," he lied. "Geez, you guys are like a little tribe or something."

"We're family," Thistle corrected him. "And we don't like people who mess with family."

"Even if they are hot," Clove added.

Landon smiled at Clove. I think he could tell she was the only one of us who wasn't overtly suspicious of him at this point.

"I just wanted to say hi," he said lamely.

"Hi," Thistle challenged him.

Landon regarded her for a second and, I swear, he shrank a little bit in her growing presence. He turned to me warily. "How is your ankle?"

"Fine. It's still a little sore, but I'm not having any trouble getting around on it anymore."

"Better than her zit," Sophie snarked.

I shot her an evil look without realizing what I was doing. Landon looked at the empty space next to me. Curiosity was written all over his face.

"You didn't answer the question," Thistle barreled on. "Why are you here?"

Landon seemed reluctant to face her, but he visibly steeled himself as he did. "I was just checking it out. That's not a crime, is it?"

"Not yet," Thistle agreed.

"Well, anyway, have a good day," Landon said, moving off hurriedly. Thistle really is terrifying when she wants to be.

"I don't like him," she said when he was out of earshot.

"He's not so bad," I protested.

"What if he's a meth dealer?"

"Then he's bad," I acquiesced.

"He's hot, though," Clove offered.

"So hot," we all murmured in unison as we watched him make his way back across the parking lot.

TWENTY-FIVE

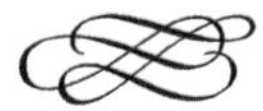

We waited at the maze for a good half an hour before we made our way inside. I saw Landon – who was keeping his distance from Thistle more than anything else, I think – studying us as we finally entered. I don't know if he considered us a threat – or just weird – but he was clearly paying a little too much attention to our shenanigans.

"He's suspicious," I said, once we were safely inside of the maze.

"Who is?" Clove asked.

"Landon," I replied.

"He's suspicious of us?" Thistle was incredulous.

"Think about it, he caught me sneaking into a corn maze – which was also a crime scene – in my pajamas after dark," I started.

"And he was also there," Thistle pointed out.

"The pajamas could just mean you're crazy," Clove added.

"He saw me talk to Sophie today," I said.

"You could have had an eye twitch," Thistle offered.

"Or some sort of seizure," Clove said helpfully.

"Every time he sees me, it's like I'm up to something," I sighed.

"You are always up to something," Thistle argued. "That doesn't mean he has the right to be suspicious."

"Besides that, he's the one being secretive," Clove pointed out. She may think he's hot, but she was still loyal to me.

"Men aren't secretive, they're mysterious," Thistle muttered blandly.

"Dude, seriously, who peed in your Cheerios?"

Thistle looked surprised at my question. "I'm still mad at Aunt Tillie."

"You tell me to let stuff go. You need to let stuff go. If we go after that woman, she will eat us for lunch." And still have room for dessert.

"Well, then I hope I give her indigestion – or the runs," Thistle countered with surprising hostility.

"Ooh, gross," Sophie squealed.

I'd almost forgotten she was here. I shifted so I could see her and Shane following behind us. He seemed nervous.

"Are you all right?" I asked him.

"I'm fine," he said. "It's just weird being here knowing that this is where my body was found."

"I know," I said. "I wouldn't make you come here unless I had to, you know that, right?"

He nodded mutely, his dark eyes clouding over.

"We're running out of time, Shane," I prodded. "We don't have a lot of options here."

"I know," he said. 'It's just ... it's just so weird to know that I was strung up on a cross here."

"It's morbid," Clove clucked knowingly.

"Yeah, well, your death is going to be a waste if you don't suck it up," Thistle grumbled. "Besides, you guys came back here on your own. This isn't the first time you have come back."

"Thistle," Clove hissed.

"What? It's the truth. We aren't here because we love cider and sneezing. We're here because we don't have a shot in hell of identifying who did this without the two of them. They need to just suck it up."

Just because it was the truth, that doesn't mean she should have just blurted it out like that. "It's called tact," I laughed.

"Please, this family doesn't have a tact gene," she argued. "We've got a busybody gene, a cooking gene, a petulant gene. The tact gene just didn't skip our entire generation; it skipped our entire gene pool."

Sometimes, Thistle just has a way with words.

Once we got to the center of the maze, we all took a deep breath and looked around. The owners had clearly come in and revamped the original theme of the maze. Now there were hay bales with smiley-faced pumpkins, colorful corn stalks and even happy little witch faces. There were no scarecrows – or crosses – in sight.

"Is this the same place?" Shane asked.

"They cleaned it up," I said.

"So ... what should I do?" He seemed nervous.

"Just walk around. Get a feel for the area. Try to listen to your head and your heart."

"You sound like a fortune cookie," Thistle laughed.

I shot a 'shut it' look in her direction, but I didn't verbally chastise her. I didn't want to derail Shane. He was doing as I told him to, closing his eyes, and wandering around the clearing.

I could do nothing but watch and Thistle and Clove could do even less. They were stuck watching me watch.

Even Sophie must have sensed the importance of what we were doing because she sashayed over and positioned herself behind Thistle and Clove. She clearly didn't want to be in the way.

After a few minutes, Shane turned to me in frustration. "They're there. I can feel them," he said. "I just can't see them."

"What if he can't see them because he never really saw them clearly," Thistle said suddenly, an idea had occurred to her.

"What do you mean?"

"The chloroform. He thought he was drugged. Maybe he was going in and out of consciousness, so he never really saw what they looked like."

"I never really thought of that," I admitted.

"That could be why Thistle's visions are all cloudy, too. She keeps seeing things from the point-of-view of those who lived it – both then and now. If the first victims were drugged, then maybe they never saw their attackers either," Clove said excitedly. "That would explain a lot of things."

"The articles never said anything about chloroform in the victims' systems," I said.

"Yeah, but did they even think to check for it back then? Is it easy to check for, period?" Thistle seemed to be warming up to her theory.

"So, what do we do?"

"I think we have to get a little help," Thistle said ruefully.

"From who?"

"You know who."

"No, no and no."

"We don't have a choice," Thistle argued. "If they can think of something that we can't – then don't we have to at least try?"

"You said yourself that we're running out of time," Clove said.

God, I hate it when they're right.

When we left the maze, Landon was still positioned outside. He met my gaze as I exited, but he didn't make a move to intercept us. He was, however, watching us curiously. He continued to follow our progression as we all filed into Thistle's car and took off in the direction of the inn. I'd have to deal with him and his issues later.

When we got to The Overlook, Thistle parked in the side lot so we could sneak in unnoticed by the guests. We all headed straight for the kitchen. We knew they would be preparing dinner.

When we entered, they all seemed surprised to see us. "This can't be good," Marnie said. "All three of them, together, and they seem to have something on their mind."

Aunt Tillie was sitting in her recliner by the counter watching. She smiled widely when she caught sight of us. "I think they're here to see me," she said haughtily.

"Think again, old lady," Thistle barked out. "Although, we will be dealing with you later. We don't have time for that now."

"Oh, really? And why not?"

"Thistle had another vision," Clove said.

"What did she see?" Aunt Tillie was leaning forward in earnest concentration. She seemed to have forgotten her joy about cursing us from just a few seconds before.

"That we're running out of time," Thistle said shortly. "We need help. We need your help." She was trying not to choke on the words.

"What do you need?"

Thistle and I exchanged suspicious glances. Aunt Tillie was never this anxious to help. She usually made us beg.

"Are you deaf, girls? What do you need?"

"Why are you willing to help so easily?" I challenged her.

"Is now really the time for that?" My mom chided me. Probably not, but I didn't think I could trust Aunt Tillie as far as I could throw her. She may be little, but she's heftier than she looks.

"I may enjoy torturing you girls, but I don't want anything really bad to happen to you," Aunt Tillie admitted grudgingly. "If one of you were to die, that wouldn't be good for any of us."

"So, you're saying you actually like us?" Clove was trying to be endearing.

"I wouldn't go that far," Aunt Tillie said shortly. "My life would just be a whole lot more boring if I didn't have you three to torture."

We proceeded to fill everyone in on the remainder of Thistle's vision – and our actions of the afternoon. Aunt Tillie looked thoughtful when we finished.

"What about a seeing spell?" She said finally.

"A seeing spell? Like to see what's really underneath the façade that people put up? Like a lying spell?" Thistle looked confused.

"We only called it a lying spell when you guys were little," Aunt Tillie corrected her.

"Why?"

"You little shits had such trouble telling the truth," she answered. "We were trying to scare you."

"So what does the spell really do?" I asked impatiently.

"It clarifies things."

"Can you be more specific?"

"Shane and Sophie may not have seen their killers clearly, but the spirits did."

"The spirits?" Not more of this crap.

"Yes, the spirits," she spat back. "We need to cast a spell that lets us see what really happened clearly."

"Well, then let's do it," I said resolutely.

I caught my mom and Marnie exchanging furtive looks.

"What?"

"It has to be done at the scene of the crime," my mom said finally.

The corn maze. Again. We should just build a house out there.

"Tell us what to do, and we'll do it." Thistle seemed as resigned as I was.

"We can't teach it to you quickly enough," Marnie said morosely. "We'll have to go with you."

"No way! We can't drag you out in the corn maze in the middle of daylight so you can do some ritual." We'd never live that down – even if we did solve a murder in the process.

"That's why we have to go after dark," Aunt Tillie said sagely.

"What if someone catches us?" I complained.

"Then we'll pretend we're lost," Aunt Tillie brushed me off. "I do it all the time."

"We're not all eighty-five," I argued. "If we try using that ruse we'll get locked up in an asylum."

"Just let me handle the police if it comes to that," Aunt Tillie said in her best withering tone. "Good grief, you three act like you've never broken the law before." Not with our mothers in attendance, that was for sure.

"Tonight is the full moon," Marnie bit her lower lip.

"You have to wear your clothes," I practically exploded.

"That's not what I meant," she said, giving me a curious look. "Your obsession with nudity is troubling, though." She had no idea. "What I mean is, didn't Thistle's first vision say that it would all happen on the night of the full moon?"

I felt a sinking sensation in my stomach as I realized that Marnie was right.

I turned to Thistle and Clove helplessly. "What do we do?"

Thistle shrugged. "We're in unchartered territory here. I don't think we have a choice. We have to go into the maze tonight. All of us. We can't do it alone."

I shook my head as I turned back to them. "Be ready to leave at ten," I finally said.

Aunt Tillie let loose of her most condescending grins. "It's going to be a fun night tonight, girls. You better suit up."

"Suit up? Like Batman?" Clove looked horrified.

"If that will make you feel better. I was talking about wearing black, though," Aunt Tillie corrected her.

"Oh, yeah, we know that."

"This isn't our first rodeo," Thistle scoffed.

"Yeah, but now you're working with professionals," Aunt Tillie said. She started to move toward the den with a clear purpose. "I think I'll take a nap in preparation for tonight," she said heavily.

"Oh, good, the head of our team needs a nap," I muttered under my breath.

I couldn't help but notice how excited my mom, Twila and Marnie appeared to be, too. Great. This was going to be one big disaster.

"Does anyone think this is going to blow up in our faces?" I finally asked.

"Oh, yeah," Thistle said. "No doubt."

"I feel like I need my own nap just thinking about it," Clove sighed.

"What we need is to just sneak away when they're not looking and try to do this ourselves," I offered lamely. I knew it wouldn't really happen, though.

"Girls," I heard my mom practically sing. "Are you hungry?"

"What are you having?" Thistle asked. I wanted to kick her.

"Lasagna."

Crap. They make really good lasagna.

TWENTY-SIX

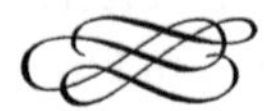

Clove, Thistle and I ate dinner at the inn – the lasagna was awesome, as always – and then we ran back to the guesthouse to get ready for the night's excursion. I slipped into my simple black track pants, black tennis shoes, a black T-shirt and a black hoodie.

When I went out into the living room, I found that Thistle and Clove were dressed in almost the same thing – although Clove's tank top had a few rhinestones on it. Thistle tossed the knit hat I had worn the first night we snuck into the corn maze at me and I offered little complaint this time when I put it on my head, making sure that all my hair was tucked up underneath it.

I paused in front of the mirror long enough to make sure that my zit was truly fading away. Yes, I know, now is not the time to be shallow. It's human nature. I can't help it.

"You can barely see it anymore," Thistle said. I noticed that she was busy camouflaging her face again.

Clove and I both followed suit and then we headed back up to the inn. Shane and Sophie had said they would get out to the corn maze themselves – they'd been practicing "winking" in and out of places – and they would wait for us there. We slipped in through the back door. I still wasn't sure that taking the four older women with us was such a good idea. That initial reluctance was only reinforced when I saw what they were all wearing.

"You can't go like that!"

"What?" My mom asked innocently, smoothing down her crushed velvet tracksuit in an attempt to eradicate any wrinkles. Priorities.

"Those are pajamas." I looked over to see that Marnie and Twila were wearing the exact same outfits – just in different colors. Marnie was in navy, my mom in gray and Twila was in a deep mauve.

"You went to the corn maze in pajamas," my mom pointed out.

"That wasn't planned," I countered.

"These aren't technically pajamas," Twila argued. "Just because we lounge around in them, that doesn't mean they're pajamas. They're meant to be worn in public. The models were wearing them outdoors in the catalog."

Thistle nudged my elbow. "It's not worth arguing about. We're probably lucky that they're not dressed like Army men – or carrying swords, or something." Or brooms and wands.

She had a point.

Marnie was looking at Clove intently. "What's all over your faces?" She reached a hand up to touch the paint on Clove's face.

"It's just some makeup to camouflage our faces," Clove said, slapping her hand away indignantly. "We're all really white – I mean really white – and that stands out in the dark."

"Oh, that's a good idea," Twila enthused. "I want some."

Thistle sighed and pulled the tin of paint out of her bag. "How did I know you'd say that?"

"Where's Aunt Tillie?" *Please say she went to bed early. Please say she went to bed early.*

"She's still getting ready," my mom answered. She didn't even bother looking up at me. She, Twila, and Marnie were having too much fun with the face paint to even register the long-suffering looks that Thistle, Clove and I were sharing. That was probably a good thing.

Clove picked up a cookie off the plate sitting on the little end table next to Aunt Tillie's chair. She's a stress eater. Actually, we all are. Thistle and I were munching on cookies before we even realized what was happening.

My mom finally noticed what we were doing – and she was frowning at us.

"What?"

"You shouldn't be eating heavy foods now," she chastised us. "It will just slow you down."

No, what was going to slow us down was them.

"Don't say it," Thistle warned under her breath. "We can't afford a big fight now and if you say it, we're going to have a huge blowup."

"All right, let's go!"

We all turned to see Aunt Tillie standing in the door impatiently. As usual, her entrance was designed for the maximum amount of drama that was sustainable for the current situation.

Clove giggled madly when she saw Aunt Tillie's outfit.

Since she was so short, Aunt Tillie usually had to have her pants professionally altered so they would fit her. I had no idea where she had managed to find what looked to be black parachute pants in her size. Maybe they were Corey Feldman's castoffs?

She had thrown a black sweatshirt on, as well, and she was wearing military combat boots. The best part of the outfit, though, was the combat helmet she had secured on her head – complete with a strap under her chin.

"Where did you get that hat?" Thistle asked.

"Forget the hat, where did you get those pants?"

Aunt Tillie didn't look like she was enjoying our mutant mixture of horror and merriment. "I'm prepared for all occasions, at all times. When are you going to realize that?"

"But what other occasion did you need a hard hat for?" Thistle couldn't stop staring at the hat. I found it a lot less objectionable than the pants, which made a shuffling sound every time she moved.

"In case it gets hairy out there, I want to protect my head," she said, her tone bland.

"But why do you have it?" Thistle wasn't going to be deterred.

"Maybe I just like it."

I had a feeling Aunt Tillie might have been indulging in the family pot a little more than anyone realized.

"Where did you get it from?" I asked finally. It was a rational question for an irrational woman.

"I found it in a catalog when that Army supply guy stayed here a few months ago," she sniffed.

Ah, that explained it. Aunt Tillie had never met a catalog that she couldn't find something to buy in. We still had a closet full of mousetraps, and no mice.

"You can never be too prepared, you know," she continued. "And now I'm ready in case we have a nuclear war."

"The hat is going to save you from a nuclear war?" Thistle was still dumbfounded.

"No," Aunt Tillie said derisively "The underground bunker that's being built in the spring is going to save me from that. The helmet is just for when the roof caves in on us. When everyone else has a concussion, I'm going to be the only one with my mental faculties still intact."

Oh, well, at least she'd thought it out.

Marnie handed Aunt Tillie the canister of face paint. "So your face doesn't stand out in the dark."

Aunt Tillie waved the canister off. "My face stands out regardless. Paint isn't going to change that."

Isn't that the truth?

"Besides," she added. "I don't trust anyone who hides behind that much makeup. That's what strippers and prostitutes do."

Whatever.

We all agreed that the only vehicle we were all going to be able to fit in was Marnie's Range Rover. Thistle got behind the wheel and Aunt Tillie got in the passenger seat. My mom, Marnie and Twila got in the backseat, which meant Clove and I had to sit in the cargo area in the back.

"This is ridiculous," I grumbled when Thistle hit a big dip in the road and we bounced up and almost crashed our heads into the roof of the vehicle.

"I think it's fun," my mom giggled.

"You would," I muttered.

"What did you say, dear? I can't hear you mumble insults when the radio is up so loud."

Despite the fact that it would have been more pragmatic to park farther away from the maze, there was no way we could do that with Aunt Tillie in tow. She's spry for eighty-five – but she's still eighty-five.

When we were all outside of the vehicle and checking to make sure we had all of the supplies that we would need in a duffel bag, Thistle couldn't help but complain. "We're going to get caught."

"Probably," I agreed.

"People in town are going to think we're even weirder than we are," Clove said.

"Oh, what, seven women sneaking into a corn maze at night is suspicious? Three dressed in black, three dressed in velvet track suits and one dressed in riot gear – that's not suspicious at all."

"Sarcasm is never your friend." I wasn't sure if my mom or Twila let loose that little pearl of wisdom, but it was a regular refrain in the Winchester house.

"Can we just get this over with?" If we were going to jail tonight, we might as well get the ball rolling. I could use a good night's sleep – even if it was on a stiff jailhouse cot.

Thistle and I took the lead. Clove wasn't happy about bringing up the rear by herself – but she admitted she would much rather be behind everyone else than in front of them. She still remembered our first nighttime trek into the maze – and she wasn't eager for a repeat. We all hated to admit it, but we felt a little better with Aunt Tillie there. She was far scarier than any murderer – or murderers, in this case.

"Where are Shane and Sophie?"

"They're probably waiting in the center of the maze. We told them we would be out here as soon as possible – but it took a little longer than any of us thought. They probably got bored waiting."

By this point, Thistle and I could have maneuvered our way through the maze in the dark – which was a pretty good thing since the only person we allowed to have a small flashlight was Aunt Tillie.

It took us a little longer than we expected, mostly because Aunt Tillie had decided to be as disagreeable as she could possibly be during the walk.

"I don't understand the point of a corn maze."

"It's just fun for families," I answered her testily.

"They why do they have hay bales?"

"I don't know. Ambiance?"

"How is hay ambiance?"

"You use hay when you're decorating for Thanksgiving up at the inn," I countered. She was just trying to be a pain.

"That's cute."

"Maybe they think this is cute," Clove offered.

"Somebody should tell them that they're wrong," Aunt Tillie said.

"Why don't you call them and tell them that tomorrow – if we're not in jail, that is," Thistle suggested.

"That's a good idea."

Sarcasm is truly lost on Aunt Tillie. Still, it might be fun for her to irritate other people in town for a while. Her family deserved a respite – however brief it might be.

I think we were all relieved when we made it to the center of the maze. Thistle dropped the duffel bag on the ground haphazardly and immediately started pulling things out of it. She handed Clove the candles and instructed her to light them in a circle.

My mom and the aunts were busy looking around the clearing. "This isn't very festive," my mom said finally.

"It was meant to be scary," I said. "But they took all the scarecrows out when Shane's body was found."

I looked around the clearing. At first I didn't see them, but then Shane and Sophie solidified in front of my eyes. "That's a neat trick," I told them.

"We've been practicing," Sophie said proudly.

"What's all that stuff?" Shane was watching Thistle rummage through the bag with genuine interest.

"It's for a ritual," I told him.

"To make us remember?"

"Not exactly. We think, maybe because you guys were drugged, that your memories are always going to be blurry. You might not have intact memories – and we can't wait any longer. We have to remember for you."

"So what will the ritual do?"

"We're hoping it will show us what happened here. Like an echo."

"So, you're trying to make the maze remember?" Shane asked. He didn't fully understand. I didn't blame him.

I considered the question for a second. "Actually, that's about the best way you could put it. Certain locations can tell us what happened there, and that's what we're trying to do."

"Will we all be able to see?" Sophie asked.

"We should," I said. "I can't guarantee what you guys – as ghosts – will be able to see. I don't think you should be any different than anyone else, though. We're in unchartered territory. I guess we're all about to find out together."

"So, it will be like watching television?" Shane asked. He still wasn't truly grasping the situation.

"No, it will be more like being in the television – but not being able to interact with the actors," I clarified. "In theory, we'll see what happens, but we won't be able to change anything."

"And the murderers won't be able to see us?" Sophie asked nervously.

"No," I soothed her.

"That sounds cool." Shane was excited, despite himself.

I didn't think he'd feel the same way when he saw himself being strung up like a scarecrow – but we were beyond protecting him at this point. I think we always had been.

TWENTY-SEVEN

It took us about five minutes to get everything set up. It probably would have taken longer if my mom hadn't distracted Aunt Tillie from micromanaging the setup. Once the candles were all lit – there were twelve in total – we all took our usual circle positions.

"It's so pretty," Sophie sighed.

"Yeah, it's great for a murder scene," Aunt Tillie sniped.

Sophie glared at her. "You don't have to be so mean."

"We need to concentrate," Aunt Tillie admonished her. "It's quiet time. Just embrace it."

I smiled at Sophie. I didn't chastise Aunt Tillie, though. She was right. The longer we stayed here, the likelier the chance that we would be caught. And, as much as Chief Terry liked my mom and her sisters, he probably couldn't ignore the fact that the seven of us were out here acting like idiots. And, in jail, we wouldn't be able to get any space from each other.

Aunt Tillie started to chant. She started by calling to the four corners. We all concentrated. We knew how important this circle would be. No one could half-ass the effort.

Magic started to swirl around us. You couldn't see it, but you could feel it. Even Shane and Sophie seemed surprised. Sophie's eyes widened in mystified shock. "What is that?"

None of us answered her. We were all too intent on our task. Marnie started intoning next. We all took our turns. As each person took on the repeating refrain, the tapestry of power we were starting to weave strengthened – like an extra-strength cobweb.

Slowly, the vision in front of us became clear. We all watched as a dark figure stumbled into the maze. I had to remind myself this was the past, not the present, and to control my heartbeat.

The dark figure was wearing a large gray jacket. It looked like any typical work jacket. I could see he was wearing gloves. The back of his head was facing us, so we couldn't see his face yet. He was dragging something into the clearing. I swallowed hard when I realized that it was Shane's body.

"That's me," Shane whimpered.

Another figure entered the clearing. It was a smaller figure, but just as furtive. The smaller figure was wearing a wool mid-length trench coat. It was clearly a petite woman. She was wearing a dark winter hat. I couldn't see her face yet. All I could see was hints of blonde hair sticking out from under the hat.

We all watched the scene unfold in silence. The only noise that could be heard was our breathing – which was dramatically increasing as the garish tableau continued in front of us.

"Grab his feet," the male voice ordered.

"That's gross," the female complained.

"I can't do it by myself. Stop being such a bitch."

"Don't you dare talk to me that way!"

The figures were getting closer to us. The man was almost on an even level to me. He was looking down as he dragged Shane's body past us – but I managed to get a good look at his face. I gasped when I saw it – and recognized it.

"Who is it?" Clove asked. She was on the other side of the circle and she couldn't see as well as I could.

"It's that guy from the inn," I said.

"Our inn?" My mom looked horrified.

"Which guy?" Clove asked.

"Ron."

"The newlywed?" Thistle asked.

"Yeah."

"That must mean …"

We all turned and focused harder on the woman. She trailed behind Ron, making sure not to touch the body. When she got closer, my suspicions were confirmed. "It's Emily," I breathed out harshly.

"That nice couple? It can't possibly be." Twila looked horrified, even though the scene was playing out in front of her, too.

"Well, it is," I said simply.

We continued to watch as Ron struggled to hoist Shane's body up onto the cross. I cringed involuntarily when I saw the body tumble to the ground when he failed at his first attempt. We could hear the sickening thud the body made as it hit the ground.

"You have to help me," Ron grumbled. "I can't do it alone. He's too heavy – and it's awkward to try and do it myself."

"I don't want to," Emily's petulant pout was disgusting.

"We can't afford to stay here forever," Ron pointed out. "We'll get caught – and I don't think you'd like prison."

"Will you buy me a nice dinner when we're done?" Emily asked.

"I'll buy you whatever you want if you just come over here and help me," Ron growled.

Emily sighed dramatically. "Fine. What do you want me to do?"

"Grab his feet."

Even though we had all the information we needed, we all continued to watch in grim curiosity. I couldn't make myself look away. I was so involved in watching what had happened in the past that I didn't notice what was actually happening in our suddenly perilous present.

"What the hell is this?"

We all froze. The voice we just heard was familiar – but it was also solid, not like the hollow memory voices we had been listening to for the past few minutes. We all swung around to find Ron and Emily standing inside the clearing watching us – rampant disbelief etched on their chalk-white faces.

Oh shit.

Emily looked surprised as she took in the scene. "Are you guys really witches or something?"

None of us answered her. We were all still shocked by the situation we found ourselves in.

Ron was watching the ghostly memories still play out around us. He seemed intrigued, despite himself. "That's a pretty cool trick," he said. "How did you do that?"

"They're magic, stupid," Emily interjected. She was watching the scene curiously, though. "Remind me not to wear that coat again. It makes me look fat."

I finally managed to find my voice. "Why are you here?"

"We saw the car outside the maze when we drove by. We were understandably curious. Who sneaks into a corn maze in the middle of the night? Only freaky people."

Says the guy who dragged the body of a mutilated teenage boy in here under the cover of darkness.

"I knew something was fishy about all of you," Emily said snottily. She was wandering around the maze – but she didn't get too close to us. "I thought all this magic stuff with the town was all fake, but when I met you guys, I knew you were different. I didn't think you were really witches, though. I just thought you were all nutcases or something."

If she was fishing for accolades for her superior intellect, she wasn't going to get them here.

"I was suspicious of you guys right away," Emily continued. "I just couldn't figure out why you were so involved. So I decided to sit back and watch. It wasn't easy. You guys are all over the place."

"That was a nice way to divert attention from you guys, being the one to discover the body with me," I said, faking admiration for their purported exploits. I wanted to keep them as calm as possible for as long as possible.

"Yeah, that was a nice touch," Emily smiled.

"Why did you risk going to the maze that morning?" I felt the need to stall – although I didn't know what benefit that would bring us.

"We just couldn't stay away," Emily said. "Ron didn't want to come at first, but he can never resist seeing how the public reacts to his work."

His work? Did this guy think he was an artist or something?

"Didn't you think it was risky to actually be one of the people who discovered the body?"

"Not really," Emily shrugged. "Especially since I wasn't alone. I was actually just waiting around to see if someone else would discover it. When I saw you looking, I just couldn't resist."

"Glad to be of assistance," I said wryly.

Emily regarded me seriously for a second, her green eyes were speculative. "I knew that we should have checked out of the inn when I realized you were investigating the case with the police. We didn't want to act suspiciously, though. So, instead, we just kept watching you. All of you."

"Did you enjoy the show?" Thistle was looking at Emily with genuine distaste.

"You're all very amusing, I'll give you that. Of course, I'm betting now that you wish you would have stayed out of this."

"On the contrary," Thistle shot back. "We like to know when we're living amongst monsters."

I was surprised that Aunt Tillie hadn't started spouting off yet. She just seemed to be taking in the scene, though. She didn't look particularly worried. I didn't know if that was a good sign or a bad sign. My mom, Twila and Marnie had moved subtly closer to one another, but they weren't saying anything either.

"Can I ask you a question?"

Emily seemed surprised by the request. I noticed that Ron seemed content to just let her run the show. I didn't know what he had planned, but I doubted it would be pleasant. "By all means, ask away. You might as well have your curiosity sated – while you still can."

I ignored the veiled threat and plowed on. "Why?"

"Why what?"

"Why did you kill Shane and Sophie?"

The ghosts, for their part, had remained silent. They seemed enthralled by what was happening, but helpless to affect it in any way.

"Oh, that," Emily waved Shane and Sophie's deaths off like I'd told her that her shoes were untied. "We didn't have anything against them specifically. They were just a means to an end."

"What end?"

"Rebirth, of course," Emily answered simply, but there was a malevolent glint in her eye.

"Rebirth?"

"They were a sacrifice to Osiris," Emily explained.

"The god of life and death? You were making a sacrifice to him? Why?" All practicing Wicca – and *Buffy the Vampire Slayer* fans – were familiar with Osiris, the Egyptian god that was usually referred to as the lord of the dead, or the afterlife.

"To regenerate themselves," Aunt Tillie said. I was surprised that she had finally spoken. She seemed to be grasping the situation fairly easily – despite the danger we were obviously in.

"Very good," Emily seemed pleased.

"I don't understand," Thistle said honestly.

"You were right," Aunt Tillie said. "The murders thirty years ago were done by the same people. These people."

I looked at Ron and Emily – who both looked to be in their mid-twenties, early thirties at the most – and felt doubt wash over me. "I don't see how that's possible," I said finally.

"It's dark magic," Aunt Tillie said simply. "Every thirty years they sacrifice two teenagers – one male, one female – and they absorb their life force. It's pretty advanced black magic. Most people today haven't even heard about this type of magic, let alone tried to harness it."

"She's smarter than she looks," Emily laughed. "She's also spot on. Tell me, how did you figure that out?"

"I've been around for a very long time. Though, not as long as the two of you, I would imagine."

"Probably not," Emily giggled. "It's too bad, really," she lamented.

"We could probably learn a lot from you. We just don't have the time to stick around. We've already stayed too long. We just have to finish the rituals tonight, they have to be done under the full moon, and we're out of here."

"Well, have a nice trip," I offered brightly.

"They're going to kill you," Shane said sadly.

I know. Oh, boy, did I know.

Ron reached into his coat and pulled out a gun. It shouldn't have surprised me, but seeing it pointed directly at my head caused the breath to hitch in my chest.

"How do you think you'll get away with this?" I managed to keep my voice even. Now was definitely not the time to panic. From the sound of Clove hyperventilating behind me, I didn't think we could afford for us all to fall apart.

"We won't be here," Ron said. "We'll be gone long before you're discovered. And why would anyone suspect the nice newlyweds from the inn? What would our motive be?"

He had a point.

"Do you really think you can get us all?" I had hope that everyone else would be able to at least try to make a run for it through the maze. There were too many of us for Ron and Emily to get all at once.

"That's why I'm going to kill you and your cousins first," Ron said smoothly. "I figure it won't be too hard to track four old ladies down once you three are gone."

"Who are you calling old?" Marnie asked indignantly.

Now was so not the time.

I was still running possible scenarios of survival through my head – none actually involved mine – when the situation even got more complicated.

"What the fuck is this?" The voice was deep. The voice was male. Oh, and the voice was pissed.

Now what?

TWENTY-EIGHT

No matter how many times I thought about how this night would end, this is the one scenario that never managed to enter my mind.

The new voice belonged to Russ. Yeah, biker Russ – who knew heroes had beer guts and wore motorcycle chaps? And he wasn't alone. He had at least three of his cohorts with him – including Landon.

I met Landon's gaze. I felt a surge of hope. They couldn't kill us in front of witnesses – and there was no way that Ron could take out all of the bikers. Landon seemed calm – ridiculously calm given the situation. He stepped into the clearing and looked around. If he was surprised to see all of us, he didn't acknowledge it.

"Who are you guys?" I noticed a certain tone of worry creep into Ron's voice. He obviously wasn't expecting this either.

"Who are you?" Landon challenged Ron and Emily. He seemed oblivious to us, at this point.

Emily seemed genuinely perplexed. "Why are you guys here?"

"Why are you here?" It was nice to see that it just wasn't my questions that Landon refused to answer.

"We asked you first," Emily said.

Landon turned to me. "What are you doing here?"

"Oh, just taking a walk," I said with faux breeziness.

"They're witches," Emily scoffed. "They were doing witchy things. They're the killers. We came upon them in the maze and we decided to take them in to the police."

She was a much better liar than we were. Landon looked doubtful, though. "They're the killers? An old lady in a combat helmet and three women in tracksuits are killers?"

Emily shrugged. "It takes all types."

Ron was busy looking the bikers up and down. I think he was wondering if they were armed. I was kind of curious about that, too, truth be told.

Landon looked at me again. "Why are you here?"

I honestly didn't know what to tell him. "We were trying to figure out who the killers were when, well, the killers kind of stumbled upon us."

"And why do they think you're witches?"

Because we are. "They're crazy. Who knows?"

"Oh, please," Emily muttered. "You were the ones who brought candles and were casting a spell to see the past."

"It wasn't technically a spell," my mom corrected her. "We don't like the term spell. We were doing a ritual."

Now she opened her mouth?

Landon looked at the seven of us in disbelief. "You're witches?"

"Hey," Thistle barked. "Witches are people, too."

Could this situation get any more surreal? "Is that really the important thing right now?"

Landon shifted his gaze to Ron's gun, which was now pointed at Russ. "I guess not," he acquiesced.

"You haven't answered the question: Why are you guys here?" Ron was speaking to Russ. Even though Landon had been the one to do most of the talking so far, he obviously saw Russ as the leader.

"We were conducting business," Russ said. His voice had a harsh quality to it. He was clearly annoyed.

"What kind of business?"

"The kind that doesn't concern you," Russ said.

"Meth," Thistle said. I shot her a dark look. Did she really think that was going to help us?

"Who told you that?" Russ was eyeing Thistle with his own brand of malice at this point.

Thistle regarded him haughtily. "It's common knowledge. Everyone in town knows." That was a slight exaggeration.

Landon regarded me for a second. "Chief Terry told you that, didn't he?"

"I don't know what you're talking about," I lied.

Russ turned to Landon and whispered something to him. Landon nodded grimly. "I'll take care of it."

"All of them?"

"All of them," Landon agreed in a low voice.

Uh-oh.

"All of them what?" Ron was understandably nervous. He knew he couldn't get everyone in the clearing.

Russ regarded Ron with a truly evil smile. "We're going to have to take care of all of you."

"Take care of us?" Emily's voice had risen an octave.

"We can't afford for our interests to be disrupted."

"We don't care about your stupid drugs," Emily promised. "We'll just leave you with the witches and go on our way and you'll never see us again. You'll actually be doing us a favor."

"I don't do favors," Russ said.

"How are you going to hide all of our bodies?" Ron was starting to visibly panic now. "They're all family. It's not as suspicious if they disappear. If we disappear with them, that's going to raise a lot of questions."

"Not if the police believe you're the ones who got rid of them," Russ tilted his head toward us.

I noticed that Landon was slowly moving closer to me as the conversation went on. His body was rigid with concentration – and his right hand had disappeared inside of his leather jacket. Was he really going to kill us? I can't believe I ever thought he was hot.

"Why would the police believe we killed them?" Ron was grasping at straws now.

"You were going to kill them."

"That's not the point."

"What is the point?" Russ was becoming increasingly bored with Ron's questions.

"Look, there's got to be a way to make this beneficial for all of us," Ron wasn't done trying to wrangle for his life. Emily had moved to his side.

Russ and Ron were so focused on each other they hadn't noticed Landon move up to my side. "You have to run in to the maze," he said in a low voice.

"You don't think they'll notice?"

"I'll do what I can to cover for you. Just get out of here as fast as you can – and don't go back for the car. They'll expect that."

"How do you think we're going to be able to get Aunt Tillie through this maze without them catching up?"

Landon glanced at Aunt Tillie and smiled grimly. "Something tells me she's stronger than she looks."

I glanced over at my mom. She seemed to understand what was about to happen. She was herding Marnie and Twila toward one of the pathways that led into the maze. Thistle and Clove were edging over, too.

"Why are you helping?"

"Maybe I like witches," Landon winked with as much bravado as he could muster. I knew he was scared shitless, though.

I saw that Marnie, Twila, Aunt Tillie and my mom had disappeared into the maze. Clove was going now. Thistle was giving me a hard look. She wasn't going to leave without me.

"Go," Landon whispered. He pushed me toward them.

I didn't hesitate. I broke into a run. I didn't look back, even when I heard Russ yell. Thistle and I caught up to the others. "Take them ahead," I ordered Clove.

"What about you two?"

"We're going to slow them down," Thistle said resignedly.

Clove looked uncertain. "We should stick together."

"We have to buy them time," I insisted.

Thistle shoved Clove hard. "Go!"

Thistle and I looked at each other. We only had one shot at this. We raced a few passageways down and waited until Clove had managed to get everyone else through it. We climbed up on the hay bales that were placed there and pushed hard, toppling them over. They cascaded down and blocked the pathway. It would take our pursuers a few minutes to get through there – which was a good thing. We were now cut off from the rest of our family, though.

Thistle and I both jumped when we heard a gun go off. The sound of a woman's shriek followed it. Emily.

"They must have killed Ron," Thistle said.

We heard another gun shot. Emily had gone eerily silent.

Thistle shrugged. "It's not like they didn't have it coming."

I kneeled down and motioned for Thistle to climb over me. "I'm not leaving you alone here," she argued.

"You have to help Clove," I ordered. "I'll be able to hide easier if it's just me. I'll be fine."

Sophie and Shane had appeared at my side. "The ghosts will be able to help," I said. I was relieved to see them.

Thistle still looked dubious, but she did as I ordered. She looked back at me over the tower of hay bales, pausing for a second before racing off into the dark. "Good luck," I murmured.

"They're coming," Shane warned.

I skidded off into a corner and pressed myself into the wall trying to hide. I could hear footsteps closing in. I kept backing down the passageway, trying to be as quiet as I possibly could. I was stunned when I felt a warm body move in behind me. I involuntarily opened my mouth to scream, but it was cut short when a hand clamped over my mouth.

"It's me," Landon breathed in my ear. "Do not scream."

I turned to him in surprise "You're alive."

"That surprises you?" His eyes twinkled in the moonlight.

"Do you think now is the right time to flirt?"

"If we die in the next few minutes you're going to be glad to have one final good memory," Landon whispered, pulling me closer to him and pinching my butt. "Shh," he cut me off when I started to protest.

"Be quiet," Sophie whispered. "They're coming."

I heard a variety of different epithets as Russ and his other cronies apparently happened on the toppled hay bales. "They can't get back through this way," he ordered. "Go back around front. We'll catch them when they try to go back to the car."

The car. I mentally smacked myself. I had forgotten to warn them away from the car.

When he was sure they were gone, Landon relaxed his grip on me. He didn't entirely release me, though. "They won't go back to the car, right?"

I looked at Landon helplessly.

"Crap," Landon swore. He scanned the immediate area quickly. "Why does a corn maze have walls made out of bales of hay?"

"Ambiance?"

"Don't be cute."

It was hard to be cute when I was terrified for my family. Landon grabbed my hand and started moving in the opposite direction from Russ.

"Where are we going?"

"There's an emergency exit somewhere over here," Landon muttered. "I saw it when I was here the other day."

"You were scoping out emergency exits in a corn maze?"

"I look for emergency exits everywhere."

I watched Landon search the far wall for the hidden exit for a few minutes. When he found it, he pushed it open and raced through it. I followed soundlessly. I had no idea what his plan was, but it had to be better than the mind-numbing fear that was clouding my brain.

When we stumbled out into the open air, Landon paused to get his bearings. "They'll exit at the back, right?"

I nodded.

Landon took off in the direction of the rear of the maze. I wordlessly followed him, struggling to keep up. I didn't want him to slow down, though. Not if it meant that he could save my family – even Aunt Tillie.

I pushed the lingering pain in my ankle out of my mind. Landon now had a decent lead on me. I saw him disappear around the corner of the maze. A few moments later I followed – coming up short when I saw the scene in front of me.

Russ had a grip on Aunt Tillie's arm. Landon had stopped a few feet in front of me. No one else was in sight.

For her part, Aunt Tillie was having none of this. "You let me go right now you piece of shit!"

"Shut up, old lady."

Russ was glaring at Landon. "I knew I shouldn't have trusted you."

"You should always follow your instincts," Landon said smoothly.

"It's all ruined now," Russ screamed.

"The others got away?" Landon asked.

"Yeah, it's pretty pathetic when the only one you can catch is the old one in a combat helmet."

"Where are Gunner and Diesel?"

"I sent them after the others."

Fear was knotted in the pit of my stomach. I moved to Landon's side, eyeing Aunt Tillie warily. "Leave her alone. She's just an old woman."

Aunt Tillie glared at me. "You shut your mouth. I'm so sick of your mouth."

"Now is not the time for you to be ... you," I ordered her.

"Did you ever think it wasn't the time for you to be you?"

"Not really."

"That's your problem. You have a definitive lack of foresight." If Aunt Tillie was scared, she wasn't showing it.

"And you look before you leap."

"The whole family does that," Aunt Tillie countered.

She had a point.

"We're probably going to die," I said finally.

"That's your other problem," Aunt Tillie chided me. "You have no faith."

"Since these are probably our last few minutes, I want you to tell me the truth." Stall. Stall. Stall.

Aunt Tillie waited for me to ask the question.

"Did you start the pot field?"

"That's the question you wanted to ask?" She seemed surprised.

"I didn't figure you'd tell the truth any other time."

"I didn't start it," she said. "Your Uncle Calvin did."

"Uncle Calvin?" Now I really wished I had been able to meet the man.

"He liked his pot," Aunt Tillie shrugged. "He liked his potato chips, too. He finally found a hobby that brought the two together."

"Is that why you let them keep it?"

"This may come as a surprise to you, but I'm not as rigid as you think." I could believe that.

Russ was making a move on Aunt Tillie. I had to do something.

"Wait!"

Russ turned to me expectantly. I saw Landon eyeing me curiously. I think he was even interested to see what I would do next.

"I have one more question," I said. I was desperate. I didn't know what else to do.

Russ looked at me expectantly and waited.

"Did you curse Thistle, Clove and I yesterday?"

Aunt Tillie smirked to herself. "I don't curse people. You know that. I don't need to," she added. "I don't need magic to win."

With those words, Aunt Tillie lifted her tiny leg higher than I would have imagined possible at this point in her life and kicked Russ as hard as she could in the balls.

Russ crumpled forward, screaming in pain.

Landon raced forward, tackling Russ. Aunt Tillie took a step away. I raced over to her. "Are you all right?"

"I'm fine," she waved me off. "That boy with you would be good looking if he didn't have hair like a girl," she said after watching them wrestle on the ground for a few seconds.

Landon and Russ were grappling for the gun. We both jumped when it went off. I saw Landon slump on top of Russ.

Aunt Tillie and I were frozen in our spots. He'd shot Landon.

Russ shifted Landon's body off of him. I could see Landon's blood splattered on his shirt. Russ was gripping the gun in his hand and climbing to his feet. There was nowhere for us to run. And boy, did Russ look pissed.

"You guys have been more trouble than ... well, just about anyone I've ever met." Russ huffed.

I slipped my hand in Aunt Tillie's. It was the only measure of comfort I could offer her.

I screwed my eyes shut when I saw Russ raising the weapon. I tried to move in front of Aunt Tillie as much as I could, to shield her. I knew it was a fruitless move, but I didn't know what else to do.

I felt Shane and Sophie move in beside me. "We don't know what to do?" Shane whispered.

"There's nothing you can do," I said. My eyes were still closed.

When the gun went off, my heart stopped. It took me a full five seconds to realize that I didn't feel any pain. I must be in shock.

After another five seconds, I finally opened my eyes. I was surprised to see Russ lying on the ground next to Landon. He wasn't moving.

I swung around to see Chief Terry standing beside me. His gun was out and he was moving toward Aunt Tillie.

"Are you two okay?" He seemed concerned, but he didn't stop as he continued on toward Russ and Landon.

"I'm fine," I said. Then I passed out.

TWENTY-NINE

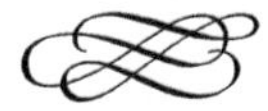

Aunt Tillie's face swam into view. She was leaning down over me. She looked more irked than concerned.

"Am I in hell?"

"Not yet," she scolded. "You're embarrassing me, though, so you probably will be later."

A hand was reaching down for me. I grabbed it and found myself face-to-face with Chief Terry.

"What happened?"

"You passed out like a ninny," Aunt Tillie supplied.

Chief Terry smiled and shook his head. "How do you feel?"

"I'm fine," I started. Everything came rushing back to me. Landon.

I swung around to see a group of paramedics had arrived and were working feverishly on Landon. No one was buzzing around Russ.

"Is …?"

"Russ is dead," Chief Terry acknowledged. "They're still working on Landon."

"Will he survive?"

Chief Terry read the concern on my face. "It's too soon to tell."

The paramedics had moved Landon onto a gurney and they were rushing him toward the ambulance. I heard one of them barking out orders on his radio: "We're en route to Northern Michigan Hospital," he barked. "We have an injured FBI agent with a gunshot to the chest. We'll pump him full of fluids on the way, but he's going to need to go into surgery."

I watched as Landon was wheeled past me. His face was ashen and motionless. He already looked dead. Then, what the paramedic had said into the radio, sunk in. "An FBI agent?"

Chief Terry looked momentarily embarrassed. "I wanted to tell you," he protested. "I really did, but I didn't think you would be able to keep your mouth shut and the minute Thistle and Clove found out, then everyone in town would find out."

"You told me to stay away from him," I countered.

"I didn't want you to mess up his investigation," Chief Terry explained. "He's been undercover with these guys for months."

"But you told me he was a bad guy," I argued.

"He's an FBI agent, not Gandhi," Chief Terry said. "Besides, I don't like the Feds. They're always full of themselves."

"How long have you known?"

"Not long," Chief Terry said. "I thought I recognized him that day out at the corn maze, but I couldn't be sure. We met at a training exercise more than a year ago. He came to my office to fill me in, though, that morning you showed up. He didn't want me to blow his cover."

"So you lied to me. I knew he wasn't just there to answer questions."

"I didn't lie. I just didn't tell you everything. There's a difference."

"I didn't realize we were able to use elementary school logic," I grumbled.

"Oh, get over it," Aunt Tillie interrupted. "He had a job to do. You had a job to do. Everything turned out fine, like I told you it would."

"Really? Now you're going to pull out the 'I told you so' card?"

I heard a commotion behind us and turned to see what was going on. I was relieved to see Russ' cohorts being led out in handcuffs. It looked as if the state police had gotten a little overzealous with them, given the bruises that were becoming apparent on their faces under the bright police lights that had illuminated the area.

"I see they put up a fight," I smiled.

"Not with us," Chief Terry laughed.

"Than how …?"

I saw a group of people walk around the corner of the maze and exhaled a pent-up sigh of relief when I saw Mom, Marnie, Twila, Thistle and Clove come into view. They looked a little dirty and unkempt, but otherwise unharmed.

"They're the ones who subdued them," Chief Terry said.

"They did? How?" Thistle and Clove had caught sight of me and were rushing to my side.

"Thank the goddess, you're all right," Clove said, throwing her arms around me.

Thistle merely smiled. We weren't big on public displays of affection. "I was worried about you guys."

"We had everything under control," Thistle said.

I saw that the two bikers were giving all the women in my family a wide berth, casting wary glances at them – along with the occasional glare – as they were led to the patrol cars.

"What happened to them?"

Thistle smirked. "Our moms got a little, um, overzealous."

"With what? A car?"

"No, more like a rake and shovel they found on the far side of the maze when we exited."

I saw that a couple of officers were carrying a rake and a shovel toward the police cars. The ends were bagged to preserve evidence. I was hoping that was just a formality and that my mom and aunts weren't going to be charged with anything.

"How did you get separated from Aunt Tillie?"

Thistle glowered at her. "She purposely separated from us. I couldn't control her. She was like a banshee. She kept saying she had to wait for you. I made a choice to get our moms away and leave her. I figured she was fairly indestructible."

"You did the right thing," I assured her. "In fact, Aunt Tillie is the one who hobbled Russ so Landon could make a run at him. Oh, and Landon is an FBI agent."

Thistle looked surprised while Clove looked relieved. "Good. I knew someone that good looking couldn't be a drug dealer."

Thistle was watching grimly as the police zipped Russ' body up in a body bag. "She didn't shoot him, did she?"

"No, Chief Terry did that. She just kicked him in the balls."

"Oh, well, it's not like he didn't have it coming." Thistle would have probably kicked him in the balls herself if she had the chance.

I was watching my mom, Marnie and Twila cautiously. "They seem okay."

"Yeah, they beat the shit out of those guys," Thistle said. She looked proud, despite herself. "When the cops showed up, they were begging them to arrest them and get them away from the crazy witches."

"I don't blame them." I turned to Chief Terry expectantly. "So, now what?"

"Now? Now you go home."

"That's it?"

"For now. I'll send officers out to the inn to question you guys, but that is pretty cut and dry. We've already hauled the other two bodies out of the center of the maze."

"Emily and Ron?"

"You know them?" Chief Terry looked surprised.

"They admitted to the killings," I said evasively.

"Did they say anything else? Like who they really were and why they came here?"

I shook my head no.

"Well, hopefully, we'll be able to dig up something on them," Chief Terry said.

Thistle and I exchanged dark looks. I couldn't help but wonder what, if anything, they would be able to dig up on two people who were a lot older than they appeared. It's not like we could tell them, though. Not only would no one believe us, but then we would also be exposing ourselves and what we had been doing out here tonight. And no one wanted that, believe me.

Chief Terry watched the unspoken exchange between the two of us. "They're not going to find anything, are they?"

I held my palms up in front of me. "I honestly don't know, but I doubt it."

Chief Terry pursed his lips as he watched the state police congratulating themselves on a good bust that was bound to make national news. "Let them waste their time," he said finally. "They're assholes anyway."

THIRTY

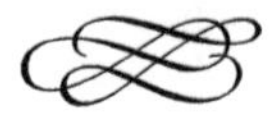

We went back to the inn to get cleaned up. While we were eating breakfast, the state police showed up to question us. We were all exhausted, but that didn't stop my mom and aunts from plying them with food to distract them.

"So, what were you doing out there?" One of the officers asked despite a mouth full of pumpkin donut.

"We like to walk for exercise," my mom lied. Well, they were wearing velvet tracksuits. Of course, Aunt Tillie was wearing a combat helmet, but we could always explain that away by saying she was senile.

"It was a full moon, we like to walk under the full moon and absorb her strength and convene with nature," Aunt Tillie told the officers.

Or maybe they would figure out she was crazy all on their own.

Once the officers were gone, I excused myself to go to the hospital. Landon had pulled through the surgery, and he was expected to wake up in the next few hours. I had a few things I wanted to discuss with him.

When I got to the hospital, Chief Terry was parked outside

Landon's room in a vinyl chair. "What are you doing here? I thought you hated Feds?"

"I figured I owed him to check on him," Chief Terry shrugged. "He did save your life, after all."

"He saved all our lives," I admitted. "He's the one who got us out of the maze in the confusion."

"I figured."

"So, he's going to be okay?"

"The doctors said he was incredibly lucky that the bullet didn't hit any major arteries. He should actually be able to walk out of here in a couple of days. It's something of a miracle."

I quirked my eyebrow. "More like divine intervention," I laughed.

"Someone was definitely looking out for him," he grunted in agreement.

Chief Terry cast a sideways glance at me as I took a seat next to him. "I got off the phone with the medical examiner a few minutes ago," he said nonchalantly. "They're in a tizzy over there."

"Oh?" I honestly didn't know where he was going with this.

"Yeah, it's weird, the two bodies that were found in the maze, something happened to them."

"They didn't disappear did they?" I was panicked for a second, wondering if Ron and Emily could somehow actually stop death and resurrect themselves.

"No, they're still dead," Chief Terry looked surprised at my question. "They don't look the same as when we found them, though."

"What do you mean?"

Chief Terry rubbed his chin tiredly. "Well, for one thing, when they opened the body bags they were filled with what looked like mummified remains."

"Mummified?"

"Yeah," Chief Terry plowed on. "The medical examiner couldn't explain it. He said, if he had to guess, that the bodies belonged to people who were more than a hundred years old – not two twenty-somethings. He also estimated they'd been dead for a really long time – at least fifty years."

Uh-oh.

"He didn't know how to explain it," Chief Terry continued. "Do you?"

"No," I said honestly. I had an idea, but no one would believe me, especially Chief Terry.

"The medical examiner figures that some unknown substance must have gotten into the bags and contaminated the bodies," Chief Terry said innocently. "They'll probably never find out what really happened, will they?"

I didn't say anything. I didn't know what to say. I had noticed, with relief, that a doctor was walking purposely toward us. We both got to our feet and waited expectantly.

"He's awake," the doctor told us. "He's asking for someone named Bay."

Chief Terry looked at me speculatively. I smiled at him nervously and then followed the doctor to Landon's room.

I was surprised to see him propped up in bed. He still looked paler than usual, but some of the color had returned to his cheeks. He actually smiled when he saw me walk in.

"I'm glad you're okay," he said. His voice was a little weak, but I was just so relieved to see him alive that I brushed the concern bubbling to the surface away.

"Did you doubt it?"

"Not for a second. How is your aunt?" His smile was faint, but it was there. He was probably remembering the combat helmet.

"She's fine. She's probably taking her afternoon nap a little early today, but she's fine. She'll be ready to wreak havoc by dinner tonight."

"And the rest of your family?"

"They're fine, too."

"And Russ?" He grimaced when he asked the question.

"No one told you?" I was surprised.

"No one has told me anything."

"Chief Terry shot and killed him. He saved us."

"Good," Landon leaned his head back on his pillow. "I was worried he didn't get the text I sent him. It was dark. I couldn't be sure my message would go through."

"You contacted him? He didn't tell me that."

"I texted him before we even went in the maze. I didn't recognize the vehicle. I just had a feeling it was you."

I was struggling with what I had to say next, but I plowed on anyway. "You could have told me that you were an FBI agent. I would have kept it a secret."

"From your cousins?" He looked doubtful.

Probably not. "I wouldn't have told anyone else."

"We couldn't risk that."

He was probably right. I decided to change tactics. "I want to say thank you. You saved us."

"I just gave you a diversion. You saved yourselves." Landon brushed my statement off like I hadn't even said it.

"Still, I don't know if we would have all survived without you," I argued.

"I think you guys probably would have found your own way," Landon sighed.

"Can't you just say you're welcome?" He was starting to irritate me again.

"You're welcome," he said.

We lapsed into silence for a few minutes. "So, now what?" I finally asked.

"What do you mean?" Landon had opened his blue eyes and was regarding me with an emotion I couldn't quite identify.

"Now what happens to you?"

"Oh, I'll go back to working out of the office until I'm cleared for field duty."

"So, you're leaving?"

"I work out of the office in Traverse City," he said. "So, I wouldn't worry, I won't be that far away."

"I wasn't worried," I scoffed.

"You were worried," he laughed, closing his eyes again. 'You were worried you'd never see me again and you didn't think your heart could take it."

"Oh, please, you're awful sure of yourself."

"Women love me, what can I say?"

"Cocky, isn't he?" I looked up to see Chief Terry standing in the doorway.

"Yeah, well, I don't feel like I can argue with a guy who got shot protecting me," I said. "I'll have to wait until he's feeling better."

I got up and moved toward Chief Terry. "I'm assuming you want to talk to him?"

"Yeah," Chief Terry said. "We have a few things to go over."

I cast a glance back at Landon. "I'll see you when you're feeling better."

Landon smiled knowingly. "I'm sure you will."

I shook my head and turned to Chief Terry. "Why don't you come out to dinner tonight? I'm sure everyone would be glad to see you."

"Do you think they'll be up for that?"

"Oh, yeah, they're all excited," I laughed. "They were talking about making pot roast when I left."

"I love their pot roast," Chief Terry's face took on a dreamy look.

"So, see you at 7 p.m.?"

"Absolutely."

I heard Landon and Chief Terry talking as I left. "You eat dinner with them a lot?" Landon asked curiously.

"Those are some fine women," Chief Terry said gruffly. "And they can all cook. Of course, eating dinner out there is like going to the circus, but the food makes it worthwhile."

"I'll have to check it out some time," Landon said.

"Yeah, they're not going to like you," Chief Terry grumbled. "Aunt Tillie will eat you for lunch."

"I'll wear her combat helmet for protection."

I couldn't help but smile to myself as he left. He might have saved our lives, but that wasn't going to make Aunt Tillie like his hair.

THIRTY-ONE

I slept most of the afternoon. I really wasn't planning it, but the guesthouse was quiet when I got back. Thistle and Clove hadn't even shut their doors. I checked on them both, but they were happily slumbering away. I planned on just laying down for a few minutes, but I didn't wake up until late afternoon.

When I went back out into the living room, Thistle and Clove were sipping tea and watching television.

"Anything good on?"

"We're the lead story," Clove said excitedly.

I glanced up at the television and saw they were broadcasting a picture of the three of us – taken at last year's town fall festival. "Where did they get that?"

"I don't know," Thistle said. "At least we all look good. I forgot how much I liked my hair when it was pink."

"Are you going to dye it back?"

"Not right away. It's worth irritating my mom with the blue for the next couple of weeks. Maybe I'll dye it back for Christmas."

"Well, that will be festive."

I poured myself a cup of tea and joined them on the couch. We all watched the news coverage for a few minutes. The perky newscaster said that police were still trying to ascertain Ron and Emily's true identities – an endeavor that was going to be mostly impossible given the state of the bodies – and they had no idea why the couple had killed Shane and Sophie.

"Where are they?" I looked around. Neither one of them were present.

"Maybe they moved on," Thistle said hopefully.

"They wouldn't do that without saying goodbye." Or at least I hoped they wouldn't. I wanted them to find happiness, but I would miss them.

"So, how was Landon?" Clove was eyeing me mischievously.

"He was fine. He should be out of the hospital in a few days."

"Did he ask you out?"

"He's in the hospital."

"So he didn't ask you out?" Clove looked disappointed.

"He said he would be working out of the Traverse City office, so he'd be around," I said. I bit my inner lip to make sure my smile wouldn't be too wide.

"Well, that's something," Clove giggled.

I didn't tell either of them about his comments regarding family dinner. The thought of that would drive them to distraction, and I wanted Thistle to bring Marcus out to soften our moms up before I brought Landon to dinner. What? I'm not selfish. Well, not entirely.

We all went up to the inn a little before 7 p.m. We had munched on cereal at the guesthouse, but we were all starving.

"I thought you were becoming a vegetarian?" I asked Thistle.

"Not on pot roast night," she said.

I was surprised to find Shane and Sophie waiting for us outside of the inn, on the back patio. They looked like they knew we were coming.

"Hey guys, I was wondering where you went off to."

"We didn't want to wake you up," Shane explained. "You were all sleeping pretty soundly."

"Are you coming in?"

"No," Shane said quietly. "We already said goodbye to them."

"Goodbye?"

"We're going to go now," he explained. "You know, move on."

"You are?"

"We can feel it pulling us," Sophie answered. "It's been a struggle to stay here long enough to say goodbye to you guys."

"You're being pulled?" Clove looked confused.

"I can't explain it," Sophie said. "I think, now that we know who killed us, there's no reason left for us to stay."

"We both went and said goodbye to our parents, even though they couldn't see us," Shane added. "I think my mom is going to be okay."

"I hope so," I said truthfully. "I hope you guys find what you need – on the other side."

"We will," Shane said knowingly. "We also know that we wouldn't have the chance to move on if it wasn't for you."

"Thank you," Sophie said earnestly. "We'll never forget any of you."

"We won't forget you either," I said. I held back tears as I saw them start to disappear. They joined hands and waved at me. Then, they were gone. "Good luck," I told the wind. I hoped they heard me.

When we entered the inn, we found Aunt Tillie watching *Jeopardy*. She didn't even acknowledge we'd entered the room. Her focus is profound sometimes.

"It looks like things are back to normal," Clove laughed.

We all went into the kitchen. We weren't surprised to see our moms bustling about as they doled out the variety of entrees and sides onto serving dishes.

"Oh, you're here," Aunt Twila greeted us. "We were worried you would sleep the day away."

"We were tired," Thistle protested.

"If your hair wasn't so depressing, you probably wouldn't be so tired," Twila said knowingly.

Thistle gritted her teeth and turned to me. "I'm never dying it back. Never."

We helped carry the serving dishes out into the dining room. I was surprised to see a full house waiting for us. "Doesn't look like all the news coverage has hurt the inn," I said.

"Oh, no, we're booked through Christmas already," my mom said. "People think we're celebrities now."

"Well, that's good for business, I guess."

I saw that Chief Terry was already seated. I couldn't help but smile when I saw Marnie and Twila start to argue over who was going to sit next to him. My mom took advantage of their momentary distraction and slid into the open seat next to Chief Terry. She smiled at him warmly.

Aunt Tillie joined us a few minutes later, sitting at the head of the table, and regarding everyone assembled. She didn't look happy to see the new guests. "I thought we'd get a break," she grumbled.

"You don't work anyway, so why do you care?" I never think before I speak.

Aunt Tillie glared at me. "I see you haven't learned anything."

"What do you mean?" I was spooning a generous helping of potatoes onto my plate. I was only half listening to her.

"I am more than just an inn owner."

"Oh, we know that," Thistle said.

"I'm the head of this family," she continued.

"We know," Clove sighed.

"I am to be loved and revered, not mocked."

"Mocking is the Winchester way," Thistle argued.

"It looks like you're getting another zit, dear," she turned to Thistle. "You really should wash your face better."

Thistle looked panicked as she tried to catch her reflection in a spoon. "Why do you do this?"

"So you'll remember just who is in charge."

Like we could ever forget.